THE EDGE OF DESTINY

The Destiny Series Book 3

EMMA EASTER

The Edge of Destiny
by Emma Easter

Paperback Edition

CKN Christian Publishing
An Imprint of Wolfpack Publishing

6032 Wheat Penny Avenue
Las Vegas, NV 89122

Paperback ISBN: 978-1-64734-705-5
Ebook ISBN: 978-1-64734-704-8

THE EDGE OF DESTINY

ONE

Lily finished cleaning the kitchen and washed the cleaning rag. She still had a lot of cleaning and dusting to do as Sofia's house was big and filled with many beautiful but delicate souvenirs from her multiple trips abroad. After hanging the rag up to dry, she headed to Sofia's bedroom to continue her cleaning and then paused in the hallway when the doorbell rang. She turned around and went to open the front door. She grinned.

"You're back, Sofia," she said, opening the door wide so her friend could enter the house.

Sofia dropped her suitcase and threw her arms around Lily, a huge smile on her face. She hugged Lily tightly and then let her go. Walking into the living room, she flung herself onto the sofa, her smile still in place, and giggled.

"I'm guessing you had a good trip," Lily said, going to sit beside her.

"I had a wonderful time in Europe, Lily. It was even better than the last trip because George came with me. We didn't go to Paris or Rome this time.

We went to Saint Tropez and then on to Barcelona and then Prague. We stayed in gorgeous hotels and did nothing but laze about and…" She stopped talking as a mischievous smile took over her face.

Lily didn't know where any of the places Sofia had mentioned were. Even though she yearned to ask Sofia about them and maybe, if she was lucky, visit those places one day, it was not the immediate thing on her mind. Her stomach twisted with concern for her friend, especially at the naughty grin on Sofia's face. She voiced her concern, knowing Sofia would call her old- fashioned. "I didn't know you traveled with George. And you both stayed in the same hotel room?"

Sofia looked at Lily and laughed. "You should see the way your face looks, Lily. You would think I just told you I joined the mafia."

"But you shouldn't stay in a hotel room alone with George. You're not married to him. The temptation to…"

"Oh, stop it, Lily! Why shouldn't I share a hotel room with George? He's my boyfriend. And as for the temptation to…"

Lily's stomach lurched, and she shook her head to try to get Sofia to stop talking. Sofia laughed again. "You do know we've been together for a year now. And yes, we have been sleeping together for most of that time."

"It's wrong, Sofia!" Lily said. She didn't care what Sofia thought. She grew up believing that it was a sin for a woman to sleep with someone she was not married to. Even though she now knew that there had been a double standard in what she'd been taught in Fallow Creek, she had her personal relationship with God now. What Sofia was doing was wrong for both men and women. But how could she convince her friend about that when Sofia didn't even seem to understand the concept of...?

"Lily!" Sofia intruded into her thoughts. "Stop looking at me like that. You're so old-fashioned. Sometimes I think you unknowingly entered a time machine that transported you here from 1920. What you need is a boyfriend of your own. In fact, I think I'll start looking for one for you. You will understand when..."

Lily stuffed her fingers into her ears, cutting Sofia's words off, and shut her eyes. This was not the first time in the eight months she'd lived in Sofia's house that her friend had brought this up. And it was usually with some crude statement that shocked her every time. She opened her eyes again when Sofia tapped her shoulder and sighed loudly when her friend pulled her fingers out of her ears.

"I don't understand you, Lily. You come from a weird community where men marry multiple wives, and yet you are such a prude." She shook her head slowly. "I know it was a religious community and women weren't allowed to do what the men did... but surely you've had a boyfriend before?"

Lily pursed her lips.

"Even a secret boyfriend?" Sofia asked, her face full of disbelief.

"I've already told you, Sofia. I've never had a boyfriend, and I don't plan on having one until I'm ready to get married. And I don't think I ever will. After years of living in a place like Fallow Creek, I cherish my freedom now above all things. I'm not letting it go for anyone."

"You don't have to get married, silly. I was talking about dating, relationships without the bonds of marriage. In spite of what your strange town says, even women have needs that…"

"Sofia, please stop!"

Sofia chuckled. "Okay. Tell you what — I will stop bugging you about getting a boyfriend if you stop complaining or even squirming every time I talk about spending time alone with George."

Lily tried to reason with Sofia again. "Do you love George?"

Sofia's smile melted off her face, and she sighed loudly. "Umm… I guess I do."

"Then marry him. What are you waiting for?"

Sofia turned away from Lily. "It's not that easy."

"What isn't easy? You get married and then you can live together." Her stomach twisted with worry again. She wanted her friend to be happy, but where would she live when Sofia married George and moved to his house? She had no job and no money and had been living off Sofia's goodwill since she'd left the hospital months ago.

"It's complicated, Lily."

Lily turned Sofia around to face her again. "Why is it complicated?"

Sofia shrugged and said, "Because he's already married."

Lily blinked and her mouth fell open. Her stomach turned in revulsion. She'd left Fallow Creek extremely relieved that she would not have to deal anymore with the polygamous lifestyle there. And yet here she was, living with someone who, for all intents and purposes, was practicing the same thing. Sofia might tell herself it wasn't so since she wasn't married to George, but the women in Fallow Creek who weren't first wives were not legally married either. Lily shifted away from Sofia. "So you tease me constantly because I come from a polygamous community, but you are a 'sister wife' as well."

"It's not the same!"

"Yes… yes, it is!" Lily shuddered and pressed her lips tightly together as she remembered how she'd almost been forced to marry Dennis Hamilton, the leader of their community.

"No, it's not. I do whatever I want without George's permission! And if I ever decide to marry him, which I'm sure I never will, he would have to divorce his wife before we could get married. So, dear Lily, it is not the same thing! Okay?"

Lily shuddered again. She hated that lifestyle with all her heart. How could Sofia be involved with a married man?

"Stop judging me, Lily! I know what you're thinking, but I really don't intend on taking George away from his wife. I'm just having fun."

"Then end it, Sofia. If you're really not planning to take George away from his wife, then end the relationship. It is very wrong… especially in God's sight."

"God again!" Sofia ran her fingers through her hair. "I don't believe in God. At least, not the way you do." She held up her hand as Lily began to protest. "Don't try to preach to me anymore. You've done enough of that." She shut her eyes. "I just came back from a long trip, and I'm tired. I don't want to argue. Can't we talk about something else?"

Lily studied Sofia. Being angry would not solve the problem. Sofia couldn't see she was doing the wrong thing. To her, it was just harmless fun, but Lily knew it was anything but. Still, Sofia had been so kind to her, taking her in when she had no place to live and very little money. The girl had just returned from a long trip. She had to give her time to rest and pray that Sofia would change her mind and break up with George soon. She sighed and gave Sofia a reconciliatory smile.

Sofia smiled back. "What's for dinner? I'm starving."

"I'm sorry, I haven't made dinner yet. I didn't know you were coming back today." Sofia pouted and Lily chuckled. "Okay... I'll get started with dinner now." She stood up.

"Please make me your delicious spicy grilled steak. We were in Italy sampling different kinds of foods, and all I could think of was your grilled steak and rice."

"Okay, ma'am." Lily laughed. "I'll be back with your dinner soon. Just put your feet up and rest."

Sofia smiled and Lily left the living room. She went to the kitchen and began to make their dinner. She hoped Sofia would not decide that they needed to drink wine this evening to celebrate her return or something like that. She'd never tasted alcohol until Sofia made her drink it three months ago. She had hated it. It was the last time she touched the stuff, but Sofia liked her alcohol and from time to time drank in the evenings. She didn't like who her friend became when she drank... especially too much. She'd heard that some people got excessively angry or violent when they were drunk, but Sofia never did. She just became a bumbling idiot who needed to be carefully watched so she didn't run out of the house naked.

As she cooked, she thought about Sofia's dreamy look when she was telling her about her trip to Europe. She remembered what Sofia had said about sharing a hotel room with George, and her heart squeezed tight again.

She sighed and tried to brush off her discomfort. It was definitely wrong for Sofia to sleep with a married man, but what if George wasn't married? Would it be wrong? Sofia had told her Lily was overly worried about that because she'd never had a boyfriend before. Everyone was taught from childhood in Fallow Creek not to have sex until marriage, but what if, along with all the things she'd learned were wrong about Fallow Creek, that was also one of them?

Why am I even thinking about all these things? she scolded herself.

It wasn't like she was going to take Sofia up on her offer and let her friend find her a boyfriend. She didn't want one, and she certainly wasn't going to sleep with anyone she wasn't married to. And since the idea of marriage made her sick, that would never happen. In Fallow Creek, marriage had been the ultimate goal for women and yet the ultimate bondage. Now that she'd left that awful town, she was a free woman. Her goal now was to be independent in every way. She wanted to travel the world like Sofia... but alone. Or with Sofia, if she would come along. She wanted a job and financial independence so she could get a place of her own and control her life and destiny.

She inhaled the tantalizing aroma of the steak she was grilling, but it brought her little comfort. Other people had controlled her life from the time she was born until nine months ago, when she had been banished from Fallow Creek. She was twenty-six but had never lived on her own. She'd never gotten a paid job or had any money. She'd thought she could finally do all that now that she was out of Fallow Creek, but she was still living off someone. She was free to go and come as she pleased, but her movements were largely dictated by Sofia because she didn't have any money. She wasn't totally independent.

Sofia had told her she would ask George, the CEO of some large company, to get her a job, but that had still not happened. Whenever she mentioned going out to get a job for herself, Sofia always discouraged her, saying she would not get a good job and promising to talk to George on her behalf. Lily always wondered if Sofia had already asked him and he'd refused, or if Sofia never remembered to. But it didn't matter anymore. Now that Lily knew George was married, she wasn't sure she wanted anything from him.

She began to dish the food onto two plates and sighed with worry. At the rate she was going, she would never be able to go back to Fallow Creek and try to get her parents out of there so they could come and live with her in Tucson. It was another thing she'd dreamt about since the day she'd left her insane hometown. But if she didn't get a house of her own, that would never happen. She had to find a job and stop letting Sofia talk her out of it.

Lily placed the plates of steaming food in small

trays and went to set them on the dining table. "Dinner's ready," she called.

Sofia stretched and stood up from the sofa. She walked to the dining room and gave Lily a huge smile. "It smells divine. I can't wait to tuck in." She sat down and immediately began to eat. She nodded slowly. "Yum!"

Lily sat on the chair next to Sofia's. "You didn't wait for me to pray over the food again."

Sofia grumbled and dropped her fork. "Okay then. Pray."

Lily breathed a quick prayer and then opened her eyes. Sofia already had her knife and fork in her hands again. She teared into her steak once more.

"Thank God there is no wine anywhere near," Lily whispered.

"What did you say?" Sofia looked up at her.

"Nothing important."

She began to eat and couldn't resist asking Sofia about her trip again. She prayed Sofia wouldn't mention George as she excitedly told Lily about the interesting people she'd encountered and sights she'd seen. Thankfully, Sofia only mentioned him in passing. She talked and talked, and Lily listened with longing. Finally, when the conversation died down again, Lily said to Sofia, "I really have to start looking for a job tomorrow. It's wrong for me to keep living off you. You've done so much for me, but I need to take care of myself."

"But I told you I would ask George to get you a job in his company."

Lily shook her head. "Don't talk to George about it." She wanted to ask Sofia why she hadn't spoken to George about getting her a job already, but she thought better of it. She said instead, "I want to get a job for myself. I have to move out of here and start living my own life."

Sofia frowned. "I don't want you to move out, Lily. I need you."

"For what? You were doing just fine without me eight months ago. Besides, I told you about my parents. I need to get my own apartment if I hope for them to move in with me one day."

"But you told me how difficult it is to leave Fallow Creek. How will you get them out... that is, if they actually want to leave?"

"I know it'll be hard to convince them to leave with me, and even harder to find a way out of there, but it can be done. I never knew I would be able to leave there as soon as I did, but here I am."

Sofia chuckled. "You told me you were kicked out."

"Yes. I think if my parents are willing, we could come up with a reason for them to be kicked out as well."

"Still, Lily, I don't want you to move out. Even if you get a job, can't you stay here?" She gave Lily a sideways smile. "It's rent-free."

Lily didn't answer. Sofia didn't understand her deep need to get her own place and to live her own life. If she stayed here, even with a job, she would still partly live on Sofia's goodwill.

"I promise to talk to George tomorrow about..."

"No! Don't do that!" Lily frowned. She wanted nothing from George. He reminded her of the men in Fallow Creek, and she never wanted to have anything to do with those kinds of men ever again. She stood up and avoided looking at Sofia as she began to clear the plates. She headed towards the kitchen with the plates and then turned. "Sofia?"

"Yes?" Sofia looked at her.

"Tomorrow, I'll start looking for a job. Even if I find one, I promise to stay, at least for a while, but please don't try to talk me out of getting a job myself and don't ever mention anything about it to George."

Sofia sighed loudly and then nodded.

"Thank you," Lily said and left the dining room.

TWO

Taylor sat in his vast living room, sipping his coffee and staring out of the huge open windows. He loved how enormous his windows were. They were almost as big as his door. He opened them wide in the mornings, sat in his favorite chair while sipping his coffee, and watched the majestic view outside. Mornings like these gave him time to catch his breath and let his thoughts run free before the madness of the day started.

His eyes roamed the rugged terrain upon which his new house had been built, and he reveled in the bare natural beauty outside his home. He loved everything about this new house. Maybe it was because of how different it was from his house in Fallow Creek. For one, there were no other houses anywhere around, unlike in Fallow Creek where he'd been surrounded by neighbors and couldn't leave his house without someone calling to him, greeting him, or wanting something from him. This house was a true solace. When he wasn't at work, he could be alone here with his kids. And fully alone in the mornings, before Joshua came rushing out to hug him and Bree's cries sounded over the intercom.

He'd moved into this house a month after he'd left Fallow Creek. He'd been living in a rented house with Josh and Bree and had hired Felicia, a fifty-three-year-old, sour-faced woman, to be his housekeeper. She'd moved here with them. She also took care of his children when he went to his numerous business meetings, but she was not a nanny and was overworked.

He'd mentioned looking for a real home to one of his regular clients, and the man had laughed. "You own a construction company and you don't have a real home?"

Taylor had told him that apart from the fact that he'd only moved to California months ago, he'd been too busy to actually start building his dream home. And that was partly true. But the main reason he'd not started doing so was because the thought of building a permanent home without Faye was excruciating.

"I have a house I'm looking to sell," the client told him. "It's rather old and a little far from everything... but you can come look at it if you want."

Taylor had taken him up on his offer and had fallen in love immediately. It was a five-bedroom stone-and-wood house, and the rooms inside were large, like halls rather than living spaces. There was another, smaller building to the left side of the main house that he decided would be great for any house staff he hired. Since he was a builder, the worn state of the house had not bothered him at all. He had spent about three months renovating the house and had moved in with Josh and Bree after that. The housekeeper and driver lived in the smaller building.

He took a deep breath and stood up and went to the window, still looking out. Massive trees surrounded the house, shading it from the summer sun. The ocean stretched out before him. Hills stood like giants watching over the grounds. The house merged in with the landscape and the property looked slightly foreboding, which he liked. He'd gotten himself a small plane so he could get in and out of 'civilization' quickly.

He took another sip of coffee and sighed when his phone trilled in his pajama pocket. Plucking it out, he frowned when he saw a message on the screen. The serenity that had enveloped him a moment ago vanished. The message was from Rachel. Once again, she was probably asking him to come back to Fallow Creek because the place was changing and she needed his help. But he'd sworn never to go back there, no matter what. He wasn't really interested in how changed Fallow Creek was or what was happening there. Besides, he knew a bit more than she thought he did about what had happened in Fallow Creek. Whatever he did not know was not his problem. There was nothing there for him anymore.

He deleted her message without reading it as the familiar pain swept through him again. The pain of losing Faye. It was one of the reasons why he'd made up his mind never to return there. It would remind him way too much of her, and of the person he'd been before he'd left. But Rachel kept sending these messages, insisting he return. He never read any of them, and he didn't care to. He had given Rachel charge of his house and sent someone to bring him all the things that really mattered to him, like pictures of himself with Faye and Josh.

The man he'd sent to bring his things here had given him a picture he'd taken with Sarah Lowery and her father, Andrew. He had sucked in a sharp breath and torn the picture to shreds. Guilt had grabbed him by the throat for days after that. Maybe if he'd not been so busy planning to take another wife, he would have been more attentive to Faye and maybe brought her out of Fallow Creek for regular medical pre-natal check-ups when he was told that her pregnancy was high-risk.

He turned away from the window, his heart heavy. "I'm so sorry, Faye. Never again will I let that happen." Of course, he couldn't raise his wife from the dead, but he would make sure nothing and no one distracted him from the people he loved now. The people he had — his precious children. He'd let his heart be ensnared by Sarah's youth and beauty, and even though he knew Faye had been upset by his decision to marry Sarah — though she'd never said so — he'd ignored her feelings. After all, he was a man. In Fallow Creek, men could marry as many women as they wanted. It was what he'd believed the scriptures had said. What was preached there.

But he did not believe in that stupid doctrine anymore. After Rachel had shared the true gospel with him, he'd given his heart completely to Christ and those beliefs had fallen away. But unfortunately, it hadn't been soon enough to get him to his senses or move him to get Faye out of Fallow Creek before it was too late.

He sat on the sofa once more and stood up again when Bree's cries filled the air. He chuckled. This was her usual way of telling him she was awake and ready to be attended to. Felicia would arrive at the house any moment now to care for Bree, but he liked to be the first person beside her bed when she woke up.

He began to head toward her room and then stopped and braced himself as Josh raced toward him. His six-year-old son jumped into his arms, and Taylor hugged him tightly. He put Josh down again and ruffled his wavy, light brown hair, so like Faye's. "Hey, you're up! How did you sleep?"

"Good."

He took Josh's hand, and they made their way to the front of Bree's room. "What grand plans do you have for today, buddy?" he asked Josh.

"I still have three months before school starts," Josh said, grinning.

Taylor chuckled. "That wasn't what I asked. And you have three weeks before school starts. Are you excited about starting first grade?"

Josh didn't answer, and Taylor looked down at him.

"I don't want to leave you, Dad," Josh said, his voice filled with fear.

Taylor blinked and then stooped down and looked into his son's eyes. "You're not going to leave me. At least, not for long. It would just be like when I go to work, Josh. You'll be at school rather than in the house while I'm at work. You will love school. You'll see."

Josh said nothing more, but his eyes still showed he was afraid. It was the same look he had anytime Taylor had to go away on a business trip. Unfortunately, he had to leave for Tucson for another one today, and he wouldn't be back until next week.

He hugged Josh again and then straightened. "Let's go see your baby sister," he said, trying to sound cheerful for Josh's sake. He looked into the room. Bree had quietened down. She had pulled herself up, holding onto the bars of her crib, and was staring at him and Josh. The expression on her face made Taylor laugh. She had streaks of tears on her cheeks and she looked like she was wondering what on earth they were talking about that seemed more important than their coming to see to her. He lifted her from her crib and kissed her cheeks. "Good morning, baby girl." She felt wet, and he scrunched his nose. "You need a bath." He began to remove her pink onesie just as someone walked into the nursery.

"Morning," Felicia grunted, her usual way of greeting him.

"Good morning, Felicia." He smiled and shook his head when she edged him away and began to remove Bree's onesie.

Josh tugged at Taylor's pajama pants. When he bent down, Josh whispered in his ear, "She's so strict. She doesn't let me play with my toys in the mornings."

Taylor's smile faded and he sighed silently. It was not the first time Josh had told him Felicia was strict. Unfortunately, he couldn't do anything about it now. Since Josh had never mentioned her being violent or abusive in any way, he would leave his kids with her as he'd done a couple of times.

However, he probably needed to start looking for a nanny as soon as possible. His children's happiness was of the utmost importance to him.

Felicia held Bree in the crook of her arm and reached out with her other hand to take Josh's. Taylor shook his head and looked up at her. "I want to talk to Josh for a minute. You can go and give Bree her bath."

Felicia shrugged and left the nursery with Bree.

Taylor stooped again to look into Josh's eyes. "Tell me, Josh, apart from not letting you play with your toys in the morning, is there any other thing Felicia does that you don't like?"

"She doesn't make my pancakes the way Mom does." Tears filled Josh's eyes. It had been really hard explaining to him that his mother had died and was in heaven, but Josh had finally accepted the explanation after months of constantly asking about her.

Pain squeezed Taylor's heart, but he brushed it aside and focused on Josh. "I'm sorry about that." He smiled. "No one will ever be able to make pancakes the way your mother does... did. But I think if you give Felicia time, you will come to like her pancakes."

Josh shrugged.

Taylor ran his hand across Josh's head. "I have to go on another business trip..."

"No, Dad. I don't want you to go."

"I know. I don't want to leave you either, but I have to. I'll be away for about five days, and then I'll come back."

"Five days?" Terror filled Josh's face. "What if you don't come back, like Mommy?"

"Shh… don't say that. I will come back. That's a promise."

"I want to go with you."

Sadness flooded Taylor's heart. Josh looked so miserable. If only he could take Josh along. But he would be away for long business meetings daily and wouldn't be back to his room until late in the evenings. "That won't be possible," he said softly. "And Bree needs you here."

Josh sighed sadly, and Taylor hugged him, his heart aching. His business had flourished even more since he'd left Fallow Creek and the restrictions he'd had to work under in the community were gone. But he had to travel to different cities regularly, leaving his kids with the housekeeper. He always dreaded leaving them, but he had no choice for now.

He stood up straight before he could dissolve into tears and forced himself to smile at Josh. "I'll get you your favorite trucks, Josh. Would you like that?" *Great. Bribing your son.*

Josh nodded, but he did not smile.

The doorbell sounded, and Taylor ruffled Josh's hair and left the room. He went to the front door and opened it. His driver was standing there and greeted him.

"I'm going out of town today, Grant. Has Dave called to say he's at the airport?"

"Yes," Grant answered.

Taylor nodded. Dave, his efficient pilot, lived miles away and only needed to make the trip to the airport where Taylor's private jet was parked. Taylor had called him the day before to tell him he was going out of town today and would need him to arrive at the airport early.

Taylor glanced at the clock on the wall. It was still a quarter to eight. He'd told Dave they would be leaving by nine o'clock but his pilot always arrived at the airport about an hour earlier. "Thank you, Grant," Taylor said.

Grant nodded and left, and Taylor shut the door again. He went to shower and then dressed quickly. He left his bedroom with his duffel bag and walked to the living room. The time was a few minutes past eight now, but they had a long drive to the airport. He strode to the middle of the living room and waited for Felicia to bring Bree to him. Josh came first and hugged Taylor again. Felicia handed Bree to him, and he kissed her short wavy hair and soft cheeks.

Bree giggled and put her tiny arms around his neck. He rubbed her back and sighed. "I will miss you, little one." He handed her back to Felicia and looked down at Josh. Once again, his heart ached at how sad Josh looked. He bent down and said to his son, "After this trip, I'll take a long vacation until school starts so I can spend time with you and Bree."

Josh's eyes lit up. "Just us, Daddy?" He glanced at Felicia.

Taylor nodded. He whispered, "Felicia will take her own vacation, and you, me, and Bree will spend time alone. I promise. We'll have so much fun together."

"No one else? Just the three of us?"

For a long moment, Taylor couldn't say anything, overcome with emotion. Josh was asking the same thing his mother had done when she was alive and well. Whenever he'd seemed too busy and refused to take Josh out to the only park in Fallow Creek, his mother had always comforted him by telling him they would go to the park on the weekend and spend time together, just the three of them. Bree had not been born yet.

Once again, guilt gripped Taylor. Thinking back to those days, he'd been busy not just with work, but also with Sarah and their wedding plans, which he'd had to stall when Faye had grown very ill. Faye had looked pointedly at him whenever she'd said those words to Josh, and now Taylor knew without a doubt that she'd meant more than what she was saying. Even though women were not really allowed to voice their disapproval over their husband's choice to marry an additional wife, she was reminding him that he had two people that were the most important to him, and that just the three of them was, or should be, enough for each other. He'd been too blind to take note then, but not now.

He reiterated what he'd told Josh. "Just the three of us, Josh. No one will ever come between us again." He'd promised himself that he would never remarry after his wife died because he never wanted to feel that pain again if anything happened, nor expose his kids to that kind of loss. He had done Faye wrong when they were married, carrying on with Sarah. He would honor her memory and stay single... which was as he wanted it, anyway. Josh had no need to worry about anyone coming between them.

It was why he'd hired a fifty-something-year-old plain woman as his housekeeper. He wanted to stay away from any kind of temptation. Not that he would actually feel tempted again. That part of him that wanted that kind of love was dead, buried with his late wife. It would just be him and his kids now.

He stood up again. Josh was beaming now, happier than Taylor had seen him in a long time. "I can't wait for you to come back, Dad, so we can start our vacation together. Where will we go?" Josh began to hop.

Taylor laughed. "I don't know yet. We'll talk about it when I get back, okay?"

"Okay," Josh said happily.

Bree reached out for him as he began to turn around, but Felicia held her tight in her arms. When she started to cry, Taylor smiled sadly, waved to her and Josh and quickly left the house. In his car, Taylor closed his eyes and sighed as he leaned back in his seat. *Stop worrying, Taylor. They're safe with Felicia.*

But he couldn't stop. Every time he was out of town, he worried about his children. Not just about their physical safety, but their emotional well-being. Especially Josh's. But he was slightly less worried than he usually was. Josh had seemed happy after he'd told him he would take a vacation after this trip so they could spend time together. He would have to cancel any plans he'd made for the next month because his promise to Josh had been unplanned. But he would gladly do so. It was high time he took a vacation anyway. A family vacation sounded great. Maybe they didn't even have to go anywhere. Just stay in the house and enjoy each other's company.

A bittersweet feeling went through him as he recalled Josh's words. "Just the three of us, Dad?"

He smiled. Definitely just the three of them. He, Josh, and Bree. As it would always be.

THREE

Rachel shut her eyes in despair and slowly sat down on the sofa. This was not good. This wasn't good at all. She opened her eyes and looked at Sharon, the adolescent who had just brought the news of yet another departure from Fallow Creek. "You're telling me Nathaniel Grover has left Fallow Creek with his wives? I thought he was one of the people who didn't care if a woman was now the owner of this place?"

Sharon sighed, a morose look on her face. "He left with my sister, Jane. That's all I care about. I don't know if I'll ever see her again. My parents and other siblings are gone. Jane was the only one left. Now she's gone too, and I don't even know where because Nathaniel didn't tell any of the wives where they were going."

Rachel felt sick with guilt and worry. Since the events that had led to her to taking over Fallow Creek nine months ago, things had gone completely contrary to how she'd thought they would. She sighed. Maybe not completely. After she'd taken over, a few women from the community had felt emboldened and either left their polygamous lifestyles or left their families that were trying to force them into unwanted marriages. They all came to stay in the Restoration House, which Rachel had promptly renamed the House of Refuge. She and Keith lived there fully now and had since watched helplessly from the house as a mass of people left – or was it fled? – Fallow Creek. Sharon was not the only woman here with family members who had deserted the town. And it was all because of her.

No, Rachel. It's not because of you. It's because of their foolish pride.

She sighed sadly again. It didn't matter. She had taken over from Dennis, and a mass exodus from the town had begun. And now, people like Sharon had no more family members here and didn't know where they'd gone.

"Miss Rachel?" Sharon called, sounding concerned.

Rachel turned to face her. "I'm sorry, Sharon. I wish there was something I could have done to stop Nathaniel from taking your sister with him."

Sharon nodded, and her eyes filled with tears. "Those stupid men and their pride. When I came here, I asked Jane to come with me, and she kept saying she would. But she never found an opportunity to escape Nathaniel's ever-brooding presence. And now he's taken her to..." Her voice choked up and she bit her lip.

"I should have known this would happen," Rachel said. "I should have tried to do something to stop it all from happening." But there was nothing she could have done. After she and Keith had revealed the whole truth to the elders of the town and showed them the evidence of her ownership of the place, the exodus had begun immediately, starting with the elders. They'd told her nothing. No one protested, as she had been sure they would and as her stepfather had said. No one threatened her, not even when she began to call for the reformation of the town. They all just started leaving. When some women began to leave their families to come here to take refuge, the exodus intensified, and within a few months, most people had left. There were hardly any men in town now.

Except for Mike, her ex. As far as she knew, he stayed more as a statement of defiance to her than anything else. Despite that, she was glad he was still here. She didn't know what she would do if he upped and left one day, taking Emily, their daughter, with him.

Her heart twisted at the thought, and she drew a long breath.

Sharon sat beside her and put a hand on Rachel's shoulder. "I'm sorry for burdening you with my problems," she said. "You already have so much to deal with."

Rachel could not speak. She felt like the weight of the world was on her shoulders.

Sharon said, "I'll keep praying as you taught us and believe that God will bring my sister back here somehow. But you shouldn't blame yourself, Miss Rachel. You have done so much for the women here. You should know that." Sharon smiled at her and then stood up and left the apartment.

Rachel pressed her lips together as she thought about Emily. In the past eight months, she'd only seen her daughter twice, and both times in secrecy.

"Thank you, Lord, for Olivia," she whispered. In spite of Mike's anger and the threats he'd made to teach her a lesson if she ever aided Rachel in seeing Emily again, Olivia had still found a way to help her see her daughter.

But it wasn't enough.

Rachel cried out, pouring out the pent-up sadness she'd kept hidden deep inside her for months. Because of the great responsibility the Lord had given her, and because there had been so much to do, even though she'd been hurting because she couldn't see her daughter, she'd buried her feelings in her heart. She'd done so in order to focus on bringing the change she believed God wanted in this community. But now she couldn't hold it in anymore. Everything she'd believed God would do for her and Keith because they'd left everything they had and come here in obedience to Him had not materialized. Fallow Creek was a deserted town and she still didn't have her daughter.

"Lord, why?" she cried out and began to sob. Tears poured down her cheeks like torrents of rain, all the tears she'd held inside all these months.

The front door opened, and Keith came into the living room. He blinked rapidly when he saw her and rushed to her side. He folded her into his arms and held her tightly. "Rachel, sweetie, why are you crying?" he asked, his voice ringing with alarm.

"Keith, it's all falling apart. Everything we believed in hasn't come true. Instead, I have done more harm than good in taking over the leadership of this community." She told him what Sharon had said about Nathaniel Grover and her sister, Jane.

Keith rocked her in his arms. "Rachel, it's not true, you know. A lot of things we believed in have actually come true. This place, for instance. Some women came here looking for refuge after you took over Fallow Creek, and many of them have already received Christ into their hearts. I mean, that is a huge miracle."

She pulled away slightly to look into his dear face. He had been such a pillar of strength for her during the past months. She gave him a sad smile. "I just feel so responsible for everything that has happened. I would never have imagined that Fallow Creek would be almost deserted just months after I took over from Dennis Hamilton. Now many of the women here don't even know where their families are. And, worst of all, I'm in the same town as my baby daughter, but I'm not allowed to see her. When God told us to drop the custody case and come here, I thought I would at least be able to see Emily often. But I've only seen her twice in eight months. With everyone leaving, it'll only be a matter of time before Mike decides to leave as well. Then what will…?" She broke down again.

Keith pulled her into his arms and whispered words of comfort to her. But it did little to assuage her doubts and fears. They both could have gone to Mike's a long time ago and insisted on seeing Emily, but it wasn't possible. Even though all the squad guards had left town immediately after Rachel took over, Mike had hired goons from who-knew-where. Goons that kept everyone he didn't want near his house away. And she wasn't surprised, because people like Mike with a cupboard full of skeletons always needed men like that to protect him in order to feel safe.

She said more to herself than to Keith, "And to shut people like me out of my daughter's life."

"Rachel, I know it's hard for you to still be away from Emily, but we have to keep believing that God is faithful and that He will restore all the time you've lost with her. I don't know how God will do it, but He will bring Emily back to you — to us — in His time."

Rachel snorted. "And when is that?"

Keith ran his fingers slowly through her hair. "I don't know. But His time is always the best time. That sounds cliché, but it's true."

She shook her head. "I'm just so worried, Keith. What if Mike leaves Fallow Creek with Emily? Remember those dreams I told you about before God told us to move here? I told you I used to dream almost every night that Mike took Emily away and I never saw her again. I've started having those dreams again."

"Shh… Rachel! Stop torturing yourself. They're just dreams. What did you tell me God has been saying to you every time you ask about Emily?"

She sighed wearily. "All I hear is that He will work it all out."

Keith gave her a wide smile as though those words were all the proof she needed that Emily would be returned to her soon, never to be taken away again. But they both knew it wasn't the case. "See? The Lord will work it out, Rachel." His face fell when she didn't return his smile. "You know what? Why don't we pay Mike a visit again today?"

Rachel frowned and looked at him. "You know there's no point. We've done that so many times and it's made no difference." She remembered the last time she and Keith had gone to ask to see Emily. They had not been able to get anywhere near the house. Mike's new guards had stopped them and refused to let them go any farther. Mike had come out of his house and taunted them.

"Listen, Rachel, I don't care if you now own even the skies above us, you're not coming near my house or my daughter. I suggest you forget about Emily." He had pointed at Keith with a look of disdain. "You have your pastor now. Go and have a baby with him to replace her."

Anger had boiled hot in Rachel's heart, and she had tried to force her way past the guards but had failed.

He'd said, "The next time you try to force your way into my house to see my daughter, I will take her away from this town, and you'll never see her again."

"We can't do that, Keith. Remember the threat Mike made the last time we went to his house to try to see Emily?"

"Yes, but remember how God worked a miracle and opened a door for you to see her after that day. Because we went, Olivia secretly brought her here to you so you could see her."

"Still, it's too risky. Olivia was able to bring her that day because Mike traveled and there were still shops open in the community. She convinced the guards she was going to buy some groceries and then came here with Emily. Now all the shops are locked and everyone else she knows has probably left Fallow Creek. I doubt she'll be able to do what she did last time. If she's caught, Mike will carry out his threat, and I will never see Emily again."

"Yes. But this time, we will not be going to see Emily. We will go and see Mike."

Rachel tilted her head and stared at him. "I don't understand. Why would I want to see Mike and not Emily?"

"Just like you said, asking to see Emily will only anger Mike, and we don't want that. We will send a message through someone and ask to see him to discuss something important."

Rachel shook her head. "Mike won't buy that. And he will never agree to see us. What important thing do we have to discuss with Mike except for Emily?"

"A business proposal."

Rachel frowned. "What business proposal? And what does that have to do with my daughter?"

"Rachel, you own most of the houses in this town."

She nodded. "Yes, but not the new ones like Mike's, Taylor's, or Dennis's."

"I know. But the land it's built on belongs to you..."

"I can't ask him to move out. He won't even budge. Besides, I don't want to... because of Emily."

"I'm not saying you should ask him to move out. We know Mike loves his money and property. How about you offer him the land and one or two of the houses that were abandoned, including the lands they were built on? In exchange, all you ask is to be allowed to bring Emily here and take care of her as her mother. He can still see her anytime he wants."

Rachel blinked. "But what if the owner of the one of the houses I give to Mike comes back? What will I do?"

"That's unlikely. Aside from the fact that the houses actually belong to you, most of these men left because they didn't want to be beholden to you. They fully expected you to take possession of the houses when they left. If any of them come back, we can give them another empty house. But we'll cross that bridge when we get there."

Rachel bit her lip as she thought about what Keith was suggesting. He was right. In the years she'd been with Mike, she'd learned that he did like gathering property — both land and houses — but he had a special fondness for this house in Fallow Creek. But whether he would agree to their proposal was another thing. He was a terribly proud man. He'd said she had shamed him when she'd left him and married Keith. He had mostly kept Emily from her to punish her for disgracing him. That was why he'd stayed when others had left; to let her know that no matter what she now owned, she'd never get him to leave his beloved..."

She gasped. He did really love his house. Enough to remain here when others had left, even when the ultimate punishment for her would be to take Emily away to a hidden place where she would never see her daughter again. "You might be right, Keith. I don't know if it'll work, but it's worth a shot."

"Who should we send to deliver the message?" Keith said. "We can't send any of the young women here or who knows what Mike would do with her. And we can't go ourselves because the guards have been instructed to not let us anywhere near the house."

"I know who we can send. Gertrude is Mike's

new wife's sister. We can send her along with Cecelia, an older woman, and she can ask to see her sister and then send our message to Mike."

Keith nodded and got a piece of paper and pen from the desk in their bedroom. He came back to sit beside her on the sofa, and they wrote the letter to Mike together. Rachel took the note and went to look for Gertrude and Cecilia. She found Gertrude and asked her if she would be willing to do her and Keith a favor. When she told the young woman her plan, Gertrude eagerly agreed.

She called to Cecilia as she passed by them in the hallway. Cecilia had worn the same scowl as Margaret the first day Rachel had met the woman, and she'd thought her assistant would be no different in character from Margaret. But Cecilia had proven to be loyal and dedicated to Rachel and had been a huge help to her since she'd been made the leader of the Restoration House. She trusted that Cecilia would help carry out her plan now.

After she told Cecilia what she wanted and her assistant had agreed to go to Mike's with Gertrude, Rachel sent them along. She returned to the apartment she shared with Keith and sat beside him on the sofa.

"You've sent them to Mike's with the letter?" he asked.

"Yes."

"I guess all there is to do now is wait for his answer."

She nodded, unable to speak. Her future with Emily depended on Mike's response. If he agreed to their proposal, she would finally be able to hold Emily in her arms after so many months. Most of all, she would be able to see her daughter regularly. It was all she wanted in this world.

But if Mike refused and their proposal angered him, he might leave Fallow Creek with Emily and smash her heart into tiny bits. Then, no matter how much Keith tried to love her back to normal, she was sure he would never be able to put her heart back together again.

FOUR

Lily finished cooking dinner and served it on one of Sofia's favorite china plates. Today, she had not been in the mood to cook and had asked Sofia if she would eat the leftover omelet from this morning.

Sofia had pouted and begged her to cook. "I feel like eating that spinach pie you made the other day, and something else as well. Can you cook that? A lot of it, because I really like it."

Lily had sighed and agreed to cook. She liked to cook, but she just wanted to rest this evening as she'd been cleaning the house all day. Sofia liked a spotless house even though she was kind of messy. She carried the plates of Italian spinach pie and the bowls of tomato soup to the dining table and then went back to the kitchen to get the big bowl of fruit salad she'd made.

Sofia came into the dining room dressed in a tight black dress that barely covered her behind and a low cleavage that showed way too much of what should be covered. Her dark hair was down and her blunt bangs hung over her eyes. She had on her bright red lipstick.

Lily gazed at her in confusion. "Where are you going, Sofia? You told me to cook because you felt like eating a big dinner and yet you want to go out now? And are you going out dressed like that?"

Sofia glowered at Lily. "Stop asking me all these questions! I'll wear whatever I want to wear!"

Lily blinked in surprise. Sofia had never spoken to her like this.

"I'm sorry, Lily. I don't know what came over me." She looked down at the table. "You have done it again! It all looks and smells so good." She sat down at the table and began to dish the food.

Lily sat across from her. "I thought you were going out."

"No."

"Then why are you dressed like that?" Sofia glared at Lily again, and she held up her hand. "I'm sorry. I won't ask anymore. Let's pray, though, before you start eating."

Sofia ignored her and dug into her food.

Lily sighed and prayed over the food. She opened her eyes and dished out her own food and began to eat. They both ate without speaking to each other, which was rare because Sofia liked to talk. But Lily didn't mind today. She had a lot on her mind... like the fact that she'd gone job hunting online for two days without finding anything at all and that Sofia had not cared to listen when she'd told her about it. Still, she'd only been searching for two days. She was far from discouraged. Hopefully, she would be able to find something soon and start planning her life the way she wanted.

Which is how, exactly? a voice in her head asked.

She knew she wanted to get a job and one day find a way to convince her parents to leave Fallow Creek. By then she would have gotten an apartment, but for now she'd promised Sofia she would remain here.

But before then, what do you plan to do with your life?

She had not thought that far. All she knew was that she wanted to be totally independent, find a job, and then one day travel the world. But that day seemed really far.

"Lily!"

Lily looked up at Sofia. "Yes?"

"What were you thinking about? I asked you a question, but you didn't answer!"

Lily shrugged.

"Are you going for your usual walk this evening? I need you to get some things from the store."

"What do you need me to get for you?" Lily asked

"Umm, just a white T-shirt, a toothbrush, and boxers."

Lily frowned. "Boxers?"

"Yes."

"You wear boxers?"

"Will you help me get them or not?"

Lily sighed. "Okay. Let me finish my food and I'll be off."

"Thanks," Sofia said.

Lily studied her. She looked slightly edgy, but excited at the same time. What was she up to, anyway?

After she finished eating, Lily cleared her plate. Sofia was still sitting on her chair, her empty plate in front of her, looking at the wall, a dreamy look in her eyes. Lily looked at her for a minute and then carried the plates into the kitchen. She went to her bedroom, a granite-tiled spacious room with a queen-sized bed and an ornate full-length mirror that had been what Lily liked the most when she'd first come to live in this house. In Fallow Creek, women were discouraged from spending too much time in front of the mirror, as that was considered vanity. There were hardly any full-length mirrors around.

She stopped in front of the mirror and looked at herself. She was wearing shorts and a green T-shirt, and her long, auburn hair hung down her back. She had thought Sofia's dress was scandalous just now, but hers would be too in a place like Fallow Creek. She pulled off her shorts, and pulled on a pair of jeans and her boots. She grabbed her jacket and left the room with her purse.

Sofia was now sitting in the living room, the TV remote in her hand. Lily walked up to her, and Sofia handed her a credit card.

"So a white T-shirt, your size, toothbrush…"

"No, not my size. Large."

Lily raised her brows and stared quizzically at Sofia. "Large?"

"Yes, large, Lily."

"White T-shirt, boxers, toothbrush. Anything else?"

"Umm… maybe a box of chocolates. Any kind. And strawberries."

Lily felt a slight discomfort in the pit of her stomach, but she didn't want to ask for who or why Sofia wanted her to buy these things. She sighed and left the apartment.

As she walked on the sidewalk, she glanced at the buildings that lined both sides of the street. They were now familiar to her, but the first time she'd taken a walk alone after she'd moved in with Sofia, she'd been so busy admiring everything around her and marveling at how different the busy streets were from sleepy Fallow Creek, that she had lost her way. Thankfully, the buildings and stores she'd been intently studying and admiring when she'd gotten lost had also led her back to Sofia's. Now she could probably find her way around with her eyes closed.

She tucked her hands into her jeans pockets as she walked. Her usual walks helped her focus on her plans for the future and reminded her of all she'd gained, especially on days when she felt glum because she'd been thinking about all she'd lost.

She got to the end of the street, but rather than turn left to go to the store, she turned right. She began to walk while looking at the buildings. She had only passed by here once, and she remembered she had seen a church here. She continued to walk and then spotted it. It was a small church, but it had a steeple and there were cars in the parking lot. Her heart flooded with guilt as she came closer. She hadn't been to church since she'd come to Sofia's. Every time she talked about finding a church to attend on Sunday, Sofia always had some other activity she wanted them to do.

But come to think of it, it wasn't really them. It was her. Sofia always had some chore or other Lily had to do. She knew how it would look to anyone who found out about her life with Sofia. It would appear as if the girl was using her as a maid, but

Lily didn't mind the hard work. She was used to doing many more chores in Fallow Creek. What she did mind was the lack of freedom. Yes, she had a measure, but it wasn't the complete freedom she had envisioned for herself when she'd dreamed of one day escaping Fallow Creek, before she was banished from the community.

She stopped in front of the church and gazed at it with longing. She could hear the faint sound of singing, which meant there was a service going on now. She stood, wondering whether to enter, and then turned around. Sofia would be waiting for her things. She hoped those things were not for who she thought they were for, but she had a sneaky feeling they actually were. She had only met George once, because he and Sofia usually rendezvoused in some unknown place.

He was an older man, probably in his forties. Lily had thought it strange that George hardly ever came to the house to see Sofia, but now she knew why. Apparently, George's wife had found out about them and had threatened to leave him. He'd told her he would break it off, but he hadn't. Sofia told Lily she'd found out the woman had traced him to her house. "That old bag knows where I live," Sofia had said.

"Why are you telling me?" Lily had asked, disgusted.

"I was just thinking out loud."

Lily had gotten up from the living room and gone to her bedroom. She had covered her face with her hands. "Why oh why, Lord, has the same madness that I gladly left behind in Fallow Creek followed me here?"

You can move out of Sofia's.

"And where will I go if I move out?" she'd whispered harshly to herself and then sighed. She'd promised Sofia she would stay. Aside from that, she had very little money — just a part of the money her mother had given her on the day she'd left Fallow Creek. She doubted it would be enough to get a livable apartment. As long as Sofia continued to keep George out of sight so she didn't have to deal with him, she was fine.

But what if these things she sent me to buy are for George?

Lily hoped not. She didn't know what she would do if they were.

She got to the store where she and Sofia usually shopped for their household essentials. She quickly picked up everything Sofia had asked her to. She began to head to the counter to pay and then spotted a bag of potato chips and made a beeline for it. She picked it up and smiled widely. She had not seen this brand in years. She recalled eating it regularly as a child, sitting outside her house with her friend, Rachel Dalton. During those days, her friend's brother, Taylor, would come out of the house and, once in a while, tease her and Rachel, which had always left her in a daze. He was easily the most handsome boy in Fallow Creek, and girls swooned when he was near. Her eyes would always follow him as he walked away and then Rachel would tease her about her huge crush on her brother.

"I will marry him one day," she would whisper to herself, but even as a child she'd known the probability of that happening was nil. Parents in Fallow Creek were heavily involved in arranging marriages for their kids. Thankfully, her huge crush on him had disappeared as she grew up. Soon she knew she didn't want to ever get married, especially not to someone from Fallow Creek.

She picked up a bag of chips and smiled all the way to the counter, reminiscing about her childhood. Where was Rachel, who she'd reunited with just some months ago? And where was the handsome Taylor now?

Of course Taylor was still in Fallow Creek, married, and, from what she'd heard before she'd left, on his way to get a second wife. But she yearned to know where Rachel was now. They had renewed their friendship at the Restoration House, but Rachel had been kicked out of town shortly after. She paid for the things she'd picked up and left the store.

Outside, she felt a strong desire to go back to that small church, and she gave in. She would only stay for a short time. She might not even like the service.

But she did. She had never attended any church service where God's presence was so palpable. She stayed right to the end, basking in God's presence.

After the service, she left quickly, feeling refreshed and as though she could conquer whatever came her way. She checked her phone as she hurried back to Sofia's apartment. She had no messages and she heaved a sigh of relief. Usually, Sofia sent her a hundred messages whenever she went out.

But that might not be such a good thing. Maybe Sofia didn't send you a message because she is busy with you-know-who.

Lily brushed the thought aside. She didn't want

to think of such things when she was on such a spiritual high after that church service.

She got to the apartment door and opened it slowly, hoping Sofia was alone. Again, she let out a sigh of relief when she found Sofia sitting in the living room alone. She went up to her and handed her the bag of items she'd bought. "I'm sorry I didn't come back earlier, Sofia. The truth is, I..." She frowned as George walked into the living room, probably from Sofia's bedroom. He was shirtless and barefoot. Lily's heart sank.

"Hi! Lily, isn't it?"

Lily ignored him. Men like him were all that was wrong with this world. She looked down at Sofia again. "Can I speak to you in private?"

Sofia looked tired. "What is it, Lily? You can say whatever you want to say in front of George."

"I'd rather not." Lily took Sofia by the elbow.

Sofia mumbled and then stood up. She stopped in front of George and gave him a look that turned Lily's stomach. Lily pulled her along until they stopped in front of Sofia's bedroom.

"Why is he here, Sofia?" Lily said. "I thought you would keep him away knowing how I feel about the nonsense both of you are doing."

Sofia gave a harsh laugh. "Nonsense?" She glared at Lily. "In case you've forgotten, this is my house and not yours. I can bring whoever I want and do whatever I like here."

Lily sighed wearily. "Sofia, I don't have to tell you that what you're doing is very wrong. You know it is… in the depths of your heart. The man is married. Why can't you find someone who is single? Why do you have to be involved with a married man?"

"And why are you so judgmental, Lily? This is the thanks I get for putting you up in my house and for giving you everything you need? You constantly criticize and judge me. I wish you would just mind your own business and let me be!"

"Listen, Sofia. I know how awful all this is because I come from it all. You don't understand how much damage you are doing... how much you've already done. You said the man's wife found out about you and he lied to her that he'd broken it off. Do you even know how much suffering you have caused her?"

"Stop, Lily! Stop talking! I'm so tired of your constant criticism. If it wasn't for how useful you are, I would have shown you the door a long time ago!"

Lily blinked. "What?"

Sofia waved her hand. "It doesn't matter. Just please leave me alone. And don't talk to George at all. I beg you. I don't want anything spoiling our week-long staycation."

Lily's heart sank to her feet. "Your week-long staycation?"

"Yes!" Sofia sounded exasperated. "We're spending the week together here. His wife is out of town and his children are with the nanny."

Lily said slowly, "And where did he tell his wife he was going?"

Sofia shrugged. "I don't know. To a business conference or something." She narrowed her eyes. "Anyway, just stay out of George's way until the week is over."

Lily smiled sadly and nodded. She would stay out of his way and Sofia's, not just for the week, but permanently. There was no way she could in good conscience stay here with them in this house. She hadn't left the polygamous mess that was Fallow Creek to come here and wallow in the same thing. It didn't matter that she was not participating in it. She would be a part of it if she stayed because she would be condoning it, knowing exactly what her friend and her married 'boyfriend' were doing. She said to Sofia, "Thank you for everything you have done for me." She turned around and began to walk away.

"Lily!" Sofia called.

Lily did not turn around. She hurried to the room that had been hers for months and, as fast as she could, packed up the few things she had. She had meant what she'd said. Sofia had done so much for her. Most of the clothes she had now were bought by her friend because she'd had no suitable clothes to wear after she'd left the hospital. Sofia had fed, clothed, and housed her. But it was time for her to go and try to make a life of her own. It was going to be difficult and if the Lord didn't perform a miracle, she might end up on the streets after some time. But she had to leave this place.

Sofia barged into the room as Lily zipped up her suitcase. "Where are you going?" Sofia cried. "Please don't go, Lily. I'm really sorry for the way I spoke to you."

Lily smiled at her and shook her head. "I have to go."

Sofia folded her arms across her chest. "The reason you don't want to stay is because of George, isn't it?"

"You and George," Lily said simply.

"But I don't want you to go. Please stay. I need you."

"I can't. And you don't need me, except for chores." Lily carried her suitcase to the bedroom door.

"That's not true. What can I do to make you stay?"

Lily turned to look at her. "You can do the right thing and break up with George. Let him go back to his wife... or wherever he wants to go."

Sofia hugged herself as though she were freezing. "You know I can't do that."

Lily sighed. She went and hugged Sofia tightly. "I'll miss you."

"But where will you go?"

"I don't know yet. Maybe to a motel."

"Wait here. Let me get you some money to tide you over until you find a job."

"No, Sofia! Don't..." She sighed when Sofia ignored her and left. She picked up her suitcase and hurried to the living room. She glanced at George, who was sprawled on the couch, and said softly, "You should go back to your wife, George."

She opened the door, walked out, and shut it quietly behind her.

FIVE

Rachel felt someone touching her hair and opened her eyes. She smiled at Keith, who sat next to her, gazing at her, and then gasped. She sat up straight and looked at her husband. He looked worried. "I fell asleep," she said. "Are they back? Are Cecilia and Gertrude back?"

"Yes," Keith said softly. He sighed, and her heart sank at the look on his face. "They said Mike was angry when they sent our message to him. He sent them…" Keith stopped speaking and sighed loudly again.

"Keith, what is it?" she cried. "What message did Mike send back to us?"

"He said he had warned us about trying to get Emily back. He's going to take her out of Fallow Creek in a few days and you'll never see her again."

Rachel cried out, and Keith gathered her in his arms. "I'm so sorry, Rachel. This was my plan. I have to find a way to make it right."

Rachel pushed away from him. "You can't make it right, Keith. Mike is the devil himself. If he's made this decision, nothing will change his mind. I have a feeling he might not even be in Fallow Creek anymore." Tears fell down her cheeks and she began to panic. "Maybe he's even taken Emily away already. Maybe he's..."

"Rachel, calm down. Mike wouldn't have taken her. I think there's still some hope to get Emily."

Rachel brushed away her tears and looked at him. "What hope?"

"Cecilia and Gertrude said Olivia wants to meet with you. She didn't say why exactly, but it's probably to do with Emily."

Rachel sprang up from her seat. "Then what are we waiting for? Let's go. Where does she want to meet?"

"Wait, Rachel. Sit." Keith held her hand. "I didn't want to tell you about Olivia's message because I knew you'd want to go without first thinking about it."

Rachel looked at Keith as though he were speaking another language. "What are you saying, Keith? I have an opportunity to see Emily, and you don't want me to take it?"

"I just want us to be careful. Think about it, Rachel. Olivia asks us to come to the house just after her husband says he's going to take Emily away to punish you and doesn't say why. After Gertrude left, Cecilia told me it was actually her sister, Davina, and Olivia who asked us to come to the house, and Mike was somewhere near. As you have told me before, Gertrude's sister is not exactly allies with Olivia and loves Mike. Do you think she would want to help us?"

"Are you saying that it might be a trap?"

"Yes. That's what I'm saying. Mike might have set them up to do this. I don't know what he wants to do when we get there, but it won't be to throw us a welcome party, I'm sure of that."

"But Olivia wouldn't do that to me. She's been so helpful, sneaking Emily out of the house a couple of times so I could see her. Why would she suddenly want to betray me?"

"Because she loves Mike. Maybe for once Mike paid her some attention and it made her complicit in his plan to trap us somehow. I know it sounds paranoid, but it's possible. We're talking about Mike Cadwell here."

"So what should we do, Keith? I can't just sit and wait for Mike to take my daughter out of Fallow Creek to somewhere I'll never see her again."

"I'm not suggesting you do. But just going to Mike's and being captured would be even worse. Not only would you not get to see Emily again, who knows what Mike would do to us? I think I should go... alone. You stay here. I'll go and find out if Olivia and Davina's request to see us is a trap. If I don't come back, you know something has happened to me, and then you can find help."

"No!"

"Rachel..."

"No, I won't let you go to Mike's alone. And I want to see Emily now if Olivia's plan is truly to help me see her. I wish we could go to the police in Prospect, but it would take forever to get them here, and Mike will have gone by then. I think we should send someone to Prospect and tell all the women here where we're going. We'll let Mike know we've told everyone where we are, and have a girl at the police station in Prospect to alert them if the women here don't call in an hour to tell her we're safe."

"But if Mike wants to harm us, he would do it and then disappear before any police officers got here," Keith said.

"The police would hunt him down. He knows he might not get far. I don't think he would want to risk getting caught by the police. And he fears law enforcement agents as much as he hates them."

Keith didn't say anything for a while, and then he nodded. "Okay. We'll go together. But we still don't know what we're going to do about Mike's intention to leave Fallow Creek with Emily."

"Maybe if I can tell him face to face that I'm serious about giving him the land and houses, he might reconsider. I can't think of anything else."

Keith nodded and stood up. Rachel did too, and he took her hand. She picked up her phone from the bedside table and frowned when she saw a missed call from a number she didn't know.

"Yes, I remember. Someone called while you were asleep, but I wasn't sure if I should pick up."

"Did Taylor call me back?" she asked, hopeful.

"No," Keith said.

She sighed. They could use his help, but he had refused to take any of her calls or answer any of her messages for months. She was beginning to worry about him. The only thing that calmed her heart and let her know he was okay was the fact that his phone still rang and he'd changed his voice message twice during the nine months she'd been calling him. But she wasn't sure he was well or that his family were. He had just upped and taken his wife and son away from Fallow Creek one day, before the exodus out of town had even begun.

She and Keith left their small apartment and went in opposite directions. They'd had to do this once before — tell everyone where they were going when Mike had called her for a meeting at his house. She and Keith had gone together, of course, but had not entered his house. They had stood in front while Mike had come out to meet them. That was the day he'd told her he'd found out Olivia had allowed her to see Emily again and that he would take Emily away if they tried to do the same thing after that day.

The women in the house greeted her warmly as she approached them. She told all the women she saw that she was going to Mike Cadwell's with Keith. After that, she called Cecilia to an empty room and told her about their plan.

"Sure, I'll go now."

Rachel put her hand on Cecilia's shoulder and smiled at the thirty-four-year-old woman. "Thank you, Cecilia. You've been such a huge help to me and Keith."

Cecilia bowed. "I'll go now," she said and walked away.

Rachel went to the common room and smiled when she saw women lounging and talking. The house was messier than when Margaret had run it, but the women here seemed happier. The awful renewal classes had stopped, and they had regular Bible studies instead. Women took turns reading the Bible and sharing what they had learned with everyone.

She felt someone come behind her and turned.

Keith put his arm around her and whispered in her ear, "You still think you've not done much for this place or the community? Look at how much change has happened here and how much happier all the women are. You keep worrying about the people who have left the community, but we should focus on those who are still here. The people who stayed."

Rachel smiled and turned into his arms. She hugged him tightly. "You always know what to say to make me feel better." She kissed him. "Are you ready to go?"

"Yes. As ready as I'll ever be."

They left the house together and made their way through the almost deserted town. She couldn't help feeling sad again. The bustling town she'd grown up in was now empty because of her. Yes, most of the women in the House of Refuge seemed happier, but many who had left hadn't had a choice. They left with their so-called husbands and with parents who didn't care if they wanted to leave or not.

All the way to Mike's house, Rachel stared at the abandoned homes, feeling overwhelmed and a little confused. Most of them now belonged to her, but she didn't know what to do with them. Every time she'd asked the Lord for guidance, all she'd heard in her heart was to wait for the right time. But what did that mean? When was the right time?

They finally began to approach Mike's house — the large five-bedroom home she'd lived in for four years before she'd finally left Mike. He had just repainted it, and it looked like a brand-new home. Hopefully that meant he was still planning to stay in Fallow Creek for a long time to come so she could continue to see her daughter, even if for now it wasn't as regularly as she wanted and in secret. But then again, knowing Mike, it might mean nothing, or even be a deliberate move to make everyone believe he was staying, especially her, so no one would expect it when he suddenly disappeared with Emily.

Fear flooded her heart again, and she tried to push it away. But it remained. As though Keith sensed her dread, he took her hand and squeezed it, smiling his encouragement. Today, there were more guards than the last time they were here, which didn't surprise her much. One of them, a beefy guard who she guessed was their leader, walked up to her and Keith, a scowl on his face.

"Yes, can I help you?" he asked, looking at them as though he'd never seen them before, even though they'd seen him the last two times they were here.

"We're here to see Olivia, Mike's wife," Rachel said. "She asked us to come."

The guard shook his head. "We only take orders from the man of the house, and Mr. Cadwell didn't tell us you were coming."

Keith said, "Why don't you send one of your men to go ask him?"

Rachel pressed her lips tightly together. It was a bold suggestion, seeing as it wasn't Mike who had invited them. She'd thought that Mike would be out of town this evening and that was why Olivia had asked them to come. Apparently, he was still around. She felt a slight foreboding. That might mean Keith's suspicions were right, and they were about to walk into a trap. But then, would the guards stop them from going into the house if that were the case? If Mike meant to harm them, surely he would instruct his guards to let them through immediately? Or this might just be a deflection, so they would not suspect anything was amiss.

The guard did not move. Rachel sighed loudly. The front door opened, and Olivia stepped out. When she waved her hand to them, Rachel shook her head and pointed at the guard who had refused to let them get any closer to the house. Olivia approached, and Rachel watched the expression on her face closely, trying to decipher what she was thinking; if she had set them up or not. She couldn't read anything from the woman's face. She expected Olivia to pull her aside and tell her the secret location where she would bring Emily so Rachel could see her. Instead, Olivia said loudly, "Come into the house, Rachel. And you too, Keith."

The beefy guard's scowl deepened. He looked pointedly at Olivia and said, "Mr. Cadwell did not tell us to let anyone into the house. In fact, he gave us specific instructions never to let these two near the property."

Olivia narrowed her eyes as she stared at him. "'These two,' as you call them, own most of Fallow Creek, and Mike asked me to call them here for a meeting about the town."

The guard frowned suspiciously just as Rachel did the same. He said, "Still, we have instructions to..."

"Are you saying I'm lying?" Olivia glared at the guard. "Do you want to come into the house and ask Mike if he really sent me to bring them in?"

The guard shook his head. "Okay." He eyed Rachel and Keith and glanced at Olivia before looking at them again. "You can go in."

Rachel followed Olivia, Keith beside her. She still didn't know what to think. She'd not been allowed into the house since she'd come back to Fallow Creek, and now Olivia was asking her and Keith in. If Mike found out that they had come into his house through Olivia's instructions, they would all be in trouble.

Olivia herself would be in the most trouble if that happened. Rachel was beginning to lean more toward believing that all this, including the guard's refusal to let them in, was a ploy. But she hoped with all her heart that it wasn't. She yearned to see her daughter now much more than she feared for her own safety.

They entered the house, and Rachel looked around the big living room. The inside of the house had not been repainted like the outside. Everything, at least here in the living room, still looked the same as when she'd left.

She sat beside Keith on the sofa, expecting Mike to step out at any moment with his annoying smirk and tell them they'd walked into his trap more easily than he'd thought. But Mike didn't come, and neither did Olivia go to bring Emily for her. Instead, she sat on the couch facing them and began to talk about how much Fallow Creek had changed. She talked non-stop, and Rachel knew her enough to see she was nervous about something.

Something was wrong. There was something very strange about all this. She was pretty sure now that she and Keith had walked into a trap... but there was something else as well. She wanted to tell Keith what she thought, but from the look on his face, he was already thinking the same thing. Any moment now, he would tell her they had to leave, but she didn't want to in spite of her suspicions. If there was any shred of hope that she could see Emily today, she would take it. Besides, they had their plan and had already sent someone to the police station in Prospect. If Mike made any move to harm them, they would let him know about that.

When she'd finally had enough of Olivia's prattle, she said, "Where's Emily, Olivia? I want to see her."

Olivia wrung her hands, a worried look on her face. She looked back as though she were expecting someone, and Rachel blinked.

She stood up. "Where is my daughter, Olivia? Where is she?"

Keith held her hand. "Maybe we should go."

"I'm not going without seeing my daughter."

Olivia looked back again, and Rachel screamed at her. "I know you're planning to hurt us. But it won't work because..." Her mouth fell open as Mike walked, or rather, stumbled into the room with a man holding him firmly from behind. His hands were bound behind him, his mouth gagged. His eyes bulged when he saw Rachel and Keith and he began to struggle, but the man held him tightly.

Rachel blinked as she recognized the man. His beard was even bushier than the last time she'd seen him. It was Daniel, who had been one of the leaders of the notorious Security Squad guards and Taylor's childhood friend. This time, he was dressed not in the usual squad fatigues, but in jeans and a black T-shirt. She'd thought all the Squad members had left Fallow Creek, but apparently not. She turned to look at Mike, who was still staring at her with rage, and shook her head in confusion.

Keith said, "What on earth is happening here?"

Olivia turned to Rachel and Keith and said, "There are people I want you to meet. It might be strange and..."

Rachel cut in as she looked at Mike. "What could be stranger than this?"

Olivia turned around, facing the entrance to the kitchen. "Davina! Please bring them out."

About eight women walked into the living room, their expressions fearful. Rachel recognized most of them. All of them except for Davina were Dennis Hamilton's wives.

Olivia faced Rachel. "You know them?"

Rachel nodded, perplexed.

"When you took over the town and Dennis disappeared, they all went into hiding. Actually, they were all staying in the abandoned house where you and Keith lived when you came back to Fallow Creek. I happened to find out when I saw one of them coming out from there and then discovered they all lived there, including their children. It was not a pretty sight."

She studied Rachel's face. "They told me they were living there because they were afraid you would drive them out of Fallow Creek because of what Dennis did to you and your family, or even harm them in some way out of revenge. I told them you were definitely not like that, and I promised to give them an audience with you. Their kids are upstairs with mine. Please tell them that you mean them no harm."

One of the women, whom Rachel knew as Dennis's first wife, said to her, "Please. We know our husband was cruel, and we don't deserve anything from you. But we and our children don't have anywhere to go. This town is our home and has been for…"

"Stop!" Rachel cut in. The women looked anguished. "I certainly do not hold anything against any of you. How could you think I would? I don't even hold a grudge against Dennis. I chose to forgive him months ago. But you and your kids did absolutely nothing wrong. I would never think of sending you out of town. You all can go back to your home. It is yours and your children's."

The women's faces lit up. "Thank you!" they said in unison.

Rachel went and hugged each of them. Mike grunted loudly, but everyone ignored him.

One of the women, the one who looked like the youngest, said to Rachel, "I don't want to go back to the house." She looked down and muttered, "I want to come to the Restoration House."

Another one, a girl with big, curly hair, nodded. "I do, too. I don't want to go back to Dennis's house since he's not alive anymore."

Rachel grinned. "You're both welcome to stay in the House of Refuge."

The curly-haired woman said, "Helen has no kids, but I have two children. Will there be space for them as well?"

Rachel looked at Keith, and he smiled cautiously at her.

Olivia said, "You've been telling me to leave Mike for so long and now I am ready to. I want to come and stay at the House too, but you know I have two active boys. Will I be able to live there with them?"

Mike grunted even louder, but they all still ignored him.

Rachel bit her lip as she thought about what to do. The House of Refuge only had female residents. Children didn't typically stay there, and it was not ideal for kids. An idea suddenly came to her, and she said to Keith, "You know I've been asking the Lord what to do with all those abandoned houses. I think I now know what he wants us to do with them."

Keith smiled at the curly-haired girl and looked at Rachel. "She and Olivia can stay in two of those houses with their kids."

Rachel nodded. "Yes. And other women who come to Fallow Creek with their children can stay in the houses as well. They will be extensions of the House of Refuge... but for families."

The women thanked her again, but she waved off their thanks. She said to Olivia, "Now, Mike. I know why and how you got him tied up..." She looked at Daniel, "but what do you plan to do with him? You know how he is. He'll not take this lying down."

Olivia shrugged.

Rachel stared at her. "Surely, you don't plan to leave him here tied up like this? He won't survive if you do."

Olivia looked horrified at Rachel's words. "Of course I won't leave him here! I still love him in spite of everything. And he is the father of my children." Her voice was pleading. "Maybe you can take him to the Restoration House. I will definitely not be able to manage him on my own, and I don't want to stay with him anymore. At the House, there are many people there who can hold him down so he doesn't escape."

"I can't take Mike to the House of Refuge!" Rachel shook her head vehemently. "Maybe we should hand him over to the police."

Mike grumbled, and Keith said, "On what charges, Rachel? Olivia's right. We can take Mike to the House. I'll watch him, and Daniel can come and stay there as well. We'll make sure he doesn't try to escape."

"Will you lock him up in the House?" Olivia looked worried.

"We have no choice," Keith said. "We won't bind him, but he will be confined to a room in the House until we know what to do with him."

Rachel turned to look at Daniel again. "I thought you had left Fallow Creek."

"I came back," he said and looked over at Davina before turning away.

"So, Davina. I thought you liked being married to Mike. Why did you decide to help Olivia with her plans, and are you still staying with Mike after all this?"

Davina sighed. "Two months ago, my sister Gertrude told me everything you taught about the gospel and God's real desire for marriages in the Restoration House. I gradually began to see that Mike wasn't really my true husband and that I was living out of God's will. I wanted to do the right thing but didn't know how. I knew I had to apologize to Olivia and tell her how I was feeling because she was the first wife, the one who I had usurped and treated badly for a long time because of my ignorance. I told her I wanted to leave Mike, and she confessed that she wanted to as well. When she saw Dennis's wives in that abandoned house, we knew we had to do something."

She looked over at Daniel and smiled sweetly. "Daniel had come back to Fallow Creek because…" She glanced at Mike and then looked at Rachel. "I told him about our plan and predicament, and he promised to help. He got into the house under the guise of wanting to offer his services to Mike. He helped us overpower Mike and bind him."

Rachel nodded, fully understanding everything.

"So the main question no one is asking…" Keith looked at Olivia, "…is how we are all — including the children — going to leave this house when there are half a dozen armed guards outside."

Olivia leaned forward. "I've been married to Mike for a long time. I know every inch of this house. There's a trap door in the cellar. No one knows about it except for Mike and me. It leads to a very long passageway that will take you a distance away from the house and property. There is an SUV parked near the end of the passageway. A getaway car. That was how the children and I got out when we fled from Fallow Creek a year ago on Mike's instructions." She smiled at Rachel. "Because of you."

Rachel listened in shock. She'd had no inkling about any of this when she was with Mike and lived here.

Mike began to struggle wildly, and Daniel held him down.

Olivia glanced at Mike and said, "Daniel will drive us in batches to the House of Refuge, starting with the children."

Rachel looked up the staircase. "Talking about the kids, where's Emily?"

Olivia nodded at Davina and Helen, and they raced upstairs.

Olivia said, "Daniel, please take Mike to that inner room, because of the kids. So they don't see him like this."

Daniel nodded and pulled Mike up. Mike struggled again, but Daniel held him firmly and pushed him out of the living room.

A minute later, Davina descended the stairs with Emily in her arms. Olivia's boys followed her, and Helen herded about a dozen kids down the stairs.

Rachel's heart leapt with joy. She opened her arms wide and hugged Emily to herself when Davina deposited her daughter in her arms. "Oh, my darling." She kissed Emily's cheeks. "You look so big."

Emily giggled and said, "Mama," and Rachel felt like her heart was going to burst with joy and love for her daughter. "I didn't know she was talking now."

"Oh…" Olivia chuckled. "She talks non-stop now. What she says hardly makes any sense to anyone around, but that doesn't stop her from going on and on."

Rachel laughed with happiness. When Keith came over to look at Emily, she turned and kissed him. Tears fell down her cheeks. "She knows I am her mother, Keith. In spite of what Mike did to try to separate us from each other, my Emily knows she is mine."

Keith kissed both her cheeks and wiped her tears away with his thumb. He looked down at Emily and kissed her little nose. He tickled her, and she wailed with laughter. "Hey munchkin, how are you?"

Emily smiled widely at him and then launched into a full tale in her baby talk. Everyone laughed, including the children.

Rachel's heart felt full, and she silently gave God thanks for this miracle. Now she didn't have to be separated from her daughter ever again. There was still the issue of the mass exodus and trying to help some of the girls in the House of Refuge figure out where their loved ones had moved to, but she would take everything one step at a time. She would trust that God, who had reunited her with her daughter permanently now, would do the same for those girls. No matter how long it took.

The children soon began to run around the living room while their mothers tried to quiet them down. Olivia said, "I guess it's time for everyone to go." Her eyes traveled round the living room. "I'll miss this house, but not the things I had to endure here." She said to Davina, "Go and get Daniel from the guest room. Tell him it's time to go. He'll take the kids and some of the women here to the Restoration House, which we are now calling the House of Refuge. Keith, Rachel and I will watch Mike and will leave last."

Davina nodded and left.

Rachel smiled and kissed Emily again. "Thank you, Lord," she whispered. "Thank you for everything."

SIX

The meeting with his clients finally ended, at least for the day, and Taylor strode out of the hotel conference room. It was only the second day of the series of business meetings he and his clients had scheduled for the week, but he already missed Bree and Josh terribly and was ready to go home to them.

As usual, he wished with all his heart that he could bring them on his business trips, but that would not be possible. If Faye were still alive, he would still miss them, but he would not be so worried about them, knowing they were in good hands. Felicia seemed efficient and firm, but she was hardly nurturing, as a mother would be. He'd vowed to be a mother and father to his children, but going on all these business trips would not allow that to happen.

He stepped into the elevator to go up to his hotel room and then changed his mind. He didn't feel like being alone in his room right now, no matter how luxurious it was. He glanced at his wristwatch. It was just five o'clock in the evening. He felt like going for a walk.

He punched the lobby button instead and rode the elevator down. Exiting, he walked briskly through the elegant lobby of the posh Tucson hotel he stayed in whenever he was in this city. He smiled and nodded at the concierge and shook his head when he was asked if he wanted a limo brought to him.

He began to walk down the street and then remembered he'd seen packets of his favorite brand of potato chips through the window of a department store on the day he'd arrived in Tucson. He'd been so excited to see the snack as he'd not seen it for years and had made up his mind to get some before he left for California. But the store was a pretty long walk from here.

He paused for just a second and then continued walking. Those chips were worth the long walk. From what he remembered, they were really, really good.

As he walked, he kept thinking about Josh and Bree, worrying about not spending enough time with them. Finally, too pained to continue to focus on his children, he shifted his thoughts to his sister. She had not sent him a message today, thankfully. Whatever changes were going on in Fallow Creek, it seemed she and that new husband of hers were at the center of it. He recalled the amazing story she'd told him of how God had told her and her husband to move there, and how He had made a way for them to do so, providing everything they needed. She wanted him to return to Fallow Creek now. He would be forever grateful to her for sharing the full gospel with him and leading him to the cross and away from the dead religion he'd had before that, but he was never going back to that town.

He kept walking and soon realized that the store was farther than he had thought. The buildings he passed began to deteriorate in appearance, and he entered a neighborhood that would be termed as a slum. He blinked in surprise. He'd been reading a financial journal in the limo that had taken him to his hotel the day he'd seen the store that sold his favorite chips and had not looked up long enough to realize it was in such a rundown area. There were abandoned cars and houses everywhere, and graffiti even on some clearly occupied homes and business places.

He passed a group of children playing way too close to the busy street and kept walking in the direction he remembered the store was in. He was good with directions and locating buildings, which was probably because of what he did for a living. He soon found the store and entered.

He walked down the aisles searching for the chips and finally saw the bright red-and-blue wrapper at the end of the aisle where he stood. A young woman was there, putting several bags of the chips into her cart. He hurried over, slightly afraid that there would be none left for him before he got there. But the closer he got, the less focused on the chips he became. His eyes were fixed on the petite young woman with waist-length, auburn hair and a perfect figure. But it wasn't just her appearance that drew him. She looked really familiar. She raised her head and looked at him, and he sharply sucked in his breath. It was Lily Hunter, his childhood neighbor.

He had not seen her up close in years except for the day at the construction site in Fallow Creek. He had turned around because he felt someone looking at him, and there she had been, gazing intently at him. She had walked away quickly, and he had gone back to what he was doing. But for a short while after, he couldn't get her out of his mind. He'd finally succeeded in doing so and then totally put her out of his mind. Faye had been alive then, and he'd also been involved with Sarah. There had been no space for a third woman.

His heart did a flip once more. She looked even more breathtaking than she had that day, dressed in a fitted white shirt and jeans that showed off her lovely figure. He chided himself. There was still no space in his heart now.

Her eyes were as round as saucers as he reached her, and they shone with recognition. He gave her a small smile, and she blinked rapidly.

"Lily Hunter," he said, trying not to sound too excited to see her. He cringed inwardly. He sounded a little cold. He adjusted his voice. "How are you, Lily? It's such a pleasure to see you here." *Great. Now I sound way too excited. Dial it down, Taylor.*

Lily looked shocked and she didn't say anything for a short while. And then she found her voice. "Taylor Dalton? How come you're here?"

"I should ask you the same thing," he said with a chuckle. Before he could stop himself, he said, "You look great, Lily."

Her expression turned slightly concerned, and she took a step back. She gave him a cautious smile, and he wondered why she looked like she was getting ready to flee. Did he look creepy or did he have something on his face that scared her? He impulsively touched his cheek and then quickly put his hand down.

They stood for a few seconds looking at each other in awkward silence. He pointed at her chips. "I see you had the same idea that I did. I saw these potato chips from the window when I was driving past this store yesterday. I knew I had to get them."

The smile she gave him now melted his insides, but it made him a little wary. "I was so happy the first time I saw them. It was actually in a different store near where I used to live. It just transported me back to when we were kids. I had to get a bag, and I've now developed a dangerous daily craving for them. Thankfully, I found this store that sells them, and I decided to buy a large stash." She laughed and his pulse quickened.

He smiled at her. "Do you remember how you used to sit outside the house with Rachel eating these chips, and how I used to come steal them right from your hands?"

She laughed again. "Yes. Rachel and I would chase you as far as we could, but you were always too fast for us to catch up. You were so mischievous then, Taylor."

"Says the girl who used to climb trees with all the boys and then pretend that she had fallen from one of them and died when her mom came out looking for her." He laughed and shook his head as he gazed at her brown eyes sparkling with mirth.

"I was a tomboy, wasn't I?" She put another bag of chips into her cart. "It was so weird how close Rachel and I were then, because she was such a girly girl." She stopped smiling. "Talking about Rachel,

I really miss her. I was at the Restoration House when she was brought there and we renewed our friendship. I was happy when I heard that she'd left Fallow Creek. Even though she was banished, she'd wanted to leave town for a long time. It was a blessing in disguise. It was so sudden, her banishment. I don't know where she went, though I think it might have been to a place called Destiny she told me a lot about. Do you know where she is?"

Taylor nodded. "She's back in Fallow Creek."

Lily's mouth fell open. "What? Why? How?"

He gave her a very brief version of what Rachel had told him.

"Wow!" Lily looked up with a thoughtful expression on her face. "So Rachel left Mike and married the man she loved. I'm so happy for her. But at the same time, I know she must have gone through a lot. The men in Fallow Creek are not very forgiving when they're spurned. They are such…" Lily stopped talking and turned away from him.

He sighed. He knew what she wanted to say. He had been one of those men and had believed the same things they did until just recently. "It's okay, Lily. You can say what you want to say. It won't offend me. I'll probably agree with you."

She faced him fully, a suspicious look on her face. "I'd rather not," she said. "Anyway, do you have a number where I can reach Rachel? I would really like to talk to her."

"Yes, I have her number." He brought out his phone and went to his contact list. He found her number and gave his phone to Lily. "Here it is."

She brought out an old phone from her pocket

and began to type Rachel's number in. He couldn't take his eyes away from her until she looked up at him and handed him his phone. "Thanks," she said, smiling.

He put his phone in his pocket and said, "You haven't told me why you're here… out of Fallow Creek."

She gave him that suspicious look again and said, "You didn't hear? I was banished like Rachel."

He raised his brows, a look of surprise on his face. "I didn't hear anything. What happened?"

She shifted slightly toward him as a woman holding a little girl passed by. He involuntarily inhaled her sweet flowery scent and his heart thudded.

"I didn't want to get married, but I was so tired of living in that Restoration House that I gave in to my parents' demands and told them I would marry whoever they wanted. But the idea of marrying a man I didn't love, especially one who might have other…" She stopped talking again.

"Other what?"

She shrugged.

"Tell me, Lily," he said softly.

She sighed and turned her face slightly away. "Other wives. The man they wanted me to marry turned out to be Dennis Hamilton, and I knew I couldn't do it. I was ready to go back to the Restoration House rather than marry him…" Her voice faded as she faced Taylor fully. "And please don't tell me other girls in the community would have given their right arms to marry him."

"I wasn't going to."

"He was offended, of course, and decided I had

to be sent away so I didn't corrupt other women in Fallow Creek. I would have been thrilled to leave if it weren't for the fact that he said I could never return and would never see my parents and sister again." Tears formed in her eyes and a look of anguish took over her face.

It took everything in him not to take her in his arms and try to comfort her. He knew a little of the pain she was going through. "I'm so sorry," he said. He wanted to tell her he could go back and speak to Dennis Hamilton on her behalf, but there was no use. He had tried to reason with the man and the elders on behalf of Rachel, but they hadn't listened and had still banished her. Rachel had been able to enter the community again only because God had performed a huge miracle. God was Lily's only hope to see her parents again.

"And you, Taylor. Why are you here? On business?"

"Yes." He wanted to tell her he'd moved away from Fallow Creek because his wife had died, but he didn't want to talk to her about Faye. He didn't feel like talking to anyone about Faye at this time.

Her eyes suddenly lit up and she beamed. "Can you send a message to my parents for me when you go back?"

He felt conflicted. He wanted to help her, but the thought of going back to that community where his wife had died, the place he partly blamed for taking her life, was too much to bear. A man walked by gazing at Lily, and Taylor glowered at him. The man looked away quickly, and Taylor chided himself once more. She did not belong to him in any way. Another man could look at her.

"Taylor?"

"Oh… sorry." He glanced at his wristwatch and his eyes fluttered. "Wow! We've been standing here talking for almost an hour. We should go." She did not move, and he sighed. "I don't live in Fallow Creek anymore, Lily."

Her jaw dropped, and she looked shocked. "You? How come?"

"It's a long story. I'd rather not talk about it right now."

"So you have moved your son and wife — or is it wives — out of the community? Where do you all live now?"

"Northern California." She thought Faye was still alive and she'd clearly heard about his misguided engagement to Sarah Lowery. He did not correct her assumptions. There was no use. After today, he would probably never see her again.

She nodded and he blinked. His heart skipped a beat. Was it disappointment he saw in her eyes? She'd just told him she didn't want to marry someone who already had a wife and she clearly thought he was still married. Why would she care where he lived unless she had designs on him? His guard immediately rose up and he told himself to calm down.

Get over yourself, Taylor Dalton. She probably looks disappointed because she needs you to send regular messages to her parents for her. He had to try to help her somehow. But how would he do that when he'd vowed never to go back to their old community?

She looked broken. "So you'll never go back to Fallow Creek, even to visit anyone there?"

He sighed. "I don't know when I will go back there, but give me your phone number. If I ever plan to, I will call you, and you can send me a message for your parents."

She still looked sad but slightly hopeful. "Thank you," she said.

He brought out his phone, and she called out her number while he keyed it into his contacts. "Lily...?" He hesitated as an unwanted thread of worry went through him. "Umm... is it still Hunter?"

"Still Lily Hunter," she said. "I'm not married."

He had to hide the grin that almost broke out on his face. *What is wrong with you, Taylor?* Thank God he would never see her again after today. He was way too attracted to her, and yet he'd promised himself that there would be no one else after how he'd treated Faye and after losing her. He had also promised Josh not many days ago that it would just be the three of them and that no one would come between them ever again.

He put his phone back into his pocket and grabbed a single bag of chips. He gave her a smile and went to the counter to pay. The sooner he got out of this store and back to his hotel, the sooner he could put her out of his mind.

She caught up to him. "Thank you, Taylor. Please don't forget to call when you decide to go to Fallow Creek again."

He nodded. He remembered his manners in spite of his hurry to leave the store and let her pay for the things she had bought before him. She had a bunch of things in her cart, and as she took them out, her eyes grew wide and she looked at them with a surprised look. "I didn't know I'd picked up so many things," she said to the cashier. She looked embarrassed. "I have to return some of these."

The cashier impatiently looked past her to him. "Next!"

Taylor turned to look at her as she passed by him and headed for the aisles. He paid for his bag of chips and began to head out of the store. He saw her coming toward him again, this time without a cart. She had just a bag of chips and a small box of tissues. She had put back most of the things she'd wanted to buy.

It occurred to him that she probably didn't have any money to pay for those things. She'd been sent out of Fallow Creek with nothing. He was sure that, like most people from that town, she knew no one outside of it. Maybe she'd made a few friends now, but she didn't have any qualifications to get a job, at least a good one, because Fallow Creek did not prepare women for employment. They were meant to get married and have their husband be the sole providers.

He felt sick with guilt. He had been thinking only about himself and hadn't even asked how she'd been faring since she'd been driven out of Fallow Creek. Maybe because she looked so good, it had not occurred to him that she might be in financial difficulty. And he was about to run away because he feared his attraction to her. Surely, he could help her somehow without putting his heart on the line.

He waited for her in front of the store. She came out two minutes later and stared at him in surprise. He went over to her and gave her a big smile.

"I thought you'd left," she said.

He pointed at the bag in her hand. "That's all you

bought? Why did you return the other things in your cart?"

She shrugged and said nothing.

They began to walk side by side in silence. He wasn't yet sure how he could help her, but he would figure out a way.

She suddenly stopped and turned to him. "Where are we going?"

Before he could think over his words, he said, "To your house. Where do you live?"

She blushed and he momentarily shut his eyes. Why didn't he think about how his words would sound to her? "Umm... I didn't mean..." He sighed and stopped talking. Whatever he said now would probably make things worse.

She gave him a small smile. "I know you didn't mean anything by your question. I live in an apartment near here."

"In this neighborhood?" he asked, looking around the poor area.

She nodded.

They couldn't stand in the middle of the street, looking at each other. He had to think fast. She smiled again and said, "Well, it's been great seeing you again, Taylor. I have to go now."

"Lily, tell me the truth. What do you do now?"

"What do I do?"

"Do you have a job?"

She looked down for a few seconds and then looked up at him. "No. I haven't found one yet."

He fought with himself. He didn't want to invite her into his life, but he couldn't just leave without helping her. Besides, he would be going back to California in a few days. He wouldn't exactly be inviting her in if he didn't see her after that. He didn't want to find her a job that paid minimum wage; he wanted her to be able to make a reasonably comfortable life for herself here. He wasn't sure what that would be, but maybe one of his clients who lived in Tucson could help out. In that way, he could help without being in her life in any way.

She shifted her feet and looked down again.

He realized he'd been gazing at her and turned away slightly. He dug his hand into his pocket and pulled out some business cards. He found the one he wanted and handed it to her. "This is all the business info of one of my clients who lives here in Tucson. He owes me a favor. I will speak to him about you and see if he has any job openings. I'll get him to call you for an interview."

Lily looked astonished as she took the card from him. "But I don't have any business skills or any type of skills…"

"I know you're very hardworking, Lily. And I remember how you liked to organize everything when we were kids. I think Steven will have something for you."

"I don't know how to thank you, Taylor. I've been wondering how I would survive past a week. Thank you so much. But are you sure I'll be able to do the job your friend gives me? I don't want to disappoint you or him."

"You won't disappoint anyone. I'm sure of that."

She thanked him again.

"I'm glad we met again today," he said. "It was fun reminiscing about our childhood. Now, I have to go and enjoy my chips."

She looked down at his hand and laughed. "You

only bought one."

He looked at the bag and sighed. He had been in such a hurry to leave that he had just grabbed a bag from the shelf. "Great," he said. He looked at her hand and smiled. She had bought just one, too, though for a different reason. Once again, he blurted without thinking. "Why don't you meet me here at this time tomorrow and we can buy as many of these chips as we want?" She looked a little uncomfortable, and he added quickly. "Don't worry, I'll pay for them."

She shook her head. "You don't have to."

Yes, Taylor. You don't have to. In fact, you shouldn't. You've done what you should do. She'll have a job before the week is over. Just walk away. But the thought of leaving now and never seeing her again felt painful. "I want to, Lily. For old times' sake." *Oh, Taylor! Why did you say that?*

Her eyes shone, and she nodded. "Okay." She suddenly looked worried. "Will your wives mind us spending the evening together? Will it take away from the time you spend with your family? I don't want to intrude on your family time."

It was on the tip of his tongue to tell her that Faye was gone and that he'd not married Sarah, but he thought better of it. He would be reasonably safe if she believed he was married.

But do you want her to keep believing you have two wives? You know what she thinks about that. At least tell her you're not married to Sarah. He brushed the thoughts away. It was better she believed the worst. None of it even mattered. He would see her tomorrow and then never again. "I came here for business. I'm not here with my family, Lily."

She gave him a strange look as she pressed her lips together. "Taylor, I want to thank you for everything. I really appreciate this." She looked at the business card he'd given her. "But can I pass on the offer to shop for the chips with you here tomorrow? I just... I just don't think it would be appropriate to do that with you."

Taylor didn't say anything for a short moment. He was not terribly surprised that she'd turned him down. Just at how disappointed he was... and relieved.

"Are you angry with me, Taylor?" She touched his shoulder lightly. "Please don't be."

He smiled at her. "I'm not angry with you. In fact, I think you're right." He nodded. "It's been great spending time with you. Goodbye, Lily. I promise to call you if or when I ever decide to go to Fallow Creek." A thought occurred to him. "Or better yet, since you have Rachel's number, you can call her and give her the message you have for your parents."

A huge smile broke out on her face. "Yes. I'll do that. Thanks." She came closer, and he thought she was going to hug him, but she stepped back again. "You have been a godsend, Taylor Dalton. Send my greetings to your family."

"I will."

She stood smiling at him for a minute more, and then she turned around and walked away.

He watched her go until she disappeared from sight and then gasped as a void formed in his heart. Why had he let her get past the barrier he'd set up around his heart when his wife died?

He sighed. He knew why. As children he'd had a crush on her, but he'd never told her or acted on it. It was just not the way things were done back in Fallow Creek and so there was no point. He thought he'd completely let go of that childish crush, but he'd clearly only buried it deep within him. Now it had resurfaced again, but as a burning desire. He was glad she'd walked away, even if it was because he had indirectly lied to her.

He walked back to his hotel, aching for her, but taking it in his stride. He would go back to his kids in a few days and forget all about her and the longing she had stirred up in him.

SEVEN

Lily inhaled and exhaled to try to get rid of her nervousness. She looked over at the receptionist at the front desk and clutched her purse as she shifted in her seat. She was the only one seated at the glass-and-granite reception area of the advertising company. She crossed and uncrossed her legs, looked down at her cream shirt and brown skirt, and sighed. She had to stop fidgeting and calm down. Taylor had already recommended her to the CEO. But she couldn't help feeling anxious in spite of that. She needed this job badly.

The man's secretary had called two days ago to tell her that she was scheduled for an interview today. She didn't know if it was Taylor's friend, the CEO of this company, or someone else who would interview her. She might not get a job here if it was someone else.

You don't even know what job you're going to be interviewed for.

She bit her lip. She had no real qualifications for any formal job, but Taylor had mentioned her organizational skills. Maybe the job she was going to be interviewed for would have something to do with that.

She took a deep breath and tried to calm her nerves again. Taylor's face appeared in her mind, and she sighed. Since the day she'd met him at the store, she'd not been able to get him out of her mind for more than a few minutes. She woke up thinking about him and went to bed still doing the same. She hated herself for obsessing over a married man. What kind of woman did that?

People like Sofia. But not her. She had loathed a lot of things about Fallow Creek, but the thing she had detested the most was the polygamy practiced there. Many women were comfortable living with someone who was already married and declaring they were second, third, or fourth wives. But she'd come to believe it was completely wrong, an anomaly. Why, then, was she lusting over someone else's husband, even if it was not willingly?

Lord, please erase him from my mind. But she knew the prayer was not going to be answered. She was here in this office for a job because of Taylor. Besides, he was not the kind of man you forgot easily, and spending time with him had reminded her just how charming he was. He had not changed in that respect since they were children. Apart from his devastating good looks, he was one of the kindest people she knew; and had been so even when they were kids.

Lily, stop thinking about him!

If only she had a picture of his wife, Faye, she would carry it with her wherever she went to remind herself that even thinking about Taylor was something she could not afford to do.

She prayed silently for forgiveness for her wayward thoughts; the hundredth time she'd done so since she'd seen Taylor at the store. Her prayers had not been answered at all since she'd prayed that God would remove the awful desire she felt for him. Instead, it had only grown, horrifying her. At least she was thankful for one thing: she didn't know where his hotel was. Who knew what she would have done with the way she felt and had been feeling for days. She was glad he would be leaving Tucson soon. Hopefully, she would never see him again, or at least not in the near future.

She rubbed her temples and shut her eyes. *Lord, you have to help me. Please cleanse my heart and make it pure again in Your sight.*

She opened her eyes again when the receptionist called her name. "You can go in," the middle-aged woman said. "Mr. Kilpatrick will see you now."

Lily's heart pounded as she stood up and, again, she tried to calm her nerves. At least it was the CEO, Taylor's friend, who would being doing the interview. But that did not help her. She let out a long breath, straightened her skirt, and walked into the office on her left.

A secretary who was sitting behind the only desk in a small office glanced at her and then went back to whatever she was doing. Lily looked nervously at the door in front of her. It had the name *J. Kilpatrick* etched on it in gold. She knocked once and then slowly opened the door and entered the CEO's office.

The office looked like the reception area, but with a larger desk and a clear view of the city from the wide windows. The man behind the desk was perhaps in his early thirties, close to Taylor's age. He wasn't as handsome as Taylor, but he looked suave and self-possessed. He smiled at her, and his eyes swept over her body.

She felt slightly uncomfortable at the way he was looking at her. He sat up straight and pointed at the seat in front of him. She sat down, took a deep breath, and then squared her shoulders to appear more confident, even though she felt anything but.

The man's eyes searched her face. "Taylor didn't tell me you were such a beauty," he said.

She blinked. Was he coming on to her or was this normal for interviews? She decided to say nothing. After all, he'd not asked her a question.

"So, tell me all about yourself," he said, his eyes fixed on hers.

"Umm... my name is Lily Hunter, and I'm twenty-five." She didn't know what else to tell him. She didn't want to talk about Fallow Creek or her past. She hadn't expected to be asked about herself, just what skills she had.

"I know all that," he said. "What can you do for me?" He gave her the same piercing look he'd given her when she came in, causing her to shift her eyes from his.

"I can help with whatever you want, like errands and..." She stopped talking when he got up, his eyes still on her.

"I hope you can truly help with whatever I want," he said in a tone that made her blood run cold. He came and stood next to her, way too close for her liking. When he leaned against the desk and looked down at her with a lustful smile, she shifted slightly away.

Lord, what is happening here?

He chuckled. "Don't look so frightened. I'm not going to hurt you. Just relax." He put his hand on her shoulder, and she froze. When his hand went down her arm and came to rest on her thigh, she gasped and sprang up from her seat.

"What are you doing?" she said, glaring at him.

"Why do you look so upset?" He came toward her. "I just want to..."

"Stay away!" she yelled. She threw his business card — the one Taylor had given her — in his face and ran out of the office. She didn't stop running until she was outside the building. Panting, she bent down. She felt like throwing up. What had she said that made that jerk think he could do what he did? She shook her head, gathered herself together, and hailed a taxi to drive her to her apartment.

She got to her decrepit apartment building, climbed the stairs fuming, and entered her apartment. Once she was in the tiny apartment, she collapsed on the sofa and bawled her eyes out. She had put so much faith in this awful guy Taylor had sent her to, believing that she would get a job. But not only did she not get a job, she felt assaulted.

She dashed at the tears in her eyes, furious again. How dare that man think she would become his plaything? She took a deep breath. What was she going to do now? The rent for this apartment, if she could call it that, was long overdue, and the landlord had threatened to throw her out if she didn't pay up. She didn't even have the money to pay the rent for this one-room hole she lived in.

She wrapped her arms around herself, feeling

terribly lonely and in dire need of someone to talk to. She missed her mother and her sister. But she knew what her mother would say if she saw her now. She would say she'd told Lily so. She'd wanted her independence; wanted a life totally different from the one she'd had in Fallow Creek. And she had found it, but it was not what she'd had in mind when she'd left the place.

"Lord, please help me," she said.

A loud knock sounded at her door, and she raised her head. She got up and went to the door. When she opened it, the landlord, a bald man in his sixties, barged in and looked around the room. "I have someone else who is interested in renting the apartment," he said coldly. "You have to move out today."

She gasped. "Today? But I have nowhere to go."

He shrugged. "I am not running a charity here. You'll have to leave before I come back in an hour."

She shook her head as her eyes filled with tears. "Please. Give me time to…" The man walked out of the apartment, and she stood looking out the open door, emotionally exhausted. For a long moment, she did not move, and then she went and sat down again. She held her head in her hands and bowed her head. She had no place to go or money to go anywhere. Maybe she would have to call Sofia to come get her. But the thought of calling Sofia made her nauseated.

She picked up her phone, but rather than call Sofia, she called Taylor.

While his phone rang, she scolded herself for calling him. But she told herself she just needed a familiar face to talk to. Someone she could lean on.

But it was not exactly true. She just didn't want any familiar face to talk to, she wanted *him*. It was the wrong decision, for sure. But her emotions were in tatters, and she didn't care much about making the right decision.

His voice came over the phone, and she broke down. "It went wrong, Taylor."

"Lily, what is it?" He sounded alarmed. "What went wrong?"

"The interview. Everything." She told him in a broken voice everything that had happened, from his CEO friend's lascivious designs on her to the landlord's threats just now. "I don't know what to do," she said after she finished. "Can you come over?" She gasped as soon as the words escaped her lips. What was she doing? It was wrong to ask him to come over. But she had said the words and couldn't take them back.

"I'll be right over, Lily," he said. "Just text me the address."

"Taylor, you don't have to come," she said weakly.

"Yes, I do. It's all my fault. You live near the store where we met, right? I can make it in half an hour."

The call ended, and she looked at her phone. Guilt filled her heart, but she brushed it aside. She didn't have time for that right now. She needed a friend; that was all.

She stood up, went to the mirror mounted on the wall, and arranged her hair. She straightened her skirt and went to sit down to wait for him, her emotions at war.

***

Taylor shut his eyes after the call ended and groaned. He stood up, went to his hotel room phone, and dialed the desk. After requesting that a cab be called for him immediately, he collapsed onto the bed. He thought about going down to wait in the lobby, but with his mood now, he would probably take his anger out on anyone who tried to speak to him. It was better to stay here until his cab arrived.

He stared at the wall as his emotions roiled with rage, anguish, and guilt. He couldn't hold everything in and stood up. Yelling, he swung his arms, almost throwing his phone across the room, but thankfully changed his mind at the last minute.

"What have I done?"

He had introduced Lily to a predator. If only he'd had an inkling about James. He'd considered the man not just a client, but a friend, and had had no knowledge that he was capable of what he'd done to Lily. The man was married, for goodness' sake, and Taylor knew his wife.

Guilt flooded his heart. Had he not also been married when he'd decided to marry Sarah, a younger woman? Yes, Sarah had noticed him before he did her, and he could tell himself that it was the way of the community he'd lived in, but that did not mean he was guiltless.

Thankfully, the Lord had saved him, and he'd left that life completely behind when he'd left Fallow Creek. But as a man who'd resided in that community and unknowingly perpetuated the polygamous lifestyle there that Lily had lived under, and as the one who had introduced her to James, he felt tremendously responsible.

The thought that he'd been part of the pain Lily

was feeling now was almost unbearable. He would kill James the next time he laid eyes on him. Now, he had to do everything in his power to help Lily, no matter what it cost.

He glanced at his wristwatch and barked, "Why on earth are these people taking so long to get me a simple cab?"

His room phone rang and he snatched the receiver up. "Yes?"

"Your car is waiting outside for you, sir."

"Thank you," Taylor said and replaced the phone on the hook. He strode out of the room and took the elevator down to the lobby. He found the car waiting right outside the hotel and gave the driver the address Lily had sent him.

They got to the apartment building Lily lived in, and Taylor looked up at it before he stepped out of the car. It was a rundown building in an unsavory neighborhood. A group of young men loitered in front of the building with hostile expressions on their faces. They studied him as he walked up and then the car he'd just vacated. He ignored them and entered the building, guilt and worry for Lily tearing at him.

This place was unsafe. He couldn't let her continue to stay here even if she did have the money to pay rent. He was actually glad she'd told him she didn't. It would be easier to convince her to leave with him than if she did.

But what are your plans once she leaves with you?

Surely, he could not take her to his hotel with him. That would be too risky.

But did he have a choice? It was too late to get her

another apartment today, and he didn't want to get her just any old apartment. He needed to make sure it was a place he liked and he believed she would like too.

He got to her apartment and knocked on the door. It immediately opened, and she poked her head out. His heart rate sped up as he looked at her. It was clear she'd been crying. He stepped inside, ignored the loud warning in his heart telling him not to, and wrapped her in his arms.

For a long while, he held her tightly, his heart beating rapidly in his chest. His emotions felt all jumbled up as he held her. She pulled slightly away from him. His arms loosened around her, but he still held her hands. He searched her face and said, "I am so sorry, Lily. Please forgive me. I didn't know that James was such a jerk, or I would never have let you anywhere near him."

"It's okay, Taylor. It's not your fault."

He gave her a sad smile. She smiled back, and he sighed. She looked so gloomy and weary, he couldn't resist. He reached out and wiped away the streams of tears flowing down her cheeks.

She gasped and stepped away from him as though his touch had burned her.

He sighed with regret. Maybe he shouldn't have touched her. He tore his eyes away from her and looked around her tiny apartment. The place was a dump and she had no furniture except for an old green sofa and blinds that had seen better days. He looked at her again. She was looking at him with worry in her eyes, and it pained his heart. Was she afraid of him for introducing her to James, or did she now distrust every man, including him?

He scolded himself again for touching her. She was in such a vulnerable place right now, and it would make sense if she didn't trust him. The last thing she needed was any man's unwarranted attention.

He moved farther away from her to put her at ease and said, "I'll end every business and personal dealing I have with James Kilpatrick. I promise."

"You don't have to do that for me," she said softly.

He shook his head. "There's no way I can continue to relate with that creep after what he did to you." Once again, he felt an overwhelming desire to hold her in his arms, but he immediately squashed the feeling.

He glanced around. This place was really awful. There was no way he would let her continue to live here. But how would he convince her to go with him, especially seeing how wary of him she looked?

He sighed loudly and said to her, "This place — not just your apartment, but this area you live in — is dreadful, Lily. Please come with me. I'll find you somewhere else to stay."

She took another step back from him, and he sighed again. She looked frightened, and he didn't blame her for it. With what had happened to her, it was as expected. His gaze remained on her. "Lily, you know I'd never hurt you, right? I just don't feel comfortable with you living here," he waved his hand around her tiny living room, "like this."

She shook her head. "I can't come with you, Taylor. I know you wouldn't hurt me, but..."

He frowned. "But what, Lily?"

"It wouldn't be right," she said. "You're married and your wives aren't here... in this city." She shook her head again. "It just wouldn't be right."

He blinked. If he told her the truth, that he wasn't married, he would be exposing his heart again to the possibility of loss and pain. He would become vulnerable. Confusion took hold of him. He wasn't married now, and with the way he felt about her, he was pretty sure where revealing the truth to her would lead, and it was not somewhere he was ready to go now or possibly ever again.

He didn't know what to say and, apparently, neither did she. They stood staring at each other in awkward silence for a long moment, and then he jerked his head up as the door suddenly flung open and an irate man walked in.

Lily turned to look at the man, and her eyes widened in obvious fear.

"You have to leave right now," the man said, staring angrily at Lily. He turned back and Taylor followed his gaze. Another man stood at the door, looking into Lily's living room, his arms folded across his chest.

The angry man turned to Lily again and said, "The guy who wants to rent this apartment is already here. If you don't have money to pay the rent, you have to leave."

Lily turned to Taylor, looking frightened.

Taylor sighed, looking at the irate man who was glaring at Lily. "I'm guessing this is your landlord, Lily?"

She nodded.

He searched her eyes. "Please come with me, Lily. It's not like you have a choice." She still looked scared, and he walked up to her and put his hands on her shoulders. She looked at his hands, and he immediately withdrew them and stepped away from her. "You can come and stay in my hotel… at least until I can find you an apartment." He shook his head when she blinked rapidly, an astonished look on her face. "No… I didn't mean… We won't be sharing a hotel room. You will stay on a completely different floor."

She sighed loudly, and her shoulders slumped. "I guess I truly don't have a choice."

"So are you moving out now?" the landlord asked. He looked at Taylor with interest.

"Yes," she answered, and turned away. Without looking at Taylor, she said, "Let me go and get my things. I have just a few of my belongings to pack up. I won't be long." She left the living room, and Taylor looked at the angry-looking landlord and then at the other man who was standing at the door. Both men were already walking around the living room even though Lily had not moved out yet, and that irritated Taylor. He wanted to tell them to leave as Lily had not yet vacated the apartment, but he thought better of it. There was no need to hinder this process or stir up any kind of trouble. The earlier Lily got out of this dump, the better.

Fifteen minutes later, Lily came out with a small suitcase. He was surprised that was all she had. She looked up at him and then walked to the windows. Standing on her toes, she grabbed the curtains, clearly trying to bring them down.

"Leave them," Taylor said. "They're dreadful."

She looked back at him and shrugged. Walking away from the window, she stared down at her couch. "What about this?" she pointed at the worn-out couch. "How do I move it?"

He shook his head. "Just leave it here as well. It's seen better days." He eyed the landlord. "It belongs in a place like this."

The middle-aged landlord smirked, but Taylor ignored him.

"So, are you ready to go?" he asked her.

She gave him a small smile and nodded.

"Then let's get out of here."

She began to roll her suitcase out of the apartment, and Taylor took it from her. She gave him a heart-melting smile, and he grinned back.

They made their way down the stairs in silence; she in front of him, he right behind her with her suitcase.

After the driver had put her suitcase into the trunk of the cab, he opened the door for them. Taylor waited for her to enter the car, then got in and sat beside her. She turned and stared out the window, while he tried to look straight on. But as the car began to speed down the road, he could not resist and stole a glance at her. She was still looking out the window, and he sighed softly.

Am I sure about this? Am I really doing the right thing? Lily was coming with him to his hotel. They would be in different rooms, but it would still be the same building. The temptation to go to her room and act on what he felt right now would be great, probably overwhelming. But there was no way he could have left her in that terrible place, especially after the landlord threw her out. She would have been stranded with no place to go if he hadn't asked her to come with him. But he would have to find her an apartment quickly.

They finally got to the hotel and got out of the

car. She gazed up at the hotel, and he smiled at her. "Let's go in," he said. He reached out to take her hand and then thought better of it.

They strode through the doors together, and he immediately remembered what she had said about appearances. For a minute, he worried that someone who knew him would see him here with her. He knew exactly what they would think. He was not overly concerned about his reputation, but it would not be fair to her for people to assume what wasn't true, especially as he was the one who had asked her to come here.

He walked to the front desk and shrugged off his concerns. They were staying in different rooms. Besides, what people decided to believe did not really matter. He turned back and beckoned to Lily, who was standing a few feet behind him looking around the lobby.

She walked up to him, while the concierge followed behind with her suitcase.

His heart pounded as he paid for a room for her. He could feel her gaze on him as he collected the room keycard. He turned and handed it to her, and she glanced at it before looking up at him again.

"You're in room three-oh-seven. I'm on the top floor." After he spoke, he groaned inwardly. Why did he tell her that? The way she was looking at him flooded his body with heat. He'd tried to put her mind at ease by letting her know that their rooms were far apart, but he'd clearly not succeeded. All he'd done was inform her that he knew her room number.

He smothered the urge to groan and told himself to calm down. So he knew where her room was, but that didn't mean he would do anything about it. He wasn't totally lacking in self-control.

They entered the elevator together with the concierge, and she moved to the other end away from him, while the concierge stood in front of them with her suitcase. Taylor glanced at her, but she'd turned her face away and plastered herself on the elevator. He didn't know whether to be amused or worried about that. He finally couldn't help smiling in amusement as they rode up to the third floor. What could possibly happen between them when the concierge was standing right here front of them?

The door opened to her floor, and she got out with the concierge. She smiled at Taylor just as the doors began to close again, and he told her he would call her tomorrow. He sighed as the door closed completely and then punched the button to the top floor.

When he entered his room, he sat on the bed and put his hand on his forehead. So Lily was now here in the same hotel as he was, and he knew where her room was. Her beautiful face was etched in his mind, her perfect figure. Why did he feel so drawn to her? So devastatingly attracted to her?

He groaned. He'd not felt any desire for anyone since his wife had died. He'd thought he was immune to it all, but the day he'd seen Lily at the store again, he'd known he was in trouble. And the more time he spent with her, the more his desire for her had grown, until it had become almost unbearable. He'd thought he had buried that part of him with Faye when she'd died, but clearly it was still alive and well.

"Oh Lord, you have to help me," he groaned again. He had only two more days in Tucson, but he would still have to see her tomorrow. If he knew someone in Tucson who could help her find an apartment, he would have asked for help on her behalf and he wouldn't have to see her again. But he knew no one. Even if he did, he would not trust anyone to help after what James had done. He had to find the apartment himself.

Again, the promise he'd made to Josh flashed through his mind: "Just the three of us. No one will ever come between us again."

He had told himself after the way he'd treated Faye that he would never allow any other woman into his life. At least not for a long, long time. It was the only way he knew to honor her memory. But this intense desire he felt for Lily just months after Faye had passed away felt like a sacrilege somehow. He was disgusted with himself. He had to find a way to get hold of his desires and emotions.

Surely you can manage for a day, Taylor Dalton, he scolded himself.

It was the right thing to do, trying to help Lily in any way he could. He would give her as much help as possible, but that did not have to include giving her his heart. He had to guard his heart as well as try to smother this crazy attraction he felt for her. He would spend just one more day with her and hope his feelings would not get him into trouble. After that, he would thankfully go back to the two people who mattered most to him, and Lily would be forgotten.

EIGHT

Lily opened her eyes and yawned. She sat up on the unfamiliar bed and stretched, and then switched on the table lamp beside her. Looking around the hotel room, she ran her hand across the bronze-colored satin sheets she had slept on. The sheets and the multiple pillows on the bed were so soft and so extremely comfortable, she knew she would stay in bed forever if she let herself. She had gotten into bed almost as soon as she'd arrived in the room the evening before, and even though her emotions were all jumbled up, she had decided not to engage them until the following day. She had fallen asleep almost immediately, emotionally weary.

She stretched and yawned again. She was awake now after a long, much-needed sleep, and though she'd thought the rest would help her, the troubling emotions from yesterday remained. She looked around the hotel room once more. She had never stayed in a place that looked this luxurious. Not even Sofia's apartment, with all its unique souvenirs from the countries she had visited and the tasteful furniture, looked like this. But her luxurious surroundings did not distract her from her confusion.

She grimaced as she recalled the dream she'd had during the night. She had dreamt of Taylor. The details of the dream ran through her mind, and she felt herself blushing. She threw off the covers and groaned. "Why, oh why did I meet him that day in the store?" If only she had left immediately after she'd found what she'd gone there to buy, he wouldn't have seen her and she wouldn't feel this way.

But then you'd be in trouble with no place to stay.

That was true. Where would she be right now if not for him? Maybe she would have gone back to Sofia, but that would have been awful. The thought of going back to live with Sofia made her sick. George would still be with Sofia in her apartment. She had said he would stay for a full week.

Lily sighed. She was judging Sofia, and yet was she any better? She was staying in a hotel room paid for by a married man, and close enough to his room to do something about the raging desire she now felt.

She bit her lip at her admission. Never in her life had she felt this way before. It was a very uncomfortable feeling, especially knowing that the man she felt this way about was unavailable. What had she gotten herself into? Her saving grace was that she didn't know what room he was in.

Her stomach flipped as a thought ran through her mind: he knew hers. What if he came here? He'd told her he would see her tomorrow.

She shook her head. There was no point thinking and worrying about it. Hopefully, he would have enough good sense not to come.

But what if he wasn't thinking clearly... like her?

She jumped out of bed in a panic. If he came by, she couldn't afford to let him see her looking like this.

Lily, I thought you were worried about what would happen if Taylor came here. Instead you're worried about how you would look to him. She smiled in self-mockery and hurried into the bathroom to take a shower.

Afterward, she frantically rummaged through her suitcase, looking for something appropriate to wear. After a while, she straightened, took a deep breath, and told herself to calm down. *Remember that the last thing you want to do is draw his attention to your body with what you wear.*

She bent over her suitcase again, ignored all the clothes Sofia had bought her, and pulled out a simple short-sleeved maxi dress. It was one of the outfits she had brought from Fallow Creek, the kind that women usually wore there. She hoped it would simply say she wasn't trying to get his attention or impress him in any way.

She looked down at the suitcase again. A pair of snug blue jeans and a sleeveless red top called out to her. She resisted the urge to pick them up. Normally, on other days, wearing the jeans and top would be fine. But today it would be a bad idea. If she couldn't control her wayward thoughts, at least she could try to control what she wore and how she looked to Taylor.

By the time she'd finished dressing, she longed

to see him so much that she knew wearing the very modest dress would not help at all, at least on her part, when she saw Taylor. She looked around the room again. She could not stay in this hotel room anymore. It was probably even wrong to hang around the hotel to see Taylor again. She remembered the way he had looked at her the day before, the way he had tenderly wiped away the tears on her cheeks. It was all wrong. He was married. He had no business doing that, and she had no business feeling the way she did about him. She had to leave now, before he called her or, worse, came to her door.

But where will I go? Back to Sofia's?

She gritted her teeth as she thought. George would still be there. How would she go back and stay with her friend who was living with a married man?

She sat on the bed and groaned. Now she fully understood the phrase that Sofia had uttered some time ago when her friend had had to make a difficult decision. "Between the devil and the deep blue sea." That was where she was right now.

"Oh Lord Jesus, please help me. What am I going to do now?"

She tried to calm her heart as she listened for guidance. But she heard nothing. Instead, she remembered that Taylor had given her Rachel's number some days ago. She still hadn't called her. She hadn't remembered to.

How would you remember when you've been obsessing over her brother for days?

She reached for her purse on the bedside table and just before she plucked out her cell phone, the hotel phone rang. She reached out and answered it.

Taylor's voice came on the other end, and her heart began to drum.

"Hey!" He had a smile in his voice. "You haven't had breakfast yet, have you?"

"No."

"Will you meet me downstairs in the breakfast lounge? We can have breakfast together and talk about getting you an apartment. I've already made some calls."

"That'd be great," she said, way too eagerly. She shut her eyes and moaned on the inside. Hadn't she just been planning to leave this hotel right now so she would not have to keep enduring the temptation of being here with Taylor? Now, without thinking, she had told him she would meet him for breakfast. What was wrong with her?

"Lily, are you still there?"

"Yes, when do you want to meet?" She held back another groan.

"In about half an hour. That okay?"

"Yes," she answered. She glanced at her wristwatch. It was a few minutes to nine o'clock. "I'll meet you in half an hour, then."

When the call ended, she stood up and began to pace the room. *Great! Just great! Maybe I should just pack my things and get out of this hotel.* But she had already promised she would meet Taylor for breakfast. It would be wrong to walk away — or more like run away — without telling him, especially after all he had done for her. She would have to meet him downstairs in thirty minutes.

She looked down at her dress and once again squashed the urge to change into something less plain. However, she couldn't resist standing in front of the mirror and brushing her hair. She picked up her purse from the bed and brought out a red lipstick that Sofia had gotten her on one of her many trips abroad. Swiping it across her lips, she stared at herself in the mirror.

What are you doing? She hardly ever wore makeup. Now, just because she was about to see Taylor, she was putting on lipstick, and a bright red one at that. It was a mistake.

But she did not wipe it off.

She shook her head. *So much for trying not to draw his attention to your appearance.*

She lingered in front of the mirror, scolding herself for obsessing over the way she looked. Over the way she would look to Taylor. "Do you even remember that he's a married man?" she said to herself in the mirror.

She turned this way and that, inspecting her figure, and then turned away, appalled at her behavior. She was certain now that she was no better than Sofia, who she had scolded for dating someone who already had a wife. But maybe she was even worse because she knew better.

She groaned as she glanced at her wristwatch again. It was time to go downstairs. If only she could slip away now... but she had already given Taylor her word.

She snatched her purse from the bed and left the room. Striding across the elegant lobby, she asked one of the hotel staff where the breakfast lounge was and then headed there when the lady gave her directions to the place.

She paused for a minute at the entrance of the

lounge and looked inside. There was a vast array of delicious-looking food that stretched from one end of the lounge to the other. She could smell the enticing aroma from where she stood, and it made her mouth water. She couldn't wait to eat. There were only a few people in the lounge, and it was easy to spot Taylor. He was sitting at a table for two, on the right side of the room, looking at his phone screen. He looked as delicious as the food in the lounge.

She sighed wearily. This was exactly the kind of thought that would get her into trouble.

She took a deep breath, plastered a smile on her face, and walked into the breakfast lounge. She headed toward him, still smiling. Her heart skipped a beat when his eyes lit up as he saw her, and then a huge smile broke across his face.

She came and sat across from him, and for a moment she looked down at the table to avoid looking into his eyes. After she'd gathered her thoughts together, she looked up at him again and found him gazing at her. She felt herself blush. He was looking at her intently, and now she could not take her eyes off his. She quivered as they sat gazing at each other, the food in the lounge forgotten.

Guilt flooded her. What was she doing sitting down here, about to have breakfast with him, and gazing at him as though he was part of the menu when she knew full well that he was married? This definitely looked like a date, though he had not said it was. She was violating her values. In a way now, she could sympathize with Sofia when it had been impossible to do so some days ago. But that did not make this any less wrong.

"You look great," Taylor broke the silence.

She said nothing.

"Are you ready to go get some breakfast?"

She nodded, remembering she was famished.

They went to the long table laden with different kinds of sausages, bacon, cheese, and eggs. Varieties she had never seen before. On the other side were mushrooms and hash browns and yogurts. And then a variety of salads and soups. Some foods she'd never seen before were arranged on her left side, and for a moment she wondered what she should eat. She picked up a plate and chose a simple breakfast of strawberries, toast, bacon, eggs, and cheese. A coffee pot and teacups were already on their table. She began to head to the table and then bumped into Taylor.

"Sorry, Lily," he said.

She looked into his eyes and, for a minute, she froze. She smiled in embarrassment and tried to walk around him. But he had the same idea, and they bumped into each other once more. He apologized again, and she smiled. He stood, waiting for her to pass, and this time she successfully walked past him and carried her plate to the table. She looked down at her food and suddenly found she was not as hungry as she'd been before. She doubted that she would be able to eat much, especially once Taylor returned to the table.

He came back less than a minute later, and her pulse quickened. She felt too on edge to eat. She cut her eggs and bacon into small bits and ate only a few bites, having lost her appetite. She kept her eyes averted from his and her head slightly bowed over her plate, but she could feel his eyes on her.

"Lily?"

She looked up at him. "Yes?" Her heart thudded as they searched each other's eyes.

"Will you come to California with me?"

Her jaw dropped, and her fork clattered as it fell from her hand onto the plate. Had he just asked her to come to California with him? She blinked and stared at him in astonishment.

***

Taylor's mind reeled from the embarrassment he felt. He hadn't planned on asking Lily to come with him to California. In fact, he had never even considered it. The words had just come out of nowhere.

No they didn't. You've been obsessing over her for days. Those words were a result of that.

"You want me to come to California with you? Why?" She was looking at him with a shocked expression, waiting for him to answer her question.

For a long moment he said nothing because he didn't know what to say. He searched his mind frantically for what to tell her. As he did, he realized he had spoken those words because the thought of never seeing her again after tomorrow unsettled him.

But he had made Josh a promise. Once he came back, they would spend an extended time alone — just him, Josh, and Bree. If Lily came with him, he would have to share his attention between three rather than two people. Even if he decided not to, her presence would be a terrible distraction, and his kids deserved all of him.

He sighed. But then again, she had no job. Even if he found her an apartment to live in, how would she take care of herself? He felt a tremendous amount of responsibility toward her, just as he had when he'd heard about what James had done. He could just open an account for her and send her money regularly, but she probably wouldn't like that very much. And he would understand fully. No one wanted to live like that; at least, no self-respecting person.

Finally, he decided to tell her part of the truth. The other part, the part about not being able to stand the thought of never seeing her again, would scare her away, and that would do no good when he truly wanted to help her. "I want you to come to California with me because I have a job for you. I've been looking for someone I can trust to care for my kids. My housekeeper takes care of them now, but she is overworked. I need a full-time nanny. I promise to pay you really well."

She blinked rapidly and then shook her head. "That wouldn't be possible, Taylor. I'm sorry, but I can't go to California with you. I think that would be a bad idea."

He was going in too deep. Deeper than he should. How would he guard his heart, keep the promise he'd made to his son, and honor his wife's memory if Lily came with him? She was right. It wasn't a good idea considering he was asking her to work for him as his kids' nanny, which meant she would be staying in his house or on the premises. But though he knew in his head that it was a bad idea, his heart yearned to see her every day, like he'd been doing for the past few days.

She looked like she was about to run away, and he quickly said, "You don't have to stay inside my house. There's a staff building on the grounds where the other household staff live. You could live there as well."

"I still can't come to California with you, Taylor. I'm really grateful for all you've done for me so far, but I can't accept your job offer."

"Listen, Lily, you don't have to decide right now. Just think about it."

"I don't want to think about it," Lily said. "I'm not going with you to California, and I definitely can't work in your house or on the grounds."

He leaned back in his seat, feeling terribly disappointed, and studied her face. Everything in him told him to let it go, that it was just as well. But he couldn't. "Why not, Lily? Tell me why you don't want to come to California with me."

She sighed loudly. "I can't believe you're asking me this, Taylor. You know why."

His pulse began to race at the way she was looking at him, and waves of desire ran through him. He knew exactly what she meant, and yet something in him wanted to hear her say it, even though he knew it wasn't right. He looked down at the table for a second. *Don't ask her, Taylor! Don't do it!*

He rapped his fingers on the table and looked at her again. "No, I don't know why." *Oh, you liar.*

She gazed into his eyes and then heaved a loud sigh. When she looked up at him again, she was blushing. "I like you… a lot more than I should. It's wrong," she said in a shaky voice. She shut her eyes and groaned. "I shouldn't have told you that."

He smiled in spite of himself.

She looked down again. "I can't risk it, Taylor. It would be so unfair to your wife if I came with you and something happened between us. It would be wrong and a sin in God's sight. I can't let that happen. I wouldn't be able to live with myself."

Once again, he trembled at her words and the depths of his feelings for her. Confusion raged in him at how hard and quickly he had fallen for her. He had known that she liked him and had seen the look in her eyes when they'd met at the store, but he hadn't known how intense her feelings for him were until now. It shook him to the core.

What is wrong with you, Taylor? Not even with Faye had he felt the way he did now. He felt an overwhelming urge to confess the truth to Lily; to tell her that he was not married anymore, but the very fact that he was so eager to do so also gave him pause. Faye had been dead for less than a year, and he was already ready to replace her. It was so wrong.

"Taylor, are you mad at me?"

He looked at Lily again. She seemed really worried. He said quickly, "No, I'm not. Why would I be mad at you? I understand perfectly."

She gave him a sad smile. "I'm glad you do. I wasn't sure you would since we both come from a community where having a wife already doesn't stop a man from marrying another. I'm glad you're not angry. You've been so caring and helpful to me." She reached out and nearly touched his hand on the table, and then she clearly changed her mind, shifting her hand away.

He sat gazing at her. He couldn't breathe or

think properly as his eyes swept her entire face and then settled on her lips. He sighed and forced his eyes away from her lips back to her eyes. If not for the promise he had made to Joshua and to himself to honor his wife's memory, he would be sweeping Lily into his arms right now and kissing her the way he'd been dying to since the day he'd seen her at the store.

As they had done a couple of times since that day, they sat without speaking, staring into each other's eyes. The air crackled with the intensity of their mutual attraction, and he felt like his heart would soon crash out of his chest. He imagined what would happen if he told her right now that he wasn't married and that they were free to be together. His body grew hot again, and he knew it would be a mistake to do so. Just because he wasn't married didn't mean that they were supposed to do anything they wanted to. They would both come to regret it if they gave in to their desires. It was better not to tell her the truth.

"Okay, so it's not a good idea to come with me to California, but I can't just leave you here knowing you don't have any money. Yesterday, I called an acquaintance of mine who is also into construction. He told me about a nice apartment building not too far from here that he worked on. He said there's an empty apartment in that building, so I decided to go take a look at it. I love the place, and so I told him I was interested in getting it for someone. We can go and see it together this afternoon so you can see if you like it. But I think you will. I already paid for it, but if you don't like it, we can always find somewhere else."

Her eyes flooded with tears as she looked at him, and he frowned with worry. "I'm sorry, Lily. Did I overstep my bounds?"

She shook her head. "No, I'm just overwhelmed by everything. I'm really grateful, Taylor, but you shouldn't have paid for an apartment for me."

"Yes, I should. I'm leaving Tucson tomorrow, and it'll give me some measure of peace to know that you at least have somewhere decent to live."

"But you paid for an apartment for me, Taylor. I don't know if that's right."

"Don't think anything of it. It's not a big deal."

"You know that's not true," she said. "It's a huge deal."

"It's not. It's like an investment. I bought it so —"

"Taylor! You bought the apartment for me?" She groaned.

"Please, Lily. Don't fight me on this. I know what I'm doing. Just accept it as my way of saying I'm sorry for introducing you to a creep like James Kilpatrick. And also for the sake of our childhood friendship." He gave her a mysterious smile. "You know you were like a little sister to me when we were growing up."

"Oh… that's not good!" Disgust was written on her face, and he found that funny. He laughed out loud, and she shook her head. "It's not funny, Taylor. With the way things are between us now, saying I'm like a little sister to you is so wrong."

He sighed. "I know. But, for old times' sake, please accept the apartment. It's the least I can do."

She pressed her lips together and then nodded. "Okay, but I'll pay you back as soon as I can. As soon as I get a job…" she looked pointedly at him, "on my own, I will pay you back. Okay?"

He sighed in frustration.

"Okay, Taylor Dalton? Do we have a deal?"

He nodded. "Okay, then." He held out his hand to shake hers. "We have a deal, Lily Hunter."

She took his hand and instantly a jolt of electricity went through his fingers and shot up into his arm. She quickly pulled her hand away, and he sighed. He looked down at his food, which he had barely touched and was now probably cold, and then looked at hers. It was the same. He picked up his knife and fork and began to eat the cold food while praying that the intensity of his feelings for her would gradually melt away.

He looked over at her again. She had started eating too, putting small bites into her mouth.

He continued to eat, or more like move his food around. He was too aware of her, his thoughts too jumbled up to eat much. He looked at her face. Her head was slightly bowed, but he could still see she was blushing.

If not for the seriousness of the situation they were in now, he would have laughed at how they were both acting like a pair of smitten teenagers. But this was serious for both him and for her. What they felt for each other was something neither of them could explore, no matter how overwhelming those feelings were. But the worst thing was that he was leaving tomorrow and who knew when or if he would ever see her again? The thought was painful.

As they ate, neither of them spoke. It was all so awkward and extremely uncomfortable.

His mind traveled back to when he'd first married Faye. He'd hardly known her, although he'd seen her around Fallow Creek from time to time. They had gradually grown fond of each other through the years and he had come to love her by their fifth year of marriage, even though he had not realized just how much until she'd passed away.

But what he felt now for Lily was totally new. While he'd loved Faye with a tender fondness that had grown as the years passed, his feelings for Lily were akin to a raging fire that threatened to burn him up if he gave in. He didn't know what exactly it was, but it was definitely not love. He'd never felt this before, and he wasn't sure he liked this feeling very much.

He finally gave up on his food after he ate half of his plate and dropped his knife and fork. He leaned back and turned his gaze to Lily. She had already stopped eating and was looking at him. She looked away as their eyes met.

"Are you ready to go?" he asked.

"Yes, I think I am," she answered.

They left the restaurant together and walked to the elevator. As it opened, she stepped in, but he held back. It was probably not a good idea to get into the empty elevator with her right now. He needed to walk off what he was feeling and maybe take a cold shower when he got back to his hotel room.

She raised her eyebrows quizzically as the elevator door began to close. "Aren't you coming in?" she asked.

He shook his head and gave her a small smile. Turning around, he strode off as the elevator door closed. He made his way back to the lobby again and walked out of the hotel. He needed a long walk. After that, he would go to his room, rest, and then call Lily and give her directions to the apartment. He'd thought he would go with her, but it was better not to. They would both be safer if she went alone.

His heart ached as he walked down the sidewalk, his hands in his pockets. Tomorrow, he would leave Arizona and go back to California, and even though Lily had said she didn't need his help in finding a job, he would try to see what he could do about getting her one here in Tucson. But he wouldn't see her face to face again. He could not afford to.

He recalled the surprised look she had given him as she'd entered the elevator, and sighed sadly, knowing that would probably be the last time he saw her beautiful face. Some minutes ago, he'd believed that the thought of never seeing her again was painful. Now he knew that wasn't true. It was excruciating.

NINE

Lily's heart raced as she looked at her phone and saw it was Taylor calling. "Calm down," she said to herself and answered his call.

"A car is waiting outside the hotel, Lily," he said over the phone. He sounded distracted. "I gave the driver directions to your apartment."

"Okay, I'll be right down." She hung up and straightened her dress. She brushed back her hair from her face with her hand and grabbed her purse from the bed. Bringing out her suitcase from the hotel room closet, she looked around the room to make sure she had not left anything unpacked. She had already packed up all her things as soon as she'd come up after breakfast this morning.

She left the room with her suitcase, her heart still racing. After the confession she'd made to Taylor about her feelings for him during their very awkward breakfast, she felt slightly nervous and embarrassed to see him again. Most of all, she felt frightened. They were going to an empty apartment together. She would have to remember to leave the door wide open when they went in.

She sighed. He would leave tomorrow, and she would finally be able to breathe easy again and stop being constantly guarded. She bit her lip as pain tore through her. Would today be the last day she saw him? When would she get to see him again?

She hurried to the elevator, rolling her suitcase behind her, and rode it down to the lobby. She checked out of the hotel at the front desk and hastily made her way out of the hotel. A limo was waiting just outside. She thanked the concierge as he helped her get her suitcase into the trunk of the limo. The driver came out and opened the car door for her. She took a deep breath, gathered her emotions together, and entered the back of the spacious vehicle. She blinked in surprise and disappointment. Where was Taylor? Surely, he was coming to the apartment with her.

She leaned forward as the driver got into the front seat. "Umm... where's Taylor... Mr. Dalton? Isn't he coming with us?"

"Mr. Dalton?"

"Yes," Lily said exasperatedly, trying to still her emotions. "Taylor Dalton. I thought he was coming with us?"

"No, he isn't, ma'am. His instructions were to take you to an apartment building not far from here. He gave me directions to the place."

She leaned back in her seat, panicking and feeling faint with disappointment. Here she was, dreaming of seeing Taylor again, and even planning how she would make sure their desires for each other did not take over at the new apartment, when he wasn't even coming at all.

Shame ran through her, mixing in with her acute disappointment and distress. It was probably God's way of answering her prayer for help. But the thought brought no relief to her. Neither did her guilt erase her pain at the fact that she had not known the last time she would see him was at the elevator. Maybe he would come and visit her someday when he came to Tucson again, but it was unlikely. He'd purposely avoided going to this new apartment with her. He would probably avoid visiting her when he came into town again.

"It's for the best," she whispered, and groaned when tears streamed down her cheeks. *Oh Lord, help me. I've become Sofia. I've become the kind of woman I used to loathe.*

She looked out the window and thought about Taylor as the driver wove through traffic. Their breakfast at the hotel had been so full of longing and desire for each other that they hadn't been able to eat. Now that she knew she would never see him again, that longing only increased.

She shifted in her seat as guilt threatened to suffocate her. Was she even now sinning against God just by thinking about him in that way? Hadn't the Lord said that even looking at a woman or man lustfully was wrong? It meant that she was just as bad as Sofia and women like her.

She shut her eyes and sighed. She thought she had put away the teachings supporting polygamy, which had been ingrained in her from childhood in Fallow Creek, and that she was above it all now. But clearly, they had penetrated her mind far deeper than she'd imagined. She hadn't gotten rid of the teachings she'd been raised with. She had only buried them. Now they had been resurrected to taunt her. She prayed silently for forgiveness and asked the Lord to take away everything she felt for Taylor.

The roads and buildings began to grow very familiar, and she blinked in surprise as they approached the residential area where she had lived with Sofia for months. Her heart began to pound as the driver drove straight to Sofia's apartment building. When he stopped right in front of it, she gasped in dismay. "Is this the place Taylor Dalton gave you directions to?" she asked the driver, hoping with all her heart that it wasn't.

"Yes," the man said. "This is the address I was given."

Lily shut her eyes and began to panic once again. *Lord, this can't be!* She opened her eyes and looked up at the apartment building. *Please tell me it isn't the apartment building I'm supposed to live in!* She placed her hand on her forehead as her head began to throb. Of all the places to live in this whole city, why did it have to be this one? Why did Taylor have to buy an apartment in this particular building where Sofia lived? She groaned as the driver opened the door for her. For a moment, she sat, unwilling to exit the car, and then she finally did.

The driver got her suitcase out of the trunk, and she thanked him as she took it from him. He got back into the limo, and she nearly got in with him again. But where would she go if she did? She had nowhere else to go, and it would be wrong to tell Taylor that she didn't want to stay here after all he'd done for her.

She felt like weeping as she reluctantly rolled

her suitcase to the entrance of the building and then paused in front of it. She groaned again as she entered the building and glanced around the familiar posh lobby. The apartments in this building were expensive. Why had Taylor gotten an expensive apartment for her? Not even Sofia, who worked and earned her own money, paid for the apartment she lived in. Lily had found out some days before she'd left Sofia's that George had been the one paying the rent.

Lily walked across the marble-tiled floor and smiled at Ivan, the twenty-three-year-old who manned the front desk. His eyes lit up when he saw her, and he grinned when she reached the desk and stood in front of him.

"Hey, Lily!" He glanced down at her suitcase. "You're back?"

She nodded. He had seen her the day she was leaving, and she'd told him she was moving out. Now she was back to live here again.

"I'm glad you're back," he said to her. He suddenly looked at her with interest and then looked down at the file in front of him. "Some very rich guy paid for a penthouse apartment in a Miss Hunter's name." His eyes lit up again, and he smiled brightly at her. "I should have known it was you."

Her mouth dropped open for a moment. "A penthouse apartment? Oh, Taylor, why?" She looked at Ivan, who was still smiling at her. "I didn't know it was a penthouse apartment he'd paid for." She groaned inwardly. She knew what Ivan was thinking now. That she was involved with a wealthy man who had paid for an expensive apartment that she would never ever be able to afford. That she was the kind of girl who dated wealthy men so they could buy her expensive stuff... like an apartment in this building. She suddenly grew annoyed. What had Taylor been thinking when he'd bought her an apartment here, and a penthouse apartment for that matter? She would never be able to pay him back!

"You look upset," Ivan said. "Aren't you happy you have a penthouse apartment? I would be over the moon if someone got me..."

"Ivan!" she cut in. "It's not what you think." When he opened his mouth, she knew he was going to ask her another question, and she quickly waved him off. "I'm tired, Ivan. I just want to go up to the apartment." There was no point trying to explain further. "Where's the key?"

"Of course. The key." He sounded professional again. He looked down at his file and looked at the computer in front of him. He typed something. A minute later, he opened a drawer at his back and took out a cardkey. Turning around, he handed it to her. Apartment 901. "It's a very nice apartment, Lily. I hope you enjoy it."

"Thank you," she said wearily.

He asked if she needed help with her suitcase, and she told him she didn't. She walked away, pulling her suitcase with her. Rounding a corner, she sighed loudly and covered her face with her hand. Of all the places Taylor had found, it had to be this apartment where Sofia lived. Not only would she never be able to pay him back, she was bound to run into Sofia soon, and then she would have to explain how she could afford to live in an apartment building like this. Hopefully, Sofia would not find out for a long time that she lived in one of the two penthouse apartments in the building.

She got to the front of the elevator and pressed the 'up' button. The doors opened and just as she stepped in, someone else came up behind her. They entered together, and Lily caught the scent of familiar perfume. She looked up at the young woman and gasped, her heart sinking to her feet. *Sofia!*

"Lily! What're you doing here?" Sofia stared at her with wide eyes and then looked down at her suitcase. "You've come back?" Sofia reached out and hugged her. "I'm so sorry for how things went down the day you left. I've missed you so much, Lily!" She looked Lily over. "You look a little different... More beautiful." She took Lily's hand. "You'll have to tell me your beauty secret when we get to the apartment." She pressed her lips tightly together. "George is still there, but I promise he won't get in your way."

Great! This is just what I needed right now. Dozens of people live in this building, but it just had to be Sofia who walked into the elevator. Lily couldn't utter a word, not only because Sofia kept talking and talking, but because her mind and mouth were not connecting anymore.

Sofia grinned at her as she pressed the elevator button to her floor. "We'll have such a good time this weekend. I know George is around, but we can still have our usual girls' weekend." She frowned and tilted her head toward Lily. "I know you don't like George being in the apartment, but he'll only be here for about three more days, and then..."

"Sofia!" Lily cut her off. "I'm not back!"

Sofia's eyes widened, and she looked confused. She looked down at Lily's suitcase again and said, "I thought… isn't this your suitcase?"

"It is, but I'm not coming to live with you," Lily said slowly. *Lord, please don't let her ask any more questions.*

"Then where are you going to live?" Sofia asked, frowning and looking even more confused.

Lord, do I really have to tell her the truth? Can't I just make something up?

"Lily, did you hear my question? Why did you bring your suitcase here if you aren't moving back to my apartment? Where are you going to live? Did you come to visit someone in the building?"

Lily sighed in exasperation. *Sofia and her constant need to talk and ask multiple questions all at once.* "I'm moving into an apartment in this building," Lily said in a low voice. "But it's not yours."

Sophia stared at her. "You're moving into this building?"

"Yes," Lily answered. She winced inwardly, guilt flooding her. She was no different from Sofia. George was paying the rent for Sofia's apartment in this building, and now Taylor had bought her an apartment here, too. They were both kept women. Lily grimaced. It was all so awful.

"Wow!" Sofia said. "You must have gotten a fabulous job in these few days since you left."

The guilt that had taken a hold of Lily now threatened to suffocate her.

The elevator stopped moving, and the door opened. When Sofia didn't get out, Lily stared at her. "Aren't you getting out?"

"No. I have to come and check out your apartment, Lily!"

Lily frowned. *I wish you wouldn't.* She said, "Okay, but I don't have any furniture yet, so there's really nothing to see."

"I'm still coming," Sofia insisted.

The elevator stopped, and Sofia's eyes grew round as Lily pressed the button for the ninth floor. She turned and stared at Lily with an incredulous look on her face. "This is the top floor. Are you are going to be living in a penthouse apartment?"

Lily's heart knocked with guilt and embarrassment. How was she going to explain it to Sofia? There was no way she would believe she'd gotten a job that could pay for a penthouse apartment in a building like this.

Sofia stared at Lily with suspicion in her eyes as they stepped out of the elevator. "Lily, are you staying in a penthouse suite?"

Lily cringed as Sofia's eyes pierced hers, and she turned away.

They walked down a plush carpeted hallway lined with tall potted plants and then stopped at the door with the number 901 etched on it. She took out her cardkey, opened the door, stepped in, and almost fainted. The living room was fully outfitted with furniture that looked forbiddingly expensive. She shut her eyes, wanting to pinch herself to make sure she wasn't dreaming, and opened them again. *Why, Taylor?* She felt overwhelming guilt and shame, and she couldn't turn to look at Sofia. She could guess what her friend was thinking now.

"Lily, tell me the truth! It's either you won the lottery, or you robbed a bank. Which is it?"

Lily said more to herself than to Sofia, "I didn't know he was going to do all this."

"You didn't know who was going to do all this?"

Lily walked to the snow-white sofa and sank onto it. It felt so soft and comfortable, and yet she felt dreadful and uncomfortable under Sofia's suspicious gaze.

Sofia sat next to her, and Lily sighed.

"Lily, what are you not telling me?" Sofia asked. She looked around the living room. "These pieces of furniture… that view…" She pointed at the sliding windows. From where she sat, Lily had a gorgeous view of the city.

Lily's phone rang, and she jumped. She quickly got a hold of herself and answered. It was Taylor.

"Do you like the apartment, Lily?" he asked.

"You shouldn't have, Taylor! I'll never be able to pay you back. I'm very grateful, but all this…" She waved her hand in the air. "I don't need all this expensive furniture."

"You don't have to pay me back," Taylor said.

"No, Taylor. We made a deal, remember? I told you I would pay you back." And yet she knew she could never do it… at least, not for a very long time. "Why did you have to get all this furniture?"

"It came with the apartment," he said dismissively.

"For an extra cost, I imagine."

"But worth it."

"Yes, and it increases the amount I have to pay back."

"I told you that you don't have to…"

"Taylor, I thought we had already agreed that I would pay you back?"

"Okay, Lily." He sounded slightly frustrated. "If

you insist on paying me back, you can. But you have all the time in the world."

She sighed. "And that might not be enough time to pay you back for all this." Her eyes traveled round the living room again.

"I'll call you back tomorrow," he said, sounding as distracted as he had when he'd called earlier. "Tell me you like the apartment at least."

"I love it, but..."

He cut in. "That's all I needed to hear. I'll call you later." He ended the call before she could say anything more, and she stared at her phone for a long moment.

Sofia turned around to face her. "Lily, who was that? Tell me the truth. That guy you just spoke to, he paid for this apartment, didn't he? He paid for the furniture as well."

Lily sighed wearily and nodded.

Sofia chuckled and shook her head. "So, you got yourself a wealthy boyfriend in just a few days. How did you do it?"

"It's not like that!" Lily protested.

"From what I can see, it's exactly like that." Sofia searched Lily's eyes. "There's something else, isn't there?" She began to laugh. "Lily! Don't tell me your boyfriend is married!"

"He is married, but he's not my boyfriend! He's just an old friend who..."

Sofia cut in. "So you gave me grief for dating George because he's married, and yet you're doing the very same thing." She shook her head. "Lily, Lily, Lily! I thought you said your religious beliefs were against that. But you're just a hypocrite."

Lily bristled. "I am not a hypocrite. I'm not doing

the same thing as you. I'm not involved with him like you are with George." She frowned. "What am I saying? I'm not involved with him at all. We're just old friends. I knew him back in Fallow Creek. We were neighbors as children, and he's the brother of my good friend."

"So then why did he get you a penthouse apartment in this building and then furnish it fully with expensive furniture?"

Lily shrugged, unwilling to tell Sofia anything more about her and Taylor.

"Let me tell you why," Sofia said. "No guy does all this for a girl unless he wants something from her. You might not think there's anything between you, but he sure does. He likes you — a lot — and he definitely wants something from you. And I know you know what."

Lily felt scandalized. "That's not true! He doesn't want what you're thinking. He's not like that. Besides, he's going back to California soon. That's where he lives. I promised to pay him back, and I'll try the best I can to do so."

"And how are you going to pay him back for all this?" Sofia chuckled.

"I'm trying to find a job. Once I do, I'll start to save."

"I guess you'll also not buy any food to feed yourself or do anything else so you can pay him back, because the money it will take to do so will mean exactly that. And it'll probably take forever. You have to stop lying to yourself, Lily. You won't be able to pay that guy back... except with something other than money." Sofia smirked.

"Stop it!" Lily glared at her friend.

Sofia raised her hand. "Okay, then, fine! Even if he doesn't want anything from you right now, I can assure you that he likes you a lot." She touched Lily's hand. "And I think you like him, too."

Lily looked away. "Of course I like him. He's a childhood friend."

"No more than that?" Sofia turned her face around again. "You're attracted to him as well. I know desire when I see it, and my friend, I can see it in your eyes. I saw it when you were speaking to him, and I see it right now as well."

Lily shut her eyes and moaned. "It's wrong! He's married." She sighed. "Well… thank God he's going back to California tomorrow."

"He's going back tomorrow?" Sofia shook her head. "That's not right. Listen, Lily. You should do something about the way you feel about him. Don't fight it."

Lily narrowed her eyes and glared at Sofia. "What are you saying? You want me to start an affair with him the way you have with George?" She shifted away from Sofia. "That's a sin in God's eyes. I'm never doing that."

"Where does he live… or at least, where's he staying now?" Sofia asked.

"At a hotel," Lily waved her hand dismissively, but her heart began to pound.

"And he doesn't live in Tucson?"

"No," Lily answered weakly.

"So, his wife isn't in town?"

Lily didn't answer. She already knew where Sofia was going with all this, and she felt disgusted. Not just with Sofia, but with herself. Sofia's line of questioning was stirring up a deep longing in her and conjuring images in her mind she did not want to think about.

"You want to be with him, Lily, don't you? You know you do. Just go to him right now and get whatever it is you feel on the inside out of your system. Maybe you'll forget about him after it's over, or maybe you won't. But at least you'll..."

Lily sprang up from the sofa and looked down at Sofia. "Stop it!" she yelled. "I will never sleep with a married man! It was why I was driven out of Fallow Creek. I was glad when I didn't have to marry a married man, even though I knew I would be separated from my family. I'm not going to start doing that now. And if you keep pushing me in that direction, our friendship will be over!"

"Okay, okay!" Sofia raised her hand again. "But what are you going to do about your feelings for that guy?"

"What am I going to do?"

"Yes. Because those feelings won't disappear just 'cause you want them to. Trust me, I know." She looked up at Lily, and their eyes met. "I think you might even be in love with him. So, what are you going to do?"

"I'm not in love with him, Sofia! Stop saying things like that. Just as I said, he's leaving for California tomorrow. Once he does, that will hopefully be the end of it."

Sofia laughed and stood up from the sofa. "You just keep lying to yourself, Lily. You're living in an apartment the guy paid for, sitting on the furniture he bought you, and you like him. It won't be long before you become just like me."

"Never! I will never be like you, Sofia."

Sofia snorted and walked to the door. She turned around and said, "You already are like me, Lily. You've been acting all self-righteous, and yet you're in love with a married man. The irony." She chuckled. "The earlier you admit the truth to yourself, the better." She stared at Lily for a moment more and then opened the door and walked out of the apartment.

Lily sank onto the sofa once more, dread, guilt and shame flooding her heart. Sofia was right about everything — except for one thing. In spite of how she felt, she would never give in to her desires. But that didn't make her feel any better about the fact that Taylor would be gone in a couple of hours. She covered her face with her hands and wept.

TEN

Taylor paused the football game he was watching and stretched out his legs on the bed. He picked up his cell phone and dialed Rachel's number. He had received numerous text messages from her over the past few days and a couple of phone calls as well. She'd been calling and texting for months, but he hadn't been ready to answer any of her calls or messages until now.

He still wasn't interested in hearing anything she had to say about what was going on in Fallow Creek, but he missed her. As kids, they had been very close but had grown apart as adults. After years of barely speaking to each other, they had renewed their relationship last year and become close again. He did not want to spoil their relationship because of his grief and stubbornness. He wanted to hear her voice again, and he also wanted her advice regarding his feelings for Lily. And not just his feelings for her, but his concerns about leaving her without a job. The more he thought about it, the more it bothered him.

He'd ordered room service after he'd come back from his final meeting with his client and had eaten thinking about Lily, wishing he could see her again. He leaned back on his pillow and waited for Rachel to pick up his call. When he heard her voice on the other end of the line, his mood immediately lifted.

"Taylor, I've been so worried about you!" Rachel exclaimed. "Why have you not been answering my calls or any of my text messages?"

"I'm so sorry, Rachel," he said. "A lot has happened since the last time I saw you."

"A lot has happened here in Fallow Creek as well," she said. "Did you get any of my text messages? Don't you want to know everything that's happened?"

"Rachel, to be honest with you, I really don't care about anything that's going on in Fallow Creek right now." He wanted to tell her he could guess what she had to say about the things that had happened there, and that it wasn't really that important to him, but he held his peace. "I don't want to hear about what's going on in that community. I left there for a reason. I would rather you didn't tell me anything about it."

"Taylor, what's wrong? Why are you talking like this? I'm pretty sure you would want to know what's happened in the town you grew up in. It's huge, Taylor. Really huge. I needed your advice about some things, but it's all been resolved now. Thank God."

"Well, I'm glad to hear that."

"Taylor, what happened?" Rachel asked. "Why did you suddenly leave Fallow Creek with Faye and Joshua?"

He took a deep breath to try to steady his voice as

fresh waves of sorrow poured over him. He recalled again the day Faye had lost her life giving birth to their baby girl. It was not something he wanted to recount, but he had to. Rachel had a right to know all that had happened. He said slowly, "I lost Faye, Rachel. She died ten months ago while giving birth to our daughter."

"No, Taylor! Tell me it's not true!"

"Unfortunately, it is. I miss her so much."

"I'm so sorry, Taylor," Rachel said, her voice laden with emotions. "If only I'd known. Where are you and Josh now? And what about the baby?"

"We all live in Northern California now," he told her. "And the baby's doing really well." He chuckled. "Her name is Bree, short for Brielle, and she's a handful, but I love her with all my heart."

"Well, thank God that the baby survived. Again, Taylor, I'm really sorry. Faye was such a kind person. But why didn't you tell me when she passed? Why did you have to leave town?"

"I just couldn't bear staying in Fallow Creek for one more minute after she died. I blamed the midwives and many other people there who advised me not to take her to a bigger hospital out of the community. If I had, she might still be alive today. I blamed myself. I still do. Going back to Fallow Creek would remind me of her and how that town claimed her life. I just can't bring myself to go back there again."

"I understand now," Rachel said. "Know that I will be praying for you and Josh and the baby."

"Thank you," Taylor said.

"I wish I could come over there and see you, Taylor, but a lot has been going on here and me and

Keith have so many responsibilities right now. I won't be able to get away."

Taylor sighed. As much as he didn't want or need any additional information about what was going on in Fallow Creek, it sounded as though Rachel had a lot more to tell him. He took a deep breath again and said, "Okay, Rachel. Tell me everything. What's going on in that community that I need to know?"

"It started some days before you left, I believe. I told you how Dennis Hamilton allowed Keith and me back into Fallow Creek because Keith gave him a prophetic word. But I didn't tell you exactly what that word was." She began to narrate the most amazing and distressing story he'd heard in a long time. He had thought he knew most of what she wanted to say, but he didn't know anything. Except for a very small part that he doubted she knew about.

He listened, his anger growing as she told him about finding out who Fallow Creek's real owner was. When she told him she was the true owner of Fallow Creek, as the land had been given to her by her real father and grandfather, he could not hold in his amazement.

"I can't believe this!" he said.

"I felt the same way when I heard," she said and continued her story. She talked about how Dennis and his men had kidnapped her and Keith and about the miraculous intervention.

He listened intently as she spoke. He was happy for her, but angry because he'd been lied to. He would have to deal with the liar later. For now, he focused on her news, fully pleased for her, but concerned about the difficulties she would face and was probably facing now.

"So, Dennis is dead?"

"Yes. He and our stepfather and those men that were with him."

Taylor frowned. He had never been close to his stepfather — in fact, they'd had a stormy relationship — but he certainly hadn't wished for the man's death.

She went on with her story, telling him how people had started to leave town when they'd found out she was the true owner of Fallow Creek. He was not surprised about that. The men of that town would not take it well once they found out a woman, and especially one who did not believe in their patriarchal way of life, was now the leader of the town. He had been like that himself months ago, but not anymore.

She finally told him with triumph and joy about getting her daughter, Emily, away from her ex. He was elated for her, but one thing worried him... no, two, but she didn't need to know about the second thing now. He voiced his concern. "Are you telling me that Mike Cadwell is sort of a prisoner at the Restoration House?"

"We don't know what to do with him yet. If we let him go, he'll cause a lot of trouble for us. I'm trying to speak to him every day to try to convince him to give up his vindictive ways."

"And what about his guards?" Taylor asked. "Haven't they noticed that he's not around?"

"No, Olivia told them Mike is taking a long break in the House and instructed her to tell them he didn't want to be disturbed at all."

"Okay, because I was afraid his guards would come looking for him at the House one day."

"They have no idea he's here," Rachel said.

"You should involve the police in Prospect, Rachel. You can't keep holding Mike at the Restoration House. I think it's the only thing to do."

"But they won't be able to hold him there as we have nothing for which they can charge him. And in spite of Mike's cruelty, I don't want him arrested. He is Emily's father."

"It's what he deserves, Rachel."

She said nothing for a long while. When she did speak, her voice was soft as she asked how he was managing the kids without Faye. "Maybe you should come back to Fallow Creek. Keith and I, and a host of other women in the House, will help you watch the kids, especially when you go to work or on a business trip."

"I can't come back, Rachel. At least not now."

"Okay, I understand," she said. "But I know your job can get hectic sometimes. I guess you have a nanny for your children?"

He sighed loudly. "That brings me to the question I want to ask you, Rachel. I saw Lily Hunter at the store some days ago. I actually gave her your number. Has she called you?"

"No, she hasn't. I got a call from a strange number a few days ago, but I didn't answer because I don't answer strange numbers these days. Maybe it was her."

"Yes, I think it was her. Anyway, I came to Tucson for a business meeting with some clients and went for a walk. I wanted to buy one of our favorite snacks growing up because I saw it in a particular store the day I arrived. That was where I saw Lily. I found out that she didn't have a job or any money. She was in dire financial straits, and I tried to get her a job, but that didn't turn out right at all."

He told Rachel what had happened with James Kilpatrick and then told her how he had offered Lily a job. "She refused to take the job, which was to come with me to California to be a nanny to my kids. I told her I would pay her well, but that didn't change her mind." He said softly, "But I understand why."

"Why? Why would she reject the job you offered her?"

He paused for a bit and then said, "Because she's afraid. Frankly, so am I."

Rachel sounded confused. "What are you talking about? Afraid of what?"

"Afraid of the intense desire we feel for each other." He began to tell Rachel everything, starting from how he and Lily had spent that first day at the store to the phone call he'd made to her some hours ago. He told Rachel about his dilemma; about the promise he'd made to Josh and the vow he'd made to honor Faye's memory. After he had told Rachel everything, he said, "I don't know what to do now. I feel terrible about leaving Lily here without a job. Every time I think about not seeing her again, I feel like I can't breathe." He sighed. "And yet I know that it has to happen. I have to go back to California and forget about her."

"So, you didn't tell her that you're unmarried now?" Rachel asked.

"No."

"Do you understand how she'll be feeling right

now? The guilt and shame that she'll be dealing with because she's fallen for you? I remember her telling me how she abhorred the polygamous practices in Fallow Creek. She'll feel terrible about falling for a married man."

Taylor gritted his teeth. He'd never thought about it that way before.

"You should tell her, even if you don't want to get involved with her. You should let her know the truth."

"But where will telling her the truth lead? Faye died less than a year ago. There's no way I'm getting involved with another woman now. Or in the near future, for that matter. I don't think I'll ever give my heart to anyone again."

"And yet it seems you have given it to Lily."

"I didn't exactly give it to her. It's more like she took it. Unwillingly, though, from all she said to me." He shook his head, more confused than ever. "I just don't know. All I know is that I don't want to leave her with no job or money. But I have no choice."

"Taylor, stop worrying about Lily. I know you're a kind man and you care about people, but Lily's a big girl. She'll be fine without you. You did a great thing by giving her an apartment. God will provide her a job."

Taylor heaved a sigh. "I know, but He can provide for her through me."

Rachel chuckled again. "I think you should tell her the truth and then let her know that right now you can't be in a relationship because of Faye. She'll understand. Just give it time. Go back to California and try to forget her."

"What?"

"You need some distance from her to know exactly how you feel. If you do forget about her, then what you're feeling for her now is not real. But if you can't, then you know a relationship with her is worth exploring."

"I'm afraid if I go to her apartment to speak to her, we'll do something that we might regret later."

Rachel chuckled. "Trust me, I understand. I had a similar thing with Keith. You don't have to tell her in person. You can tell her over the phone."

The thought of not seeing Lily every day as he'd done for almost a week now felt awful. He said, "How long should I stay away?"

"As long as it takes," she answered. "I would say at least six months to a year."

He gasped. "What if she finds someone else within that time?"

"Then it's either she is not for you or the relationship will be temporary and you'll find your way to each other."

"It won't be easy leaving Lily in Tucson. I think about her almost every waking moment. I don't understand how I've fallen so hard for her in just a few days."

Rachel laughed. "I don't know about just a few days, Taylor. I remember that you were very fond of her when we were kids. You liked her more than all the other girls who were always chasing after you."

In spite of himself, he chuckled.

"You felt something special for Lily, then, I remember. And I know for sure that she had a giant crush on you. I don't think either of you have forgotten about that, and even though, for a time, the feelings were suppressed, they have bloomed again now that you're together as adults."

"And yet I have to go back to California and try to forget her."

"Yes. You feel so strongly about keeping the vow you made to honor Faye's memory by staying single that you've actively been keeping the truth about her death from Lily. But you have to tell her."

His sighed. "Okay. I will."

"Good. Does she know how hard you've fallen for her?"

He groaned. "I think she does. I probably didn't do a very good job of hiding my feelings from her yesterday. We were supposed to go to the apartment I got for her together, but I decided not to. I didn't think it was safe for us to be alone together in an apartment."

Rachel burst out laughing.

"It's not funny, Rachel. It's excruciating."

"I'm sorry," Rachel said, still laughing. "I want you to be happy, and I think you will be with Lily. But since you don't want to surrender your heart to her because you feel it's too soon, you definitely shouldn't get involved with her now. You've already planned to take time off work to spend with your kids. Do that and mourn Faye some more. After that, you can start a new life with someone else if that is what you truly want."

"Thank you, Rachel," he smiled. "I'm glad I called you."

They talked some more about Fallow Creek, about Rachel's unique dilemma and the new idea she had to help the women still living there. When the call finally ended, he thought about everything

Rachel had said to him about Lily. His heart flooded with worry once more. After tomorrow, he wouldn't see her again, and he would have to leave her knowing she had no money. He was a fixer. He liked to fix things. That was probably why he'd chosen construction as his occupation. He had gotten her that apartment, but it just wasn't enough. Yes, he had stocked the fridge with food, but it would only last so long.

Stop worrying, Taylor. Remember what Rachel said. God will take care of Lily.

She was an adult. She had survived without him for all these months. She would survive without him when he was gone. He couldn't continue to treat her like a charity case anyway, or she might come to resent him.

He put his hand on his forehead and shook his head. Rachel had told him to tell Lily that Faye had died and he was single now. After that, he was supposed to leave town and try to put her at the back of his mind. He was supposed to go on with his life as though he had not spent five heart-wrenching days falling hard for her.

That would be hard. That would be very hard.

A scripture verse appeared in his mind. *Lie not to one another, seeing that ye have put off the old man with his deeds.*

He shut his eyes, imagining how she would feel when he told her. Rachel was right. She deserved to know. It had been totally wrong to keep the truth from her. Maybe she would hate him once he told her about Faye. After all, he had knowingly withheld the truth from her, putting her through a lot of emotional pain. He had to tell her now. The sooner, the better.

He picked up his cell phone from beside him and began to dial her number. He stopped for a moment and sighed. Once he told her the truth, two different things could happen. She would either hate his guts for knowingly keeping the truth from her and causing her hurt, or they would both give in to the desires that had been tearing at them for days. Dread flooded him. "Lord, please don't let her hate me for keeping the truth from her. And please help us to stay away from each other until I leave tomorrow."

He continued to dial her number and then held his breath as the phone rang. *Lord, please let it go well… at least as well as it can go considering the situation.*

But he knew that no matter how it went, he would leave Tucson tomorrow with an aching heart.

ELEVEN

Lily sat beside Sofia on the plush snow-white couch, sipping the mocktail Sofia had brought from her apartment and listening to her friend talk about her future travel plans to north and east Africa. From time to time, she gazed out the window of her new apartment. The view outside was even more amazing now that it was evening.

Sofia had invited herself back to Lily's apartment this evening in spite of their argument earlier in the day. Without apologizing, she had sat on the couch and started talking to Lily. At first, Lily had ignored her, but gradually, she'd listened with fascination as her friend regaled her with one story after another.

They had both fallen into their usual routine once more. Sofia was doing all the talking while Lily listened intently. Sofia's stories, especially the ones about her trips abroad, were always so interesting. Lily was hungry to see the world after being trapped all her life in the tiny Fallow Creek. It was what she wanted most next to finding her family and maybe being with the man she'd fallen for.

She groaned as Taylor's face filled her mind and all the feelings she had for him poured over her.

"What is it, Lily?" Sofia asked.

"Nothing."

Instinctively, she turned and stared at her phone on the coffee table. Taylor was supposed to go back tomorrow, and she had been terribly worried about that. Worried about not seeing him again. That was probably why she had let Sofia back into her apartment. Sofia's many interesting stories would sufficiently distract her. At least she had thought so. But now Taylor's face was etched in her mind, and she couldn't stop thinking about him. If only he would call so she could hear his voice for the last time. If only she could see him again... but she knew going to his hotel to see him would be asking for trouble.

She jumped when her phone began to ring. When she picked it up, she gasped. It was Taylor. Her heart began to gallop and she swallowed. *Calm down, Lily!*

"Who is it?" Sofia asked. "Your married friend?"

Lily ignored her. She tried to sound as normal as she could and said, "Hey, Taylor! How are you?"

"Umm... I'm good."

She frowned. He sounded scared. Why?

"Lily... you know I'll be going back tomorrow," he said. "I just wanted to check up on you one last time."

The ache in her heart increased, and an overwhelming longing to see him again, to be with him, washed over her. She forced a smile into her voice and tried to smother the longing. "Great," she said. "I'm glad you called to check up on me. And thank you for everything. Especially the apartment. It's beautiful."

"I can't wait to go back to California and see my kids again."

"Oh… you have two kids now. Is the second one a boy or a girl?"

"A girl. A beautiful girl." He sighed loudly. "Every time I'm away, I miss them so much, and I worry constantly about them."

"I understand, Taylor," she said, and then silently chided herself. How could she possibly understand when she had no kids? She quickly added, "I know you're a great father. If I had kids and had to leave them constantly for work, I would miss them too. But you're lucky you have Faye. I don't know her well, but I've seen her once with your son. I think she's a great mom. Since your kids are with her, they're in good hands. You shouldn't worry so much."

He said nothing for a long moment, and she began to worry that he wasn't on the line anymore. "Taylor, are you still there?"

"I have something to tell you, Lily. I haven't been totally honest with you. I should have told you the first day we met at the store."

She bit her lip, fear gripping her. What was he about to tell her?

"Faye died ten months ago, after giving birth to our daughter. It's just me and the kids now."

The floor beneath her felt like it was collapsing. She closed her eyes as a wave of weakness went through her. Sadness overtook her as her heart hurt for him. She finally found her voice and said, "I'm so very sorry, Taylor."

She suddenly felt horrified. She had not even asked how Faye was doing. She remembered the times over the past few days when she had brought up his marriage and his wife with him. She had just assumed the woman was alive and well when she had died months ago. She felt like a cad. "I'm really sorry," she said again. "I didn't know."

"It's okay," he said. "And I'm sorry for keeping it from you. I just didn't want to talk about it, and the pain is still somewhat fresh."

"I understand, Taylor."

"And Lily, you spoke about Sarah on the day we met at the store. I didn't marry her. I'm single now."

He sounded so sad and so lost. An irresistible urge to rush to his side and try to comfort him came over her, but she managed to smother it. She pressed her lips together, trying to fully process all he'd revealed to her. If he wasn't married and was available, then she could go to him. She gasped.

Go, Lily! He's not married, and you know that now. There's nothing stopping you from going to comfort him. He needs you.

She bit her lip and forced herself to remain seated. No good would come from going to him, and he didn't need her. He had the Lord. She knew exactly what would happen if she gave in to the way she felt now. They would both end up doing something they would regret later. Just because she now knew he wasn't married didn't mean she had to throw caution to the wind and give in to her raging desire. "I'm sorry," she said again, not knowing what else to say.

"It's okay," he said.

She began to imagine how lonely he must be without his wife, his lifelong companion. *You can help take away that loneliness now*, a voice in her head said. She sighed heavily and ignored the voice.

"Anyway, I'm glad you have somewhere good to stay now. At least that will give me some peace of mind."

She smiled. "Have I thanked you for the apartment?"

He chuckled. "Many times."

"Well... thank you again."

For a few seconds, he said nothing and then sighed. "So, I guess it's goodbye now. I've enjoyed every minute I spent time with you, Lily Hunter. Even though some of those times were a little awkward."

She shut her eyes as a flood of panic swept over her. He was saying his final goodbye. *Oh Lord, I can't let him go just like that.* Not now that I know he's not married. What was she doing just sitting here?

Still, she forced herself to remain in her seat. She wasn't thinking straight. The man was clearly still mourning his wife. No good would come out of rushing over to him now. Her mind went back to her past conversations with him. She'd talked about his wife casually, thinking Faye was still alive. She could imagine how much pain that would have caused him, even though he had said nothing. If only he had told her earlier.

What would you have done if he had? It was a good thing he'd held out on telling her the truth until the day before he left Tucson.

"Lily, I have to go," he said.

"Yes. Have a safe flight and kiss your kids for me."

"Will do."

He ended the call, and she wrapped her arms tightly around herself to keep from leaping up and rushing out the door to go to his hotel. Tears flooded her eyes and then streamed down her face.

"Lily!" Sofia put her hand on Lily's shoulder. "What's wrong? Why are you crying?"

Lily bowed her head as waves of sorrow washed over her.

Sofia lifted Lily's head up. "Lily, tell me. What's troubling you? Is it the phone call you just got? That guy said something to upset you, didn't he?"

Lily sighed and shook her head.

"Why are you crying, then?"

"Taylor lost his wife. She died months ago, and I didn't know. He just told me now. He sounded so sad, so hurt. With everything in me, I wish I could go to him right now and comfort him. But I can't. And he's leaving tomorrow." Fresh tears welled in her eyes.

Sofia looked confused. "I don't understand. You just found out the man you like isn't married and there's nothing in your way anymore. Why are you still sitting here, weeping? Go to him!"

"I can't!"

"Why not? You just told me his wife is dead. He's single now and so are you. What's stopping you from...?"

"I just can't! It makes no difference that we're both single. With the way I feel about him, the way we feel about each other, I know it wouldn't be safe for us to be in his hotel room alone."

Sofia frowned. "You and your weird religious beliefs. I don't understand how two single consenting adults who have such intense feelings for each other choose to do nothing about it." She shook her head as she stared at Lily. "It makes no sense."

Lily turned away from her.

"Okay, tell you what. I'll go with you to the hotel where he's staying and act as a chaperone. Will that help?"

Lily stared at Sofia as hope began to swell within her. "You'd do that for me?"

"Of course I will," Sofia said. "Call him right now and tell him you're coming over."

She immediately picked up her cell phone and dialed Taylor's number. He answered almost instantly, and she told him she was coming over.

There was silence on the other end of the line.

"Taylor?"

"Are you sure that's the right thing to do?" he asked.

"Yes, Taylor. A friend of mine is coming with me so there's no temptation to do something we'll later regret."

Again he said nothing for a short while and then said, "Okay." He sounded hesitant, which gave her slight pause, but she waved her concerns away.

"I'll be right over," she told him and quickly ended the call. She turned to smile at Sofia. "Let me go get my purse." She hurried into the next room. Taylor had also outfitted it with a bed, mattress, comfortable all-white bedding, and burgundy drapes. She grabbed her purse from the bed and hurried out again.

She immediately made her way to the front door and stopped when Sofia called out her name.

"Wait for me, Lily!" Sofia said, giggling. "You look like a lovesick teenager. I'm sure he's still going to be at the hotel when we get there. Just calm down."

Lily sighed and waited until Sofia was at her side, and they both made their way out of the apartment.

"You'll drive me there?" Lily asked Sofia as they got into the elevator.

"Yes, I will. Good thing I have my car keys here." She put her hand on Lily's shoulder, a huge grin on her face. "I'm almost as excited as you, Lily," she said. "This'll be my friend's first boyfriend. How exciting!"

"He's not my boyfriend, Sofia."

"But you want him to be, don't you?"

She wanted that and much more. But she told Sofia nothing and turned her gaze away from her. In a little while she would see Taylor, but she didn't know how things would end between them. He was leaving town tomorrow anyway. Who knew if he wanted a relationship with her, especially considering he clearly still loved his wife and was still mourning her.

The best thing she could expect was that he would want a relationship with her. A thread of excitement went through her. It would be a long-distance relationship, which was not ideal, but…

She gasped.

"What is it?" Sophia asked as they stepped out of the elevator.

"I just remembered that he asked me to go to California with him to become his kids' nanny. Of course I refused because at the time I thought he was married, but now…"

Sofia smiled. "Now you can go."

Lily frowned, worried. "But I'm still not sure it's the best thing to do."

"Why not?" Sofia asked as they strode through the lobby.

"Because of the very same reason I didn't want to go to his hotel room alone. It would be even worse living in his house or near it. Besides, I'm not sure how he really feels about me. I know he likes me, I know we have a strong physical attraction for each other, but I don't know if that's enough. He clearly still loves his wife. I don't know if he's in any place to start a relationship right now. It might be a mistake for me to hope he'll want one with me."

"This is your insecurity talking, Lily. Besides, you have only really talked about what Taylor wants. What do *you* want?"

"I will take him up on his job offer and go to California with him. I know I shouldn't, but I will. Not just because I need a job badly, but because I can't help it, Sofia. The thought of never seeing him again after today has been driving me crazy."

Sofia giggled. "So you have already gotten over your fear that you will sleep with him if you move to California and then later regret it?"

Lily rolled her eyes at the mischievous grin on Sofia's face. "No, I haven't. But I guess I'll have to ask the Lord to protect us both."

Sofia chuckled as they got into her car. "And isn't that like tempting God or something?" Lily stared at her in surprise, and she shrugged. "What? I read it somewhere. I can't remember where, though."

"You're right, Sofia." Lily pressed her lips tightly together. "That would be tempting God." She put her hand on her forehead and sighed sadly. "I guess I can't take him up on his job offer."

"But you need the job!"

"The Lord will have to provide one for me here."

"You're the strangest person I know," Sofia said.

Lily did not reply.

TWELVE

Taylor's heart drummed as he dressed in a gray sports coat over his shirt and pants and left his hotel room. Lily had sounded so eager to see him. Even though he was equally eager to see her, he felt hesitant at the same time. Yes, she had said she would bring a friend along, but still, he felt very vulnerable with her. And without a doubt it was not completely safe for them to be here in the hotel together, even with her friend.

He got to the lobby, walked to the entrance of the hotel, and took a deep breath when he saw her approaching. She was with a dark-haired woman who looked about her age. He smiled as she reached him, and she smiled back. His pulse raced as he gazed at her. She looked beautiful, even dressed simply in a loose, off-white dress.

He exhaled and told himself to calm down as he reached out to give her a loose hug. She introduced him to her friend Sofia, and he led them both to his favorite restaurant in the hotel. It was almost eight p.m., and the restaurant was packed. They sat at a private table in the far-left corner of the restaurant, and a waiter came to take their order.

He didn't feel like eating much, so he ordered a simple grilled fish and herb salad. Lily ordered a Caesar's salad with chicken, and her friend ordered a seafood platter. When she also ordered a glass of cognac, Taylor lifted his eyebrows slightly but said nothing. The waiter left to get their food, and Taylor turned to look at Lily again. She took his hand on the table, and he gasped in surprise.

"I'm sorry, Taylor," she said. "Faye's passing must have been so hard."

He sighed heavily. "It still is. I miss her every day."

Heat spread through his fingers and up his arms when she wove her fingers through his. Her hand felt soft and warm in his, and a pleasurable sensation ran through him. He was surprised that she was holding his hand, and even more so that she had woven their fingers together. His breath caught in his throat at the look of longing in her eyes.

For a long moment, neither of them could take their eyes away from the other. He looked down at the table. *Keep your wits about you,* he cautioned himself. Just because she knew now that he was single didn't mean they should lose their heads. Besides, he was leaving tomorrow. Nothing could ever happen between them; definitely not now, and maybe never.

When he looked up into her eyes again, she was still looking at him, and he knew without a doubt that she had different ideas from him. Unlike him, she was interested in pursuing a relationship. He couldn't think straight. Under different circumstances, he would have wanted that too, but as it was, it wouldn't be possible.

"How have you been coping with just you and the kids?" she asked.

He shrugged and pretended that the way she was looking at him now, coupled with the feel of her hand in his, was not slowly stealing his senses. With as much nonchalance as he could, he said, "I'm doing okay, I guess. For now, our housekeeper also acts as the nanny."

As soon as he said the words, he regretted them. He had offered her a job as a nanny for his kids, but now he knew it was not the best idea for her to come back to California with him. He groaned inwardly at the conflicting emotions he felt — that he'd been feeling since the day he'd met her at the store.

On the one hand, he wanted her to remember the job offer and tell him that she would accept it, but on the other, he did not want that. He wanted to do what Rachel had told him to do. He wanted to keep his promise to Josh and to his late wife. And he wanted to prevent the disaster that was sure to happen if Lily went back to California with him.

Her friend Sofia began to talk about a mutual acquaintance of hers and Lily's. At first, he politely listened, and then his mind strayed back to his present dilemma.

The waiter arrived with their food, and the three of them tucked in. Sofia asked him what he did for a living, and he tried to explain his job as best as he could but with as few words as possible. He didn't really feel like talking.

"So, the apartment you bought for Lily. You fully

furnished it. I have to say, you're a very generous man."

Taylor shrugged. "I don't know about that. I've known Lily since we were kids. She needed my help, and I tried to help with what I could. I'm sure she would have done the same for me if I were in her shoes."

Sofia chuckled and glanced at Lily. "I'm sure she would have."

He looked at Sofia's plate and arched his brows, surprised. She had almost finished her meal. And it had been a large one.

She glanced at her wristwatch and said, "I have an emergency. I have to go."

"What emergency?" Lily raised her brows and stared at her friend with a suspicious look on her face.

Taylor smiled in amusement.

Sofia stood. She bent down briefly to give Lily a kiss on her cheek and then gave her a mischievous smile. She turned to Taylor. "It's been nice getting to know you, Mr. Dalton." She looked down at Lily and smiled. "Now you be a good girl... but not too good. I'll see you later." She grinned and glanced at Taylor. "Have fun, you kids." She strode away.

Lily called out to her, but she didn't answer. She groaned and bit her lip. She seemed frightened, and Taylor frowned. She murmured something and finally faced Taylor fully.

An awkward silence stretched out between them as they ate. Lily picked at her food, and Taylor intermittently glanced at her while he ate. It occurred to him that the reason she seemed frightened was because her friend was gone; the friend that had been here to act as their chaperone. He searched his mind, trying to come up with a conversation that would put her mind at ease, or at least help her forget her fears. He finally remembered his phone conversation with Rachel and looked at Lily. "I have some news about Fallow Creek."

She looked at him with a quizzical expression on her face, but she also looked slightly afraid. "What is it?"

"Something huge happened there."

The panic disappeared from her face, replaced by concern.

"I finally called Rachel, and what she told me blew me away."

Lily gazed intently at him. Her lashes fluttered as she fixed her gaze on him, causing his heart to do the same. He ignored his fluttering heart and went on. He told her everything Rachel had said to him, from her and Keith's arrival at Fallow Creek to finding out that her grandfather had been the true founder of the town and that she was the owner now. He told her that Dennis Hamilton had murdered Rachel's father and about the confrontation with Dennis. He talked about the kidnapping and the supernatural flood and mudslide that had swept Dennis and several of the squad members into the river at the edge of Fallow Creek.

She listened with eyes as big as dinner plates. Her eyes were fixed on him, her mouth slightly open. When he'd finished, she shook her head slowly. "Unbelievable! How have things changed so quickly within the past ten months since I left? Wow! I wish I'd been there to witness all that. So

Dennis Hamilton is gone, and your sister is now the leader of our community?"

Taylor nodded.

"Wow!" she exclaimed again. "Did you know that I was supposed to marry Dennis Hamilton?"

He laughed, but she shook her head. "I'm serious, Taylor. When I left the Restoration House, it was because I'd made a promise to my parents that I would marry anyone they wanted me to. I was tired of that House and wanted to get away from it. My plan was to find a way to escape Fallow Creek one day, but when I found out it was Dennis Hamilton they wanted me to marry, I freaked out. I couldn't bring myself to do it."

He shook his head slowly, shocked. "I didn't know that," he said, loathing the man who had tried to force Lily into marrying him. "So then he kicked you out of Fallow Creek for refusing to become his wife?"

"Yes. He said he didn't want me to 'pollute the minds of the other women in the community.' He said I was already lost. I was sent out of town with nothing but what my mom was able to secretly give me, though it wasn't a lot." The amazed look on her face returned. "So I can go back to Fallow Creek now," she said, sounding excited. "I can finally see my parents. I probably won't stay there because I don't want to stay in a small town anymore, but I'll…"

He interrupted her. "Lily there's something else," he said.

She arched her eyebrow. "What is it?"

"Rachel told me that shortly after she took over leadership of the town, people started to leave. She said that almost everyone has left now except for the women who were at the Restoration House already and a few who joined the House later."

Lily pressed her lips together as a look of dread appeared on her face. "What about my parents?" she asked in a shaky voice. "And my sister? Did she leave as well?"

"I don't know, Lily." He took her hand again on the table. She looked so worried that he wanted to take her in his arms, but that would not be a good idea. "We can call Rachel together and ask her right now." He looked around. The restaurant was still full and as noisy and rowdy as ever. "Let's step out of the restaurant for a minute."

They walked out of the restaurant together and stood in a corner that was empty of people and less noisy. He dialed Rachel's number, and she answered on the second ring. Putting her on speaker, he said, "Rachel, Lily Hunter is here with me."

Rachel's voice came on the other end of the line. "Lily! How are you? Taylor told me you live in Tucson now."

"Yes," Lily said, a smile on her face. "I called you once or twice, but you didn't answer."

"I'm so sorry," Rachel told her. "A lot has happened over the past few months, and I stopped answering calls from unknown numbers."

The smile melted off Lily's face, and she looked worried again. "Taylor was just telling me that you said most of the people in Fallow Creek have left the community. Do you know if my parents and my sister, Stella, are still there?"

For a few seconds there was silence over the line, and then Rachel answered, "I really don't know, but my guess is that they have left as well."

"Maybe you can help me check their house to see if they're still there," Lily pleaded.

"I will," Rachel said, "But to be truthful, I think they've left. I know all the people who are still in this community."

Taylor silently sighed. *Not all.*

"Most of them now stay in the Restoration House where my husband and I live. If your parents and sister were still in town, I would know."

Lily bit her lip and said nothing for some seconds. She looked like she was about to cry. Taylor took her hand and squeezed it encouragingly, and she gave him a sweet smile. "You don't know where the people who left went?" she asked.

"I have no idea," Rachel answered. "I'm sure they are all spread in different places now."

Lily's shoulders stooped, and she bowed her head.

"Listen, Lily, now that everyone, including the elders who threw you out of Fallow Creek, have left, you can come back."

Lily said nothing, and Rachel added, "Please think about it, Lily."

"What's the point?" she asked, raising her head again. "If my parents and sister aren't there, then there's no point going back. There's nothing for me in Fallow Creek anymore. Besides, I don't want to live in a small town any longer. My plan was to go back, find a way to get my parents and sister from Fallow Creek, and leave again."

"But now that I'm the leader of this place, people can do whatever they want. Things aren't the way they used to be." She sighed loudly. "The town is deserted now."

Lily shook her head, looking depressed. "No, Rachel, I can't go back. Not knowing where my parents and Stella are bad enough. Going back to Fallow Creek would only make me more depressed. I'll just stay here." She pressed the phone to her ear. "Besides, I have plans to see the world one day. Living in tiny Fallow Creek is the last thing I want to do."

Rachel chuckled. "You have plans to see the world?"

Lily did not smile. She shrugged. "I guess I caught a bit of a travel bug from my friend Sofia. She's a world traveler, and it's what I want as well. But I also need to find my parents and my sister." Her voice choked up, and she didn't say anything for a few seconds. Finally, she spoke again. "I need to find them, Rachel. I need to find them now. I miss them so much."

Taylor's heart went out to her. He knew how it felt to wish every day that a loved one was still around so you could see them. Not knowing where her parents and her sister were was no doubt extremely painful for her. An idea entered his heart, and he pushed it away immediately. He had to follow Rachel's advice because it was right, especially as Lily had said now that she wanted to see the world. With Faye passing away, he didn't want to bring anyone into their lives who was just going to leave at any moment. His children, especially Josh, had already suffered enough with the loss of their mom. Lily had other plans than settling into one place and watching or being responsible for kids that were not even her own. He couldn't ask her to do the very opposite of what her dreams were.

"Please, Rachel, if you hear anything about the whereabouts of my parents and sister, or if they come back to Fallow Creek, please call me immediately," Lily said, still sounding dismayed.

"I will, Lily. I promise."

A small smile touched Lily's lips. "And Rachel, I'm really happy for you. I'm glad you've taken over the leadership of Fallow Creek. You can now make all those changes you told me you would make in the community if you had the power to. It's a shame that a lot of people have left, but there are still people there who need your help."

"I know, Lily," Rachel said. "More often than not, this 'power' I have feels more like a burden than a blessing. It's been hard trying to figure out what to do for the good of this town every day. I felt so guilty after the mass exodus… I still kind of do. But I know that whoever the Lord has planned to remain here will remain. Anyway, let's not talk about me anymore. I'll try to ask around and see if anybody knows where your parents and sister went."

"I really appreciate that."

They talked a bit more about the state of the community, all the abandoned houses and what Rachel planned to do with them. Taylor was proud of her for taking control of the place in spite of so many obstacles and hardships that had come her way.

"I'll call you once I get to California," he told Rachel.

"Okay. Say hi to my niece and nephew. And Keith sends his greetings."

After the call ended, they went back to their seats inside the restaurant. Taylor looked at Lily, and his pulse spiked with worry when he saw tears in her eyes. He couldn't help taking her hand on the table and giving her a sympathetic smile. "I'm sorry about your family, Lily."

"Here I was, dreaming for months of getting enough money so I could go back to Fallow Creek and get my parents and Stella, when they've been gone for a long time." She sighed and said brokenly, "Where am I going to find them, Taylor? Where?" Her eyes shone with tears and then they ran down her cheeks.

He reached out and took· both her hands. He knew he had to help her in spite of his decision to stay away. She was in distress, and he understood how awful she must feel. "Listen, Lily," he said softly, "when I go back to California, I'll make some calls and try to find out where your parents and sister are. There has to be someone in Fallow Creek who I can call; someone who knows where they went."

She looked up at him with sad eyes. "But most people in Fallow Creek don't even have a cell phone; at least, they didn't when I left."

"I know a few people who smuggled cell phones in, and a few like me who were allowed to have one. They might know where your parents are."

A glimmer of hope entered her eyes, but just a glimmer. She gave him a smile, and then once again she wove their fingers together. She looked at him in a way that made his insides melt, and he felt as though, if he kept looking at her, he would take her in his arms right now and kiss her right here. He averted his eyes and pretended to look down at his food again.

"Taylor?"

He looked up at her again, and from the look in her eyes, he knew what she was going to say. But he couldn't allow her to say it. They'd had five amazing but difficult days together, and they were both not thinking as clearly as they should. They needed time apart. He needed time to process his feelings for her and to spend alone with his kids. He had to give himself time to know if he could enter into another relationship. But he was sure he didn't want to open his heart to more pain, and he certainly didn't want to expose his kids to the kind of pain Josh had felt when his mom had passed.

Lily wanted to see the world; she only thought she wanted a relationship with him now because of their intense attraction to each other. But some time apart from him would help her settle her priorities again.

"Taylor, I know you feel what I've felt these past few days..."

He interjected quickly before she could finish her sentence. "I know. I'll miss you too, Lily. The days we spent together were great, but all good things have to come to an end. I'm definitely glad to go back to my kids, finally. I'll call you when I get to California, especially if I have news about your parents."

His heart twisted with pain at how hurt she looked. The expression on her face turned from dismay to anger. She pulled her hand away from his, got up abruptly, snatched her purse from the table, and hurried out of the restaurant.

Regret and worry flooded him as he sat there

looking after her and wishing with all his heart that he could change what he had said. But then again, there was nothing else he could have said to her. Conflicting emotions warred in his heart. Maybe it was better this way. At least she might suffer less if she thought of him as a jerk once he was gone.

And yet, he was appalled at the thought.

His thoughts were all jumbled up as he fought himself, trying to figure out what he should do. His heart told him to go after her, but his head told him to let her go. He remembered Rachel's advice. It was the best advice for him now. *Let Lily go, Taylor.* In time, he would probably forget about her and she him.

He groaned. That would probably never happen. Still, the best thing was for him to let her go. He looked down at his empty plate, feeling miserable.

"I can't," he muttered. *I can't let her go.* Not when she was so terribly sad because she didn't know where her family was. And not when the last thing she would remember about him was that he was a heartless jerk. Even though he still could not start a relationship with her because he had to protect his heart, and because it was not the right thing to do, he couldn't just let her go when she was suffering so much.

But what are you going to do? It's not as if you can give her what she wants.

He ignored the warning in his heart and stood up. Quickly, he paid for their meal, strode out of the restaurant, and out of the hotel.

THIRTEEN

Once she got to her apartment, Lily collapsed on the sofa and began to weep. She scolded herself for crying over Taylor, but she couldn't stop. She had gone to his hotel telling herself that she could protect her heart, her feelings. But she had not been able to because she wanted so much more than to be just a temporary source of comfort for him. But what she wanted, he was not willing to give.

What am I saying?

He wasn't just unwilling to give what she wanted, he didn't want to give anything. Yes, he'd given a lot of stuff, but she wanted his heart and not those things. She angrily dashed at the tears that poured down her cheeks. He had promised to help find her parents. She was grateful for that, but at the same time, it grated on her. Now she was sure that he thought of her as nothing but a charity case. He was kind and generous, and all she was to him was an opportunity to give to someone who was suffering, someone who was a childhood friend and had fallen on hard times. Yes, he liked her, but not in the same way that she liked him.

Her eyes pooled with tears again as she thought of how he had looked at her with such desire, especially at that breakfast they'd had together at the hotel. And he had held her so tenderly on the day she'd moved out of her old apartment. But clearly, it was all part of his kind nature. She looked around her posh apartment. Sofia had said that he'd done all this for her because he liked her, but she wasn't so sure anymore. In fact, she was sure that wasn't the case, at least not the kind of 'like' that she wanted.

She remembered the look on his face when she had gone to the hotel and the way he had looked at her when she had taken his hand. Now she knew it all meant nothing. She had gone to comfort him because of his wife's death, and clearly, he was still grieving for the woman. He was still in love with his late wife. She did not blame him for that. His wife had been dead for less than a year and she had only been reacquainted with him for a few days.

But that did not change how much she was hurting. Even though they had only been reacquainted for a few days, all the feelings she'd harbored for him when they were growing up had come rushing back and were much stronger and more mature now. He'd said he would miss her, but that did not mean much considering his thoughtful personality. He had his kids to think about, his late wife to grieve. Lily sighed sadly. He would go back to California and forget about her. She had seen it written in his eyes.

What did you expect, Lily? That Taylor Dalton, the richest and most handsome man in Fallow

Creek, would fall hopelessly in love with you within just a few days and then confess his undying love for you? She smiled in self-mockery. That happened in fairy tales, but not in real life, at least not to people like her. She'd thought they couldn't be together because he was married. But finding out he wasn't had made no difference, because he might as well still be. His heart was closed to every woman except his late wife.

Why, oh why had he told her he was now single? Maybe if she still believed he was married, the fact that he was leaving tomorrow would hurt less. Now that she knew he was single, she would never be able to forget him. She would not be able to get out of her mind what would have been if only his feelings had matched hers.

Fresh tears fell down her cheeks, and she wiped them away again. No matter how difficult it would be, she would have to learn to forget about him. She had no choice.

She pressed her lips tightly together as pain twisted her heart. When he left for California tomorrow, she... Her mouth fell open as the door opened and Taylor walked in. She blinked and stared at him. She had not considered that he would come here looking for her. But here he was. He looked worried as he gazed down at her, and she could not take her eyes off his.

"Lily, you've been crying," he said. "I'm sorry for what I said. I know I hurt you." He walked over, sat beside her on the couch, and pulled her into his arms.

She closed her eyes, buried her head into his chest, and wrapped her arms around him. *Lord, why did he come?* This would only make things worse when he left tomorrow.

He stroked her hair while she held him tightly. His heart was beating fast against her. She sighed, wishing she could remain in his arms forever but knowing she had to pull away after what he'd told her. Their mutual physical attraction had clearly not disappeared. There was an element of danger with him here in her apartment. It was better he left now since he was not genuinely interested in her. She pulled back slightly from him and looked into his eyes. The look he gave her sent her pulse racing.

She trembled as they sat gazing into each other's eyes, his arms loosely around her. She wanted to tell him it was best for him to go now, but she couldn't bring herself to do so. She gazed at his lips. Everything in her wanted him to hold her tightly and kiss her. She wanted to hear him say that he had fallen hopelessly in love with her. But she knew it was just a dream. She'd been wrong about his attraction and desire for her, though it seemed real and palpable now. But her feelings for him were definitely different from his for her. Their intense physical attraction and desire for each other were not enough.

He suddenly drew her close and held her tightly in his arms. She gasped and looked into his eyes, and then knew she was in trouble. They both were.

But this time, she didn't care. She was itching to draw even closer to him even though she could now feel his heart beating against hers. Waves of pleasure washed through her as he kissed her nose and her temples. When he brushed his thumb across her lips, she trembled. Her heart began to pound in anticipation as he bent his head and brushed his lips against her cheeks. His lips lightly touched hers, and she groaned in disappointment when the door flew open and he pulled away.

"Lily!" Sofia called her name. "You won't guess...!" Sofia's eyes grew wide as she looked at Lily and then at Taylor. "Oh, I'm sorry. Did I interrupt something?"

Lily shifted away from Taylor and frowned at the look in Sofia's eyes. Sofia smiled and winked at her. "Well, I guess I did interrupt something." She waved her hand. "I'll be on my way. Carry on."

Lily's face grew hot with embarrassment. She knew what Sofia was thinking now, and the worst thing was that if Sofia had not interrupted them, she and Taylor would have done exactly what Sofia had in mind. Lily shifted to the edge of the couch.

He gave her a rueful smile, and then the smile melted off his face. "Tell me, Lily, why did you run away during our dinner?"

The best thing would be to give him a random excuse so he would not go back to California feeling guilty or thinking that he owed her anything. But the words in her heart were fighting to burst out of her mouth, and she let them. "You know why, Taylor. I want a relationship with you. But you don't have to worry. You don't owe me anything."

"Lily!"

"No! I understand. You still love your wife and you're still grieving for her. Really, it's wrong of me to want something from you that you clearly cannot give." She smiled sadly. "I'll miss you terribly when you go back to California, but we'll survive. *I* will survive."

He reached out to take her hand, but she held it away from him. "It's best this way. Let's just keep our distance."

"I'm truly sorry, Lily."

"You have no reason to be sorry. You've done nothing wrong."

"I can't leave you like this."

She wanted him to go back to California without feeling as though he had to say or do something in order to make her feel better for his rejection. And she didn't blame him in spite of it. He had the right to still love and grieve for his wife. He owed her nothing.

"I'll be fine. I just feel sad because of my parents. I miss them terribly, and now that Rachel has told me that they aren't in Fallow Creek, I just don't know what to do, where to start looking for them."

The distress she had felt when Rachel had told her that her parents had left Fallow Creek returned. A sob rose in her throat. "Oh, Taylor, where are they? What if I never see them again?"

"No, Lily. You will see them again. I promised you that I would do what I could to look for them. I'm reiterating that promise now."

She shook her head. "It's unlikely that the few people you can call to ask about them know where they are. I don't know how I'll remain in Tucson when my parents and my sister have moved to somewhere I don't even know. They don't know where I am, and I don't know where they are. How will we ever be reunited? And who knows if my sister is even with them or if she moved somewhere different with her husband? And what if they're hurt?" She couldn't stop thinking about the different awful things that could have happened to them. "Where can they possibly be?"

He moved close to her and pulled her into his arms again. "Shh... you'll find them soon, Lily," he said.

She pulled away from him and said, "How do you know?"

He blinked, and then his eyes brightened. "I have an idea."

She raised her brows. "What?"

"If we're going to find your parents, maybe the best place to start looking for them is in Fallow Creek. That is the only place we are sure they've been."

"You want us to go back to Fallow Creek?"

"Yes. We can try to trace their steps from there."

"You'd go back to Fallow Creek for me?" she asked, astonished. "I thought you said you would never go back there because of what happened to your wife."

His face contorted in anguish, and she wished she hadn't brought up his wife. "Taylor, it's okay if you can't go with me."

"No! I want to go with you. I want to help you find your parents." He looked at her with a thoughtful expression on his face. "And in truth, I still feel awful about leaving you here without a job. Plus, I still need a nanny for my kids. Since I already told my son, Josh, that I would take time off work so we could spend time together, like a mini-vacation, I think we can take the opportunity to all go to Fallow Creek. You can help me take care of Josh and Bree." He smiled at her. "What do you say,

Lily? Will you accept my job offer?"

"What about this apartment you just bought me?"

He waved his hand. "I'll find a use for it." He smiled at her. "And now you won't be living here anymore, you don't have to pay me back."

She smiled back. "That's a relief." She grew sober again. She was silent for a full minute, considering his offer. He was offering her two of the three things she wanted — no, needed — most right now. A relationship with him was the third, which he clearly wasn't offering. However, she would be a fool to reject his offer, even if it didn't include a relationship.

She sighed. It would be difficult working for him and seeing him every day when she knew he didn't share her feelings and didn't want a relationship with her. But she would have to be content with what he was offering her.

He tilted his head, his eyes studying her face. "What do you say, Lily? Do you want to come work for me and go back to Fallow Creek to search for your parents?"

"Yes," she said.

He nodded and she frowned. Considering he was the one who had offered to help her search for her parents and had given her a job, she was surprised that he didn't look too pleased she'd accepted. Was he already regretting his offer? But she said nothing about it. He had made her a promise. Even if he regretted doing so, he was bound to his word now. Tomorrow she would leave Tucson with him, and together they would try to find her family. She would have to give up what she hoped would develop between them and focus entirely on that.

"So are you ready to leave for California tomorrow?" he asked.

She shrugged, trying to mirror his nonchalant look. "I guess I'm as ready as I'll ever be." She gazed at his handsome face for much longer than she should have and then looked away, silently reprimanding herself. There was no point dwelling on what she could not have. She had to focus on what she did have. He had done so much for her and was still doing so much. She was grateful to God for him. Hopefully, they would find her parents soon, and then once she had saved enough from her job, she could start to fulfill the other dream she had — to travel the world.

FOURTEEN

Taylor settled into the back of the limo that would drive him and Lily to the airport. First, they had to drive to Lily's to pick her up. As the limo driver started the vehicle, Taylor turned and looked out the window. He felt conflicted and had been so since yesterday when he'd had dinner with Lily. He had tossed and turned in his bed, his mind repeatedly going over the promise he had made to Josh before he'd come to Arizona, his thoughts taunting him. Josh would be disappointed that he was bringing someone else on their family trip, that it would not be just the three of them.

His mind went back again to what Rachel had told him. He was ignoring all of it now: his promise to Josh and Rachel's advice. But he had no choice. He would not be able to live with himself if he left Lily in the state he'd seen her yesterday.

But you know that's not the only reason you asked her to come with you! a voice whispered in his mind. *You didn't ask her to come with you just because you're concerned about her.*

He groaned, feeling slightly ashamed and weary of the constant war going on in his mind because of Lily. In spite of the fact that he'd agreed to take Rachel's advice because it was the right thing to do, he had still gone ahead and asked Lily to come to California and then Fallow Creek with him. But he couldn't stand the thought of never seeing her again. He would have to try to protect his heart and keep his hands off her, but at least he would get to see her regularly.

You know that isn't right.

He could easily have gone to Fallow Creek to look for her parents without her. Now, his vow to honor his wife's memory and keep the promise he'd made to Josh were in jeopardy. He could have gone to Fallow Creek with only his son and daughter, and they could have enjoyed each other's company while he also tried to discover the whereabouts of Lily's parents and sister. Instead, he'd asked Lily to come with him and she had agreed.

He sighed as he remembered how Lily had bared her heart to him yesterday, the way she had looked at him as she did. He felt like a jerk. She had told him plainly that she wanted a relationship with him, but all he could tell her was that he was sorry. The hurt in her eyes still haunted him. It was bad enough that she now knew he was single. He also now knew that, not only did she like him, she was interested in a relationship with him.

Maybe you should just give in, Taylor. You know that is what you want, too.

His heart nearly stopped at his admission. He had never admitted to himself that he wanted a relationship with her. But there was no point dwelling on it. Rachel was right about him keeping his distance from her. His decision to not be involved with any woman at this time was the right one. And yet the thought of being in close proximity to Lily in the coming months left him out of sorts because it threatened that decision.

He groaned and then raised an eyebrow when the limo driver stared quizzically at him through the rearview mirror.

He turned to look out the window again while telling himself to stop thinking about Lily. In a few minutes she would be in this car, sitting right next to him. The more his thoughts centered on her and his growing feelings for her, the more likely it was that he would throw all caution out of the window. He could already imagine how soft her lips would feel on his when they kissed and...

Stop it, Taylor! His mind was going in the direction it should never go. He looked around him for something to read to distract himself, but he found nothing. He had to get a hold of his feelings now, or the hours they would spend together in the plane would be torture.

The limo wove through traffic, and Taylor momentarily put Lily out of his thoughts. He smiled as he imagined Josh's small arms around his neck as they hugged, and Bree's smile that amusingly now resembled a smirk. He could not wait to finally get home and see them again — his precious kids. He was excited about their coming vacation. They would be able to spend an extended amount of time together, just the three of them.

Not the three of you anymore. Now Lily will be there, too.

Great! He was back to thinking about her again. His mind traveled once more to Rachel's advice. How would he be able to properly process his feelings for Lily if she was physically in his house? How could he give himself a chance to forget about her if she was right there with him? And how long would they both be able to hold out before they gave in to their untamed passions?

He shuddered. It would be a disaster for so many reasons if that happened. And it ultimately would if he didn't find a solution for it, the way he was pining over her. His kids would be around. It was bad enough that he would have to explain to Josh why he'd brought someone else home. He didn't want to have to explain any kind of physical affection to his son.

They couldn't afford to get as carried away as they had yesterday at her apartment. If her friend had not shown up when she had, they would be dealing with awful regret now, and he probably wouldn't have been able to ask her to come with him today. As his children's nanny, she was supposed to live in the main house, but she would have to live in the staff building. He wasn't going to take any chances. In two or three days, they would leave for Fallow Creek. He wasn't yet sure of their living arrangements there, but he would figure it out later.

They got to the front of Lily's apartment building, and he sucked in his breath sharply when he saw her standing in front of it, her suitcase by her side. She was wearing a fitted royal blue dress which showed off her perfect figure.

"Calm down or you'll have a heart attack," he muttered sarcastically.

But his heart didn't stop racing, even as the driver got out and put her suitcase into the trunk of the car. When she got in beside him, he gathered up a smile for her.

"Good morning," she said to him. She sounded more upbeat today than she had yesterday.

"Good morning, Lily." He deeply inhaled her floral scent and then turned away to look out the window so she would not see how much she affected him. No one had ever affected him in this way. He had never felt anything close to this. Maybe it was too late, anyway. Maybe he was already falling in love with her. But it was all too soon. He felt awful. He had already replaced Faye with someone else... at least in his heart. And what he felt for Lily was a burning desire, not just physically, but emotionally. He had loved Faye, but never had he felt this way about her.

Lord, help me, he thought. The admission he had just made strengthened his resolve to keep away from Lily if he wanted to honor his wife's memory. He turned to look at Lily again. He couldn't keep his eyes off her. He knew for certain that he was falling in love with her. He had vowed never to go back to Fallow Creek because of Faye, but just the sad look in Lily's eyes when Rachel had told her that her parents had left the community had been enough to change his mind.

"Taylor?"

His heart skipped a beat, and he took a deep breath before he turned to her. "Yes, Lily?"

"I'm afraid of what your kids will think of me," she said with worry. "What if they don't like me?"

He blinked. How could she think that? Without

meaning to, he reached out and took her hand. She looked at their joined hands and gave him a small smile.

"Bree is still really a baby and won't mind your presence. Josh is another matter since he really misses his mom. But I'm sure he'll come to like you, Lily. It might take a bit of time, but he will warm up to you. You'll see."

Her smile widened, and she looked relieved. He squeezed her hand and then let go of it. *Remember, Taylor. Keep a physical and emotional distance as much as you can.* He turned away again and stared out the window, but even though he wasn't looking directly at her, her face remained etched in his mind.

She didn't say anything more until they got to the airport. Neither did he, but his mind stayed on her and his emotions remained raw and all jumbled up.

The driver opened the door for him, and they stepped out of the limo. The driver had driven them into the private hangar where his plane was waiting. He turned when Lily came to stand at his side.

She looked around and then looked back at him with an amazed expression on her face. "How come we're here?"

He blinked. "What do you mean?"

"Well, I was expecting us to be at the airport… you know, the public airport where other people are checking into their flights."

Taylor chuckled. "Well, we're checking into our flight now as well. Only we will simply be going straight onto the plane."

He began to walk to his plane, and she followed him. She pointed. "That's a private plane," she said, and her mouth dropped open. "You own a private jet, Taylor?"

He shrugged. "Why do you look so surprised? It's not a big deal. I need it for my business trips."

"Wow!"

He was slightly amused as he walked up the steps of his small plane. He went into the cockpit to briefly greet his pilot and then stepped out again. Lily was standing in the middle of the plane looking around. She shook her head and said, "You travel in style, Taylor Dalton."

He laughed and sat down in his favorite seat up front. The plane could seat several people, but she came and sat down next to him. He tamped down a groan and ignored the way his heart rate increased.

She was still looking around the plane, and then she turned to him. "I think I might take a nap at the back of this plane later." She smiled at him. "This is impressive, though."

He chuckled. "It's not that impressive, Lily. It's a small plane and mostly for business."

"So you've never used it for pleasure… like flying with your kids to Europe, maybe?"

"I bought it some months ago. I've been too busy to travel anywhere except for my business trips, and mostly within the United States. I haven't had the chance to take my kids on vacation, but this trip to Fallow Creek will act as our first vacation together in a while."

"You must really miss them," Lily said.

"I do. I always miss them when I travel. I can't wait to see them again."

She turned around again, and her shoulder grazed his, sending sparks through him. He sighed. If only she would find a seat somewhere else so he could give his heart and nerves a break. As it were, he was on edge with her so near. He had to distract himself somehow. He looked around once more, and this time he saw a business magazine on the back of the seat in the other aisle. He stood up and went to get it, and then decided he might as well sit down in this seat. She might be hurt, but she would get over it.

He opened the magazine, but he didn't see a word that was written on it. He could feel her eyes on him, and once again he felt like a jerk. But it was too late to go back and sit beside her. Besides, he felt better already. This was for the best. Their trip would be less uncomfortable if they sat separately.

He buckled his seatbelt as the pilot announced that the plane was ready to take off. He looked out the window again while the plane taxied out of the hangar and along the strip. The plane gradually lifted off, and as it flew higher and higher, everything grew small and smaller and then disappeared as they flew above into the clouds.

He finally couldn't stop the overwhelming desire he felt to see her face again and turned to look at her. She was looking out the window, her slim legs crossed. She had a smile on her face. He watched her for a long moment. He would give anything to know what was on her mind right now. She began to turn around, and he quickly looked away, but not before she caught his eye and raised her brow quizzically.

You also have to keep your eyes away from her,

he thought to himself as he looked down at the business magazine again. Gradually, he focused totally on what he was reading, though her face lingered at the back of his mind. Soon, he felt himself drifting off. He put the magazine aside and closed his eyes.

His eyes flew open when he felt rather than heard a loud thud. He looked out the window and saw that the plane had landed. Instinctively, he turned to look at Lily. Her eyes were closed, her head resting on the back of her seat. The plane taxied into the hangar and stopped, and he unbuckled his seatbelt again. Standing up, he went to Lily and, with all his might, resisted the urge to smooth her hair back from her face. He placed his hand on her shoulder and gently shook her awake. "Lily, we've arrived."

She opened her eyes and looked up at him. She blinked and rubbed her eyes.

"We're here in California," he said, and walked away. His excitement was growing now. In a little while, he would see his babies again. He couldn't wait. He began to worry a little about what Josh would think about Lily and then shrugged his worries away. He couldn't think about that right now. He would have to deal with anything that came up when he got home.

They got into his car and, after he'd greeted his driver, Grant, he picked up the magazine he'd been reading on the plane and continued to read. He felt really bad for ignoring Lily, but he didn't want his thoughts to be absorbed with her.

But once again, he could not avoid looking at her, and he put down the magazine. He turned toward her to ask her if she was okay, but she was looking out the window. He turned around again and went back to his reading.

They approached his house about an hour later. The closer they got, the more relaxed and happier he became. They finally entered his property, isolated from the busyness of the city, and he sighed in relief.

Lily turned to him and said with wondering eyes, "This place is beautiful, Taylor, but it's so far from everything."

He nodded. "I like it this way. My home is sort of my refuge from all the noise on the outside."

They approached the front of the house, and he turned to gaze at the ocean. It glistened as the sun shone down on it, and he smiled at a flock of birds taking flight. After the busy week he'd had and the commotion of staying right in the heart of the city with all its hustle and bustle, he was glad to finally be back here, away from people and traffic, at least temporarily. Soon they would go back to Fallow Creek. But since Rachel had told him most people had left the community, it might not be so different from this place.

Lily got out of the car just as it stopped and took off her shoes.

He watched her in amusement as she ran and then stopped in front of the still ocean. She dug her feet into the sand, bent down, and scooped water into her hands, and then she threw it up in the air. He couldn't help but smile as she sat in the sand, uncaring of her pretty dress. A gust of wind blew her hair around her face, and she brushed it back with her fingers.

He felt a sweet ache in his heart as he watched

her looking up at the sky and then cupping water into her hand and pouring it back like an offering into the ocean. He couldn't resist and walked over to her.

She looked up at him and said, "If I lived here, I would sit right in front of this majestic ocean every single day. From morning until evening."

He laughed. "No, you wouldn't. Not if you have kids to take care of."

The dreamy look in her eyes disappeared, replaced by guilt. She immediately stood up. "I'm sorry, Taylor. The first thing I was supposed to do was to go find the kids I'm supposed to take care of. Please forgive me."

She began to move past him, but he held her hand. She turned to him and he said, "Stop worrying, Lily. You just arrived. You're allowed to wile away some time before you start working. I'm sorry if I made you feel like I was reprimanding you."

She gave him a small smile. "Thank you. Still, I think I should go in now and meet your kids." She walked away, and he looked after her for a few moments before following. She looked up at his house when they got to the front door. Her eyes held wonder and awe. She looked back at him and said, "Taylor, this is not a house, it's a castle. It's amazing."

He chuckled. "I'm glad you like it," he said. "I wanted a peaceful place where I could hear myself think when I'm not at work." He smiled. "Though it's not like my kids ever let that happen."

"It's a pity we have to leave immediately for Fallow Creek," she said. "When exactly are we going?"

"As soon as possible," he said. "Probably the day after tomorrow."

She nodded. "Thank you again, Taylor. I really appreciate you taking the time to help me find my family."

"It's nothing," he said. He opened the door for her, and she stepped into the portico. Wildflowers lined the place, and the swimming pool to the right glistened like the ocean, though it was bluer. Her heels clicked on the tiled floors as they walked down the long hallway. They finally entered his living room, and he immediately left her to go find his children.

He was at the top of the stairs when Josh came flying toward him. He opened his arms wide, and Josh flew into them. He folded his son in his arms and held him tightly. "You're back, Dad!" Josh hugged Taylor tightly. "I'm so happy you're back."

He held Josh close for another minute and then put him down. He ruffled Josh's hair and grinned. "How are you, my boy? Have you been a good boy since I left?"

Josh nodded and took his hand. "Bree was crying in the morning. I think it was because she missed you."

Taylor smiled. "Where's Felicia?"

Josh shrugged. "I think she's in the kitchen with Bree." Josh kept pulling him along the corridor.

"Where are we going, Josh?"

"I want to show you my LEGO. I made a new building today."

Taylor followed Josh to his room and inspected the LEGO building his son had made. "It's fantastic!" Taylor said, looking at the high stack of

LEGO. "Let's go and find your sister."

Down the stairs, they both strolled to the kitchen and, for a moment, pain twisted Taylor's heart. Faye would have loved this big kitchen, much bigger than the one in their house in Fallow Creek. But then again, if she were still alive, they would not be here.

Felicia was stirring something in a small pot on the burner. It smelled delicious, but he ignored the food and went straight to his beautiful baby daughter. Bree was sitting on top of the island, small pink pillows around her, looking at him with a huge grin on her face. When he got close to her, she held out her hands and he immediately scooped her up into his arms. "Oh, how I've missed you, Bree," he said, kissing her cheek.

Felicia turned and greeted him before turning back to her cooking. Josh tugged at his pants. "Dad, let's go outside and play," he said excitedly. "Remember you promised that we would spend time together, just the three of us, when you got back."

Taylor's stomach did a flip, and he took a deep breath. He had to tell his son now that he had not been able to completely keep his word. He would still take a vacation, and they would still spend time together, but it wouldn't just be the three of them. He put Bree down but held her hand so she wouldn't fall. Bending down to Josh's level while holding on to Bree, he said, "Josh, I have something to tell you. I met a childhood friend of mine in Arizona, and I asked her to come and be you and Bree's nanny."

Josh's eyes grew wide. "A nanny? What about

Felicia?"

"Felicia is a housekeeper. She's just been working as a nanny because we didn't have one yet. But now we do. She's very nice, Josh. I want you to come meet her."

"Will she stay here? Will she be with us during our vacation?" Josh looked worried.

Taylor said truthfully, "Yes, she will."

Josh frowned. "I thought you said it would just be the three of us, Dad."

"We'll still spend as much time together as we want. She won't stop us from doing that."

"But what if she doesn't let me play with you or Bree as much as I want?" Josh said and glanced at Felicia.

Taylor chuckled. "I'm sure she'll let you spend time with me and Bree. As much time as you want. Besides, I'm at home now, and she can hardly stop me from spending time with my two little babies."

Josh looked away. "I'm not a baby, Dad."

He ruffled Josh's hair. "I know you're not." He looked at Bree, who was staring at Josh with an amused expression, and grinned at her, wondering what was going on in that mind of hers.

"Let's go and meet her," Taylor said to Josh.

"I don't want to."

Taylor groaned. *Great!* Josh was already acting up, and he hadn't even seen Lily yet. "Josh, please. You'll be spending a lot of time with her since she's your nanny, so it doesn't make sense not to meet her now. Just come and see her. You'll see that she's nice."

Josh grumbled but let Taylor take his hand.

With his children's hands in his, he left the

kitchen. Josh sulked as they walked, while Bree staggered like a drunk person. She tried to pull her hand from his, but he held on. They walked into the living room. Lily was still standing, gazing at a painting that he'd hung over the fireplace. It was a three-dimensional painting of a juicy red apple on a tree in a garden.

She turned around to look at him, and her eyes lit up as they settled on Bree. She hurried over, bent down, and grinned at his baby daughter. "If you are not the cutest little girl I've ever seen!" Lily cupped Bree's cheeks. She looked up at Taylor. "Can I carry her?"

"Of course," Taylor said. "You'll be taking care of her and Josh."

Lily lifted Bree into her arms, and Taylor wasn't surprised when Bree settled her head on Lily's shoulder and threw her tiny arms around her neck. "She has already taken to you, Lily," he said. "Bree is a good baby. She hardly cries or complains."

Lily turned her gaze to Josh, and Taylor sighed. Josh looked angry.

"And this must be Josh," Lily said. She smiled at him. "I've heard so much about you from your father and Aunt Rachel, but I'm so happy to finally see you myself. I'm Lily, and I'm your new nanny. I've known your father since we were children and..." Lily blinked as Josh snatched his hand away from Taylor's and ran out of the living room.

"I'm sorry about that," Taylor said. Lily looked astonished and worried. "He's just feeling a little down right now because I promised him I would spend time with just him and his sister once I started my vacation."

She looked even more worried. "Maybe I shouldn't have come here, Taylor," she said.

"Of course you should have," he told her. "Josh will get over his annoyance. I promise you. It's not you he's annoyed at. It's me. I am sure he feels like I broke my promise. But I know you, Lily. You're a warm and loving person, and you will be a great nanny." Taylor smiled as he looked at Bree, who was still resting her head contentedly on Lily's chest. "Just look how Bree has taken to you. I'm sure in no time Josh will come to love you like Bree clearly does." Taylor grinned at Bree. She was now playing with Lily's hair, a self-satisfied smile on her face.

"Are you sure, Taylor?"

"Yes, I'm certain of it. Don't worry."

She nodded, and he gave her an encouraging smile. "So, I'll take this little one here from you so I can bathe and change her, and then put her to bed."

"Can I come and help you with her?"

"No," he answered, holding out his hand to her. He wanted to spend this time with his kids alone, just for today, and to try to comfort Josh. He understood why his son felt the way he did, and what Josh needed right now was his father's unconditional love and encouragement. "You just rest, Lily. You only just arrived. Tomorrow you can start your duties."

"Okay," she said slowly. She looked unsure, but he didn't have the time to stay and reassure her that everything would be okay. He had to go to church. He took Bree from her, gave her another smile, and left her to find his son and try to put his mind at ease. He would have to convince Josh that he and Bree were still his priority and that they had his full and undivided attention. The only thing that troubled him was that he was not so sure that was the truth.

FIFTEEN

Lily stared out the window of Taylor's plane as it began to taxi down the runway strip. She turned to look at Taylor, who was in the other row playing with Joshua and Bree, and then turned back to look out the window again. She felt lonely and isolated — and completely useless. After she'd arrived at Taylor's house two days ago, she'd hardly seen him, or the kids for that matter.

Felicia had taken her to a two-story building at the back of the main house that housed the staff and showed her the two-bedroom apartment that would be her residence from henceforth. She had come to the main house the next day to start her job, but she'd found that Taylor was already up with his kids. Apparently, since he was on vacation, the children were too, and their regular sleeping times had been adjusted. She'd asked him what she could do since he was preparing to give them a bath, but he'd shaken his head and said, "Nothing. You can just take a tour of the house and the entire property."

She had done that for a while and then come back to see if there was anything she could do for the kids, but by then Taylor was playing a game of catch with Josh at the back of the house. Bree was sitting on an ornate stool near them with Felicia, laughing and stretching out her little hands as she'd watched the beanbag sail through the air.

Lily had watched them for a while, but none of them seemed to notice her. She'd left again, and by the time she'd come back, Taylor had left the house with his kids. She'd asked Felicia where they'd gone, but the woman had simply grunted and said, "Out."

Lily sighed. It felt like she had not seen them until this morning, when Taylor had asked if she was ready to travel to Fallow Creek. Yes, he'd told her they would leave for Fallow Creek in two or three days on the day she'd arrived at his house, but he had not told her it would be two or a specific time. She'd had to pack her things quickly. They had left two hours later.

She sighed again. Why had Taylor even asked her to come here to be his kids' nanny if he didn't need her help? Why had he asked her to come at all if he was just going to totally ignore her? She understood that he needed time alone with his children and that was why he had taken a vacation, but he'd employed her to care for them, yet he was doing everything himself. In fact, he had actively gone out of his way to see that she did nothing for them. It was clear he was avoiding her and maybe even keeping the children from her.

She looked down as the plane flew over houses, leaving for Arizona again. Soon they would be in Fallow Creek, the town of her birth. He had promised to help find her parents, but by the way things had gone these past two days, she wondered how they would work together to do that if he kept avoiding her.

She turned to look at him again. Bree was strapped into a car seat on his left while Josh sat on his right, laughing as they arm-wrestled. Her heart ached as she watched them. Taylor had actively excluded her from his family time.

She remembered what he'd said about making Josh a promise that once he took a vacation, it would only be the three of them. And though she was here now, it might as well still be just the three of them. She looked out the window again and forced Taylor out of her mind.

Her mind went back to her parents, to the last day she'd seen them in Fallow Creek. She remembered how miserable her mother had been as she'd pleaded with Dennis Hamilton to let Lily stay in town. She remembered how her father had hugged her and the pain in his eyes. She would give anything to see them again now, including patiently bearing Taylor's behavior toward her.

She pressed her lips tightly together as Taylor roared with laughter. She didn't turn to look at him or find out why he was laughing. She simply imagined herself with him and the kids now, being part of their fun and laughing with them. Her time with him in Arizona had been anything but fun. It had been full of heartache, longing, guilt, and more longing, and yet it had also been extremely memorable. If only Taylor would look at her the same way he had during those five days together.

But he hardly ever looked at her now, not even the very few times he spoke to her.

She definitely wasn't expecting a repeat of what had happened at her apartment, the day they had nearly kissed, but she would be content to see him smile at her, just once, or at least look at her when he was speaking to her.

It's only been two days, Lily. Calm down. He's not seen his kids for days, and he's just catching up with them. Once he has spent enough time alone with them, he will start to include you, too.

She smiled sardonically. More like remember that she existed.

She chided herself again. *Really, Lily, you're jealous because the man spends time with his children rather than with you. Stop being so childish!*

She glanced at him and the kids again. They had finally settled down, and Bree was now on her father's lap, leaning back on his chest. Taylor had his hand on Joshua's hair, slowly running his fingers through it, while he held Bree with his other arm. He had a smile on his face; a smile of pure contentment. She sighed sadly. It hadn't taken long for him to completely forget about her. But what had she imagined would happen when they came here? That he would carry on with her as though they were still in Tucson rather than focus completely on his children? They were his main priority now, and rightfully so.

But I'm not asking him to make me a priority. I just want him to notice me again. Surely, that isn't too much to ask.

She turned back to them when Bree began to

whimper. Taylor tried to soothe her, but she wanted to get off his lap, probably so she could be free to roam around the plane. Lily got up immediately and went to them. She smiled tentatively as she looked down at Taylor. "Let me take her so you can rest," she said. "We can both walk around the plane together if she doesn't feel like sitting down." She gasped when Josh got up from his seat and squeezed himself between her and Taylor.

"Josh!" Taylor scowled at him. "Sit back down and buckle your seatbelt!"

Lily began to back away, and Josh said loudly, "Dad. I don't like the way she looks at you!"

Lily cringed, and her face grew hot with embarrassment. Mortified, she turned around and walked back to her seat. She looked out the window as shame flooded her. This wasn't good. Even a little boy had noticed how much time she spent ogling Taylor. It hadn't been intentional, though that didn't matter. She hadn't even known that she had spent way too much time looking at him. Enough for his son to notice. She would never live down this shame.

She bit her lip. It was clear that Josh didn't like her at all. He was probably afraid that she was here to replace his mom. He clearly didn't want his dad in a relationship with another woman, and, like most children, he had said exactly what was on his mind. A fresh wave of shame washed over her. Josh had clearly read the intense feelings she had for Taylor in her eyes. She did not blame Josh for what he'd said. He was a child acting up because he missed his mom and was afraid he would lose his dad… at least his dad's undivided attention. She did not blame Taylor, either. He had gone out of his way to help her, and they were going to Fallow Creek now because of her. She blamed herself for falling in love with him even though she knew he was unavailable still. Yes, he was single now, but his heart was still attached to his late wife.

After a while, she turned away from the window and groaned when she glanced again at Taylor. He was asleep now, and Bree had slipped off his lap and was playing with Josh, who was still seated beside Taylor. Her eyes met Josh's, and he glared at her before turning back to his sister.

Lily turned away.

Five minutes later, Bree began to stagger away from Josh just as slight turbulence rocked the plane. She fell, landed on her butt, and began to cry.

Lily immediately got up to get her, but Josh moved like lightning and stood between her and his sister.

Lily said exasperatedly, "Josh, Bree's crying. She needs help. I just want to pick her up and buckle her into her seat."

Josh glowered at Lily. "Bree doesn't need your help! We don't need you!"

Lily sighed.

Taylor opened his eyes and shot to his feet. He grabbed Bree from the floor and settled her on his lap again. Glaring at Josh, he said, "You will not speak to Lily that way, Josh! Apologize right now!"

Josh grumbled and said "Sorry," in a voice that told Lily he was anything but. He went and sat down in his seat again.

"I'm so sorry for that," Taylor looked at Lily and then quickly looked away before she could respond.

Lily felt anger burning in her stomach. Not at Josh, but at Taylor. He couldn't even look at her when he spoke to her. Why had he asked her to come with him if he was going to treat her this way? She took a deep breath to try to rid herself of her anger and said, "It's okay. Josh is just a child, and I understand that I'm simply a stranger to him."

Taylor nodded without looking at her and looked down at Bree. He wiped the tears from her eyes with his thumb and kissed her cheek.

Lily watched them with longing. Would she ever have a family of her own one day? She pictured herself holding Bree, Taylor beside her, looking at her with eyes full of love, Josh grinning beside them. She sighed and went back to her seat.

She loved Taylor. She could admit that to herself now. She was desperately in love with him, but he didn't feel the same way. What she had pictured in her mind would never happen. And she would never have a family of her own if she remained with Taylor and his kids. The best thing she could do was go back to Tucson as soon as she found her parents. She would have to give herself time to forget about Taylor. When that would happen, she didn't know. But judging from how strong her feelings were for him, she doubted it would be anytime soon.

Twenty minutes later, the plane landed on a small airstrip in Prospect and taxied into the hanger. Like in California, a car was already waiting to drive them to Fallow Creek. Taylor had rented a black SUV, which reminded Lily of the ones that the security squad had driven around in. They would be in Fallow Creek in about two hours if there were no problems on the road.

They loaded their things into the trunk of the vehicle, and Taylor got into the backseat with Josh and Bree. Lily sat alone in the middle seat, directly behind the driver. She sighed sadly again and then told herself to get her feelings together. This was how it would be from now on, and there was no point dwelling on it.

But she could not shake the intense loneliness she felt. She had heard someone say that it was possible to be lonely even in a crowd, and that sometimes you could feel even lonelier than when you were on your own. She certainly felt that way. She was lonelier now than the days she had spent alone in her new apartment.

She shut her eyes to try to sleep as Bree's laughter filled the vehicle. Taylor was telling them a silly joke now, and his deep voice stirred up an aching need in her that she knew she had to smother. Sleep would be her salvation.

But she could not sleep. She kept listening to Taylor's voice as he told one silly story after another, laughing with his kids, the three of them enjoying each other's company.

You can join in, Lily.

But she knew she couldn't. Josh would say something rude, Taylor would reprimand him while ignoring her, and then not only would she not have joined in the family fun, she would have simply ruined it. It was best to stay out of it.

She focused her mind on why they were going to Fallow Creek. To find her family.

But she ached not only to find her parents and sister, but also to be a part of the family that was having fun together behind her. Without her.

Sleep finally and mercifully claimed her a few minutes later, but then she woke up startled when someone called her name. Taylor had opened the car door and was looking at her with an expression she could not read.

"We're here, Lily," he said. "We've arrived in Fallow Creek."

Lily looked out the window and conflicting emotions began to war in her mind. They were in front of the Restoration House, the House she had spent months in. The House she had been so desperate to leave that she had promised her parents she would marry whoever it was they wanted her to. This place brought back awful memories, but then the town also brought back good memories, especially of her loved ones.

She stepped out of the car, and her heart skipped a beat when Taylor took her hand and helped her out. He let go of her hand as soon as she was out of the car and turned away.

She got her suitcase from the trunk of the car and rolled it behind her toward the gates of the House. Taylor was already in front with Josh. With one hand, he rolled a massive suitcase containing all his things as well as Josh's and Bree's; in his other arm, he carried Bree. Josh had his knapsack on his back.

Just as Taylor lifted his hand to ring the bell, Rachel came bounding to the gate, a huge smile on her face.

Lily peered through the bars of the gate as a handsome man came behind Rachel. They both opened the gate, and Taylor and the kids walked in first. Lily followed behind, forgetting momentarily her loneliness and Taylor's attitude toward her. She focused on Rachel, happy to see her friend again.

Rachel gave Taylor a big hug and then looked down at Josh and gathered him in a hug as well. Finally, she looked at Bree. "Oh, Taylor, she's beautiful," Rachel said in a voice choked with emotion.

Taylor smiled and nodded. "She looks like her mother."

"Yes," Rachel said. "You're right. She definitely looks like Faye."

"I wish Faye was here to see our daughter," Taylor said. "To see how beautiful and exuberant she is."

Rachel hugged him again, gathering Bree into the embrace. Finally, she stepped away, looked at Lily, and beamed. She stretched out her arms and pulled Lily into a tight hug. "I thought I would never see you again, Lily Hunter."

Lily grinned. "I'm so happy to see you. I thought the same thing."

Rachel pulled away slightly and gave Lily a mischievous smile. "Now why wasn't I surprised when I heard that you were kicked out of Fallow Creek? I always knew it would happen eventually, knowing how stubborn you are."

Lily laughed. "If I remember correctly, you were sent packing before me. So we are both stubborn, but that's okay. It's served us well."

"That it has," Rachel said, and turned to the handsome man beside her. "Everyone, this is my husband, Keith. Keith, this is my brother, Taylor. And this is Josh, his son. This tiny little pumpkin right here is Bree, his daughter. And this is my friend, Lily."

Taylor gathered Keith in a tight hug and pounded his back. After that, Keith bent down to grin at Josh and tickled Bree's chin. Finally, he hugged Lily.

With a huge smile, Lily said, "Now I see why my friend talked nonstop about you when we were both living here. I thought she was exaggerating, but you're as handsome as she said you were." She looked at Rachel. "I'm glad you were finally able to reunite with him. I remember how heartbroken you were when you thought he was dead."

"Please don't remind me of those days," Rachel said, smiling. She wrapped her arms around Keith and pulled him close. "What would I have done without him? He's my rock." She kissed him, and Lily's heart filled with envy and pain. She glanced over at Taylor. He had a corny grin on his face, and his hand covered Josh's eyes.

Josh chuckled and slapped his father's hand away.

Bree began to fuss and, without thinking, Lily reached for her. Hurt and pain shot through her again as Taylor moved slightly away and tightened his grip on Bree.

"She's just tired. She'll be fine," he said without looking at Lily. "Once we go in and she settles down and takes a nap, she should be good as new."

Lily felt like going to a place where she could be alone and weeping her eyes out. Taylor had given her this job to take care of his kids when he'd never intended for her to do so. Why?

"So, let's all go in," Rachel said, pointing at the Restoration House. "The kids need to rest, and we adults need to catch up." She pulled away from her husband and went to take Lily's hand. "We girls especially have a lot to catch up on," she said, smiling at Lily.

Lily smiled back, feeling a little better.

Inside the House, Lily looked around the common room. Even though the Restoration House looked the same on the outside, it was now completely different on the inside. At least, the common room was. It had been empty during the time she'd stayed here, and no one ever lingered in this place, but now there were sofas around the huge room, a center rug, and a coffee table. A huge, flat screen TV was mounted on the wall. But what was most surprising to Lily was that women lounged on the sofas, some even in their pajamas, talking and laughing.

She glanced at the stairs and saw women coming up and down with smiles on their faces. This place seemed completely different now. She turned to Rachel. "Well, Rachel Dalton! I'm so happy you're in charge of this place now. The women look so much happier. Now, if I'd still been here when you took over, I would definitely not have been so desperate to tell my parents I would marry anyone just to find a way out of the House."

Keith, who was standing at the back with Taylor, said, "And this is just one of the many things Rachel has done to change the House. Everything is different now, from the food to the furnishings and the rooms."

"That's great!" Lily said, looking at Rachel, impressed but not surprised. "What about those horrid renewal classes?" She laughed. "No. Don't tell me. I know you hated those classes as much as I did. They were the first to go, weren't they?"

"Actually, I couldn't stop the classes right away.

Dennis Hamilton was still in charge of this town at the time."

"What? Dennis Hamilton was in charge when you started running the Restoration House?" Lily asked astonished. "How did that happen?"

Rachel chuckled. "It's a long story. We have a lot to talk about, Lily."

"Well, I can't wait to hear everything," Lily said. "Taylor has told me some things that happened, but I know you have a lot more to tell me."

They climbed up the stairs to go to Rachel and Keith's private apartment. Lily had never been there when it was Margaret's. She couldn't wait to see the place. She and many of the residents of the House had always wondered about the apartment that was right inside the massive Restoration House.

Many women greeted them warmly as they made their way to the apartment, and the few that where acquaintances hugged Lily. "We thought we would never see you again after you were banished from Fallow Creek," a few of them said to her.

"I'm glad I'm here," Lily told them.

They finally got to the apartment, and Lily admired the place. It was not lavishly furnished, but the furnishings were tasteful, and everything was pleasing to the eye. She sat on a cream sofa and breathed a sigh of relief. She was tired from their trip, but not enough to take a nap. She wanted to hear everything Rachel had to say.

Rachel sat beside her and took her hand. Lily turned and smiled gratefully at Rachel, glad to have a friend with her now. She felt considerably less lonely already. Rachel's presence here made her realize just how lonely she had been these past two days in Taylor's house. Never had she thought it would be the case. She had known that being with him in his house, or at least on the grounds of his house, would be difficult, that their desire for each other would be tough to bear, but she had never imagined that he would completely ignore her to focus on his kids, or that she would be consumed with loneliness even though she was in the same house as the man she deeply loved.

Taylor laid Bree, who had fallen asleep, on one of the sofas, but Keith and Rachel insisted that he put the kids to bed in their room, especially as Josh was already nodding off as well. Taylor agreed. When Lily stood up and offered to take one of the children to the room, Taylor shook his head as he lifted Josh into his arms and told her he would manage. But when Rachel stood up and carried Bree from the sofa, he did not object.

Lily felt incredibly hurt but tried to press the hurt away. Two minutes later, Rachel and Taylor came out to the living room again.

Taylor sat on the sofa beside Keith, facing both Lily and Rachel, and Rachel began to narrate everything that had gone on over the past nine months. Taylor had already told Lily some of it, but not the details. Lily listened in amazement. When Rachel told them how she and some of the other women had bound Mike Cadwell up so he would not escape, and then brought him to the Restoration House to place him under house arrest, Lily laughed loudly.

"Lily!" Rachel shook her head and smiled. "It's not funny, Lily. We didn't know what to do with him, but we knew we couldn't hold him forever as a prisoner in the House."

"I'm sorry," Lily said, still giggling. "I can just imagine how you all tied Mike up and how much he would have complained about being held prisoner."

"So, what did you do with him?" Taylor looked at Rachel and Keith. "Is he still here?"

"No," Rachel said. "We finally handed him over to the police in Prospect. We told them he'd threatened the lives of the women in the House, which he had, because he was raving like a lunatic when we brought him here. I know they won't be able to keep him for long because we have no real charges against him, but I hope they keep him for as long as possible. At least until Keith and I know what to do. I'm sure he'll make a lot of trouble once he's out, especially about Emily."

Lily leaned forward. "You have Emily now?"

"Yes."

"Oh, Rachel! I'm so happy for you! After being separated from her for so long, you finally have your daughter with you. Where is she?"

"She's sleeping in her tiny room opposite the one where we put Josh and Bree. The truth is, I'm still afraid. When Mike is released from custody, I don't know what he'll do, but I'm sure he'll try to take Emily back." Rachel turned to look at Keith with a sad expression on her face. "The truth is that we might have to leave Fallow Creek for Emily's sake. So that Mike doesn't try to take her back."

"But you can't leave Fallow Creek," Taylor said. "You told me God told you to stay here. Besides, if you run away with Emily, Mike might be able to prove in court that you kidnapped her by separating her from her father and running away to a place where he wouldn't be able to find her."

"Yes, Rachel," Lily said. "Besides, you've worked so hard to change the Restoration House and the town in general. God has used you to change the lives of many of the women here. You can't just leave when you still have so much to do."

"I would leave it all in a heartbeat for my Emily," Rachel said. She looked at Taylor. "Mike has surrounded himself with armed men that he hired from who-knows-where. If he tries to take Emily by force, we won't be able to prevent it from happening."

"That's serious," Taylor said. "You might have to go to the police station in Prospect and find other crimes that Mike can be charged for so they will keep him in custody. With Mike Cadwell, that can't be difficult. I'll probably have to hire a lawyer for you both."

Rachel looked at Keith and then back at Taylor. "I don't know if we're supposed to hire a lawyer for Emily. Remember I told you about the word Lord gave to Keith and me before we came to Fallow Creek? He told us not to go to court to fight for Emily's custody. I thought the Lord would give Emily to us quickly, but it didn't happen until recently. But I'm glad the Lord has finally done it, and we have to not let Mike take Emily away again."

"Are you sure you don't want me to hire a lawyer?"

"For now, I'll say no," Rachel said, and Keith nodded.

"Okay, then. But tomorrow I'll go to the police station in Prospect and try to see if they can hold Mike in custody, at least until you think of what exactly to do."

"That'd be very helpful," Keith said. "Thank you."

They changed topics and talked about the changes Rachel had made in the Restoration House. Finally, the conversation shifted to tracking down Lily's parents and sister.

Rachel said, "I've asked many of the women in the House if they know where your parents and sister moved to, Lily, but none of them do."

Taylor said, "I have someone around who might know where they went. He might not divulge what he knows willingly, but I might be able to get him to talk."

Lily frowned in surprise. "Who?"

Taylor turned away, but not before Lily saw a strange look in his eyes. He waved his hand dismissively. "Just some guy who lives near here. He probably doesn't know, but I'll still ask."

"Okay. Does he live in Fallow Creek?" Rachel asked.

"No," Taylor said quickly.

Lily stared at him. What was he hiding?

He stood up. "I think it's time to go," he said. He looked at Lily. "We have an early day tomorrow." He left the living room to go and get his kids.

Rachel stood up and followed him, while Lily stared after them. Taylor had assumed that she was going with him. But she wasn't going to. She was tired of feeling lonely, tired of him ignoring her, and tired of being treated like an enemy, an intruder who had come to take the place of a beloved wife and mother when that was far from the truth.

Are you sure it's the right thing to do?

She was sure it was. She would not go with him. He was determined to spend time alone with his kids, and all she'd done was come between them during their time together. There was no point going to his house with him. She would stay here with Rachel. Besides, she had missed Rachel, and her fun camaraderie made her feel less lonely and much happier. Tomorrow, early in the morning, she would go to Taylor's house, and then they could talk about ways to look for her parents and her sister. She didn't need to live in his house for that.

He came out to the living room holding Josh's hand, and Rachel came out behind him carrying Bree. "So we will see you both tomorrow." Taylor hugged Rachel and then Keith. He didn't even look at Lily. He began to walk out of the apartment and then turned around when Lily remained seated on the sofa.

"Lily, aren't you coming?" he asked her.

Josh grumbled, and Lily sighed. "No, I'm not."

He looked surprised. "Why?"

"Because I want to stay here with Rachel. I'll come to your house early tomorrow morning."

"Okay." He shrugged and then turned around and left the apartment with Josh. Rachel followed behind him with Bree in her arms.

She felt alone, hurt, and angry. Most of all, she felt disappointed.

Why on earth do you feel disappointed? You're the one who doesn't want to go to his house with him.

She sighed silently. Yes, she didn't want to go back with him because he had ignored her, but she wished he'd at least tried a little harder to get her to come. Then again, Josh had grumbled, showing that he hadn't wanted her to come along. His father probably agreed. He didn't seem bothered at all that she was supposed to be his children's nanny and yet had chosen to stay here with Rachel and Keith.

"So, Lily, Rachel told me you grew up together and were best friends when you were kids. Can you tell me how Rachel was as a child?"

Lily smiled, glad that Keith had asked her a question to distract her from how she felt. She looked up thoughtfully and began to tell him stories about her and Rachel's mischievous antics as children. Soon Rachel came back and joined in their conversation. They laughed as they reminisced about their childhood. Lily was happy for the distraction and for being with people who actually wanted to talk with her and didn't ignore her. But a small part of her still ached at how Taylor had been acting toward her, and even though he had left no longer than thirty minutes ago, she already missed him.

SIXTEEN

Mike stood in front of the Restoration House and pounded on the gate. He raised his voice and yelled, "Open the gate this minute!" He had come straight here after being released from jail. Those stupid police officers had released him because they had nothing on him. Rachel and Keith would pay for how they'd humiliated him. And he was going to get his daughter back no matter what.

Two women came to the gate. When they saw him, they fled back into the House, and he cursed them. He pounded on the gate again, but no one came to open up for him. He laughed harshly. So neither Rachel nor Keith was going to come out to face him and answer for how they had humiliated him and handed him to the police. They were such cowards.

He stalked away, walking all the way to his house. He got to his house and began to pace his living room, thinking about what to do. Rage swallowed him. Olivia and Davina had left, taking his boys with them. If they thought they could just leave him like that, they had another thing coming.

A light entered his eyes as an idea came to him. Why was he here pacing his living room when he should be doing something about the humiliation that had been heaped on him? Even though Rachel was now the so-called leader of this town, he had more power than she did. He might as well be the leader. The real leader and owner of Fallow Creek. Because Rachel actually belonged to him and not to that Keith, and as his wife, what was hers was his. Now that Dennis Hamilton was dead, there was nothing stopping him from taking over. Fallow Creek would belong to him, and he would also take everything else that belonged to him: his family.

He opened the door and left the house. He walked to the leader of his guards and glared at him. "Alan, you allowed those two into my home when I expressly told you not to!"

Alan frowned. "Who?"

"Are you dumb? Who else did I tell you to keep away from my house? That whore Rachel and the man she now lives with."

Alan shook his head. "Your wife came and threatened us. I thought they were your guests."

"My wife!" He glowered at the leader of his guards. "And when did you start taking orders from my wife?"

"I'm sorry, sir," Alan said.

"Keep your apologies to yourself. Gather the men. We're going to pay Rachel and her horde of whores at the Restoration House a little visit." He grinned. "You and your men might even be able to sample what that House full of harlots has to offer if you don't bungle this assignment."

Alan grinned lustfully. "We won't fail."

"Go now," Mike ordered. "We leave immediately."

***

The bell at the gate rang, and Rachel looked at Lily. They had just finished having a light breakfast and were chatting on the living room sofa. She glanced at the clock on the wall. It was just a few minutes past nine o'clock. "We're not expecting anyone," she said. "It's probably Taylor."

When someone began to pound on the gate continuously, she frowned. "Who on earth can that be?"

"That definitely can't be Taylor," Lily said. "He's usually mild-mannered. Maybe it's one of his kids."

"It certainly can't be Bree." Rachel smiled. "Those tiny hands couldn't pound the gate that loud. It's Josh, no doubt." She stood up from the sofa, and Lily followed her. Keith was in the bathroom giving Emily a bath. She had asked to do it, but he'd insisted that she needed to catch up with Lily. She had smiled gratefully and left him to take over their joint morning routine with her. They'd been so excited since Emily had finally come to live with them. Rachel wanted to spend as much time with her daughter as she could. Tonight, she would read Emily a bedtime story with Keith once they tucked her into bed.

She walked out of the apartment with Lily and walked down the hallway. As they descended the stairs, Rachel's eyes widened in surprise. Mandy, the petite brunette who worked as an assistant for the cook, threw the front door open, her eyes wild with terror. Rachel's heart began to pound at the look of dread on Mandy's face.

She hurried down the stairs just as Mandy reached her. "What is it? Who's at the gate?"

Mandy shook her head and pointed toward the door. "They... he... there are many..."

"Mandy," Rachel grabbed her shoulders. "Please calm down and tell me what's wrong!"

"Outside. Mike Cadwell. He's outside with about six men holding guns. He told me to send you a message."

Lily gasped audibly while Rachel took Mandy's hand. "What message?"

Mandy bit her lip and said in a trembling voice, "He said... he said I should tell his wives, Olivia, Davina, and you, to come out with his children right now, or he and his men will storm into the house and shoot everyone they see."

Rachel blinked. "What?" The room began to sway. She felt weak with fear. She held on to the staircase to steady herself. Her hands trembled, and she took deep breaths to keep herself from hyperventilating.

Mandy began to whimper, while Lily placed a hand on her shoulder. They both walked to the window, and Rachel opened the curtains slightly. That insane Mike still believed she was married to him. Now he wanted her and Olivia and Davina to come out, and he wanted Emily, too, not just his boys. There was no way she was going to bring the kids out for him. Especially with his men out there.

Lily looked out the window. "That Mike Cadwell is plum crazy." Another loud bang sounded at the gate, and then a gunshot rang in the air. Rachel started, while Mandy screamed. Several women in the house shrieked, and some of them began to run down the stairs to see what was happening. Rachel said sharply, "All of you, get away from the door! We have an emergency!"

Some of them still stood at the door, clearly frozen, while the majority stepped back.

"Get back!" Rachel ordered again.

They all moved back, dread etched on their faces. Keith rushed down the steps, Emily in his arms, and looked at her. "What was that?"

Rachel told him what Mandy had said. He opened his mouth just as another loud pounding on the door started. It sounded as if the gate had been crashed into. All the women in the common room screamed, and Rachel went to the window again. Her heart raced with fear as one of the armed guards walked in through the gate and stood just in front of the house. He yelled, "Listen, Mike Cadwell is giving his wives Olivia, Davina, and Rachel half an hour to come out of the house with all his children. If they're not out by then, he said his wives will be to blame for whatever happens to the women in this house." The guard turned around and left the property again.

The women screamed and sobbed. Olivia walked up to Rachel, holding her son's hand. "Rachel, I think we should go out."

Keith screamed in outrage, "He can't do that! He can't ask you or Rachel to come out. You aren't his wife! That man is insane!"

Rachel felt like her heart would burst out of her chest at any moment. She turned to Keith. "Calm down, honey. We have to think about what to do."

Olivia placed her hand on her forehead. "All this is my fault. There's nothing else to do, Rachel. We have to go out there and meet Mike. I know what he's capable of doing. We have no choice."

Another gunshot sounded, and Rachel gasped.

Daniel strode out to the common room as women scampered about, screaming and looking confused. He said, "Nobody's going out there." He brought out a gun from his waist and cocked it. "I'll fight them all off if I have to."

Davina rushed up to him and shook her head. "You can't do that, Daniel. There are about six men outside, and I saw more at the back of the house. Mike and his men will kill you without batting an eyelash. And then we will have no one to protect us here."

Rachel said to Daniel, "Davina's right. What you can do right now is help me get all the women to their rooms. Let them hide anywhere. Under the beds... in the closets. Anywhere they can hide."

Daniel gazed angrily at the door.

"Please, Daniel," Rachel said. "Please go now and do as I say."

Daniel looked at her for a few seconds and then turned around and began to gather the women and lead them away from the common room.

"So, what are we supposed to do now?" Keith asked Rachel. "Because there's no way I'm going to let you out of this house to meet that madman."

"There's nothing else to do!" Olivia yelled. "We have to go out now!"

"And what if he hurts you or your children?" Keith looked at her. "Rachel isn't married to him. She can't go out and meet him. And I won't allow

Emily to, either. Mike seems like he has finally lost it. I mean, he was crazy before, but now he's become a psychopath. There's no telling what he'll do to all of you if you go out to him." Keith looked at Rachel, Olivia, and Davina. "I'm sure he's furious now because of what we all did to him."

"I doubt that he'll hurt his own children," Olivia said, looking frightened. She looked down at her boys, who were looking at her with bewilderment, clearly not fully understanding what was happening. She looked at Rachel, Keith, and Lily with confusion in her eyes. Emily was bouncing in Keith's arms, completely unaware of the terrible danger they were all in.

"How are you sure he won't?" Rachel asked Olivia. "Even if he doesn't hurt his children, what about you, Olivia, or Davina, or me? After what we did to him at the house and how we brought him here, are you really sure he won't hurt us?"

A light entered Olivia's eyes, and she sighed heavily. "You're right, Rachel." She began to sob. "What have I done? I should never have called you to come to the house. I should never have left. It was so selfish of me." She hugged her boys to herself and wept, causing them to begin to cry as well.

Lily put her hand on Olivia's shoulder, and Rachel said, "It's not your fault, Olivia. You did the right thing."

Daniel came back, and Rachel said to him, "Please take the boys upstairs and find somewhere for them to hide."

He nodded.

Another loud gunshot sounded, and Rachel felt like she was going to explode. She took Emily from

Keith and hugged her tightly. Emily began to cry, and she tried to soothe her little girl. Someone yelled from outside. "Fifteen minutes left!"

Davina whimpered and paced the common room. "What will we do now? Mike's going to kill us all."

"He isn't!" Keith roared. "I won't let him."

"You can't do anything about it!" Davina screamed, tugging at her hair. "What are you going to do? Fight off all his armed men with your bare hands?"

"Davina, please calm down," Rachel said, even though she was freaking out herself. "Let's try to think about solutions rather than the problem."

"There's no solution or anything to think about." Olivia stared at her. "We have to go out and meet Mike. We have only fifteen minutes."

"Maybe I should go outside and see if I can try to talk some sense into him," Rachel said.

Keith shook his head. "No, Rachel, you're not going anywhere. You know Mike resents you. Actually, he hates you for marrying me. He's definitely going to hurt you if you go out there."

"But we can't stand around here waiting for him to come in and kill us all," Rachel said.

Olivia began to head toward the door, but Rachel pulled her back.

Lily said, "Maybe Taylor can help. We should call him."

Rachel put her hand on her forehead and shut her eyes. "Why didn't I think of that? Lily, please call him. Tell him to call the police in Prospect."

"But what can the police do?" Davina screamed. "Before they get here, it'll be too late. Mike will have massacred everyone."

Rachel sighed. In spite of how hysterical Davina was, she was right. "That's true," she said, "but we should still call Taylor so he can inform the police of our situation while we figure out what to do here. We might have to go out to buy the women some time."

Lily shifted on her feet. "Rachel, you should call him," she said, looking down at the floor. "He might not pick up my call, and we need him to answer quickly."

"Why wouldn't he pick up your call?" Rachel asked, and then waved her hand before Lily could answer. "Keith, do you have your cell phone here?"

Keith dug his hand into his pocket and brought out his cell phone. He handed it to her. She glanced at the time on the phone and almost collapsed in fear. They only had five minutes.

"We have to go out and meet Mike now," she handed the phone back to Keith. "Call him, Keith. Tell him what's going on." She turned to Olivia and Davina. "We need to go out to meet Mike."

"But he asked for his children as well," Davina said. "He might not be satisfied with just the three of us."

"You're not going out to meet that crazy man," Keith said to Rachel.

"Call Taylor, now!" Rachel yelled. She sighed and said softly, "Please, Keith."

Lily asked, "What if we send someone out to give him a message?"

"A message?" Rachel looked at her.

"Yes. We can ask him to give you guys a bit more time to come out since you have to gather the children together. That will buy us a bit of time while we try to figure out what to do."

Rachel nodded. "That's a good idea. It might not work, but I have nothing else. Who will go out to speak to Mike?"

Daniel stepped forward. "I'll go and give Mike the message. I don't have to step out of the gate. I can stay just inside and tell him what you want me to."

Rachel shook her head slowly. "No, Daniel. A man, especially a former member of the squad team, would be too threatening for Mike and his men. They will kill you as soon as they set eyes on you. That might set Mike off, and he'll storm in here in anger with his men. Besides, we need you here. I'll go."

"No, Rachel," Keith said, the cellphone pressed to his ear. "I'll go."

"Certainly not, Keith," Rachel said. "You heard what I just told Daniel. Besides, Mike despises you more than anyone else here. I'll be fine. I won't leave the premises. Mike won't try to grab me since he doesn't want just me. He wants all of us. I'll tell him it will take a bit more time to prepare Emily and the boys to come out and meet him." She went and kissed Keith's cheek and then opened the door and walked out of the house.

She walked to the gate, her heart pounding with fear. The gate was slightly open, and she knew the men would have stormed in at Mike's request a long time ago if not for the fact that the Mike she knew was even now taking obscene pleasure in his ability to make them all squirm in prolonged terror. She opened the gate slightly and stuck her head out.

"Mike," she called to him. He was standing right in front of the gate, but he turned around. When he saw her, a triumphant smile touched his lips.

"Mike, I need to speak to you."

He smirked and shook his head. "Your time is up, Rachel. You all need to come out."

"Please, just give us an hour more. You know how the kids are. They are refusing to cooperate. We need some time to soothe them and prepare them to come out. Emily's been asleep. We need to wake her up and get her ready to come out."

Mike stared suspiciously at her and then nodded. He glanced at his wristwatch and said, "You have ten minutes. There'll be no more excuses once your time is up. We'll come in, take all that belongs to me, and kill everyone else."

"Mike, why would you do such an evil thing?"

He glanced at his wristwatch again. "Nine minutes and fifty-three seconds."

She glared at him and then turned around and hurried back into the house. Everyone gathered around her, and she said "We have about nine minutes. After that, he'll come in and his men will start shooting."

"That beast!" Keith growled.

Olivia was standing near the window. She stared outside and said, "It's Mike's way. He's extremely jealous, especially over things he thinks belong to him. He believes we — his wives and children — are his property and that we were taken away from him. He has to get us back no matter what it costs." Olivia's face twisted with pain. "I should have known all this and not done what I did."

"Stop it, Olivia," Rachel said. "You did the right

thing."

Keith went to Rachel and put his arms around her. "I won't ever let you go," he said, hugging her.

She smiled sadly and then pulled away slightly to look him in the eye. "I might have to, Keith. I can't let Mike come in here and harm these innocent women. You know that would be wrong."

"I've told Taylor everything," Keith said. "He's probably made the call to the police station now. Maybe they'll be able to come before crazy Mike has a chance to do anything. Then you don't have to go out."

"You know that's unlikely," Rachel told him. "There has to be something we can do," she desperately looked around her.

"What?" Davina asked angrily. "I don't see any way out of this."

"There has to be a way," Rachel answered. And yet she couldn't think of anything. Davina was right. Unless a miracle happened and the police arrived in less than nine minutes, they would all perish or be taken captive by Mike. She would never see Keith again, even if she survived, because Mike would definitely kill him. Fear gripped her once more, but she pushed it away. *Think of a solution, Rachel.*

Keith said, "What if you all go out to meet him and, after he has you, he still tells his men to come in and kill everyone in here?"

Rachel tugged at her hair, fear and desperation overwhelming her. She took a deep breath to try to calm herself down and said, "That's very possible, but we still have no choice. Like Davina said, I don't see a way out of this except to go out and meet Mike with the kids."

"We'll find a way," Keith told her. "God will make a way."

Rachel nodded but Keith's words of assurance did nothing to calm her fears. If the Lord was going to help them, He had to do so now, before they ran out of time.

SEVENTEEN

Taylor finished making the call to the police station and began to pace his living room. His hands shook and his legs trembled, and he had to sit back down again. "No, Lord! This can't be happening!" Fear threatened to consume him. "Lily is in there, Lord. And Rachel. Please help them." He felt like storming out of the house and rushing to the Restoration House to fight off Mike and those evil men of his. But that wouldn't be possible. He felt an overwhelming helplessness settle over him and he groaned.

"Lord, all those women in the house. Lily! Why didn't I make her come with me?" He had never felt this afraid before. What would he do if he lost Rachel and Lily? He placed his hand on his forehead and shut his eyes. He couldn't bear to imagine it. He groaned again. He could not let anything happen to them. He had to do something. The police wouldn't arrive in time.

He stood up and paced the living room again. He couldn't just sit down when the life of his sister, his niece, and all those innocent women were in danger. When the life of the woman he loved was on the line.

He wanted to pass out as he thought about Lily. How would he go on if anything happened to her? *Lily, I'm so sorry.* He loved her with everything in him. Now he could admit it. He had been wrong for ignoring her. He'd thought that keeping his distance was the right thing to do because of their extreme attraction to each other. Because he didn't want to betray the memory of his wife. But he had to tell himself the truth. He was hopelessly in love with Lily, and if anything happened to her, he wouldn't be able to go on. He couldn't let anything happen to her.

"Lord, what do I do?"

An idea came to him, and he took a deep breath and mulled it over. It wasn't much of an idea. It was unlikely that bull-headed liar would help him, especially with the vendetta he had against Rachel. If Taylor had known the full story, he would not have been so quick to help that man out. He'd been lied to, but Rachel had told him the full truth. The man owed him his life and those of his men. It was the reason why he had not gone after Rachel since.

Taylor dialed the phone number quickly. It didn't matter that Dennis Hamilton had a vendetta against Rachel. He needed the man's help right now. Dennis had told Taylor he owed him a huge debt of gratitude.

Taylor sighed. Dennis owed him much more than he realized. Dennis had withheld the truth from him for a long time, not telling him that he'd nearly killed Rachel to hold on to his grip on power. If not for the Lord, Taylor would have sent that man packing from his house. The flood that had swept Dennis and his men into the river had not been accidental, as Dennis had told him, but a supernatural act to save Rachel and Keith. Rachel would be angry with him for keeping such a huge secret from her, but then again, if Dennis could help, she might thank him for it later.

He waited as the phone rang, and finally Dennis's voice came on the other end of the line. Without greeting the man, he said, "I need your help!"

"What is it?"

"The Restoration House is in trouble, Dennis. My sister, her friend, Lily, her husband and their child, and all the women there are in danger." He told Dennis in as few words as possible everything Keith had told him and said they had little time left. "You have to go and help them. You and your men."

Dennis laughed. "You're kidding, right? You know what your sister did to me, and yet you want me to help her?"

"Dennis! You kept the truth from me for a long time, and I only found out recently that you tried to kill my sister and her husband. And yet I still let you and your men stay in my house. Now, you will help me get rid of Mike."

"I won't, Taylor!"

"Did you hear me?" Taylor yelled. "Gunmen have surrounded the Restoration House and will kill all the women there in a few minutes. You have to help them. You owe me. You promised."

"You should have known better than to believe me when I make a promise," Dennis said. "Please, Taylor. I don't want to hear anything about Rachel anymore. It's enough that I'm hiding in Fallow Creek like a fugitive. A place I used to lead. I haven't bothered her at all because of you. That is the promise I made to you. But I draw the line there. I'm not going to help her or any one of those women in that House. Now if there's nothing else you want to tell me, I have to go."

"Dennis!" Taylor screamed in desperation. "Listen, Rachel told me your wives and children are in that house."

"That's a lie! You're just saying that in order to get me to help her."

"Do you want to stake their lives on it? I'm not lying."

For some seconds there was silence, and then Dennis groaned. "Fine! I'll go and fight off Mike Cadwell."

"Good," Taylor said and ended the call. Rachel had told him that Dennis's wives had come to her for help along with their children, but he was not sure they were at the House. He'd told Dennis Hamilton what he had out of desperation. Hopefully, the remaining squad members who were with Dennis would be enough to face off with Mike and his men and defeat them. One way or another, there would be a bloodbath, but he hoped the blood that was shed would not belong to any of those innocent women at the House.

His mind went back to Lily, and then to Rachel, and he held his head in his hands, his heart pounding. "I can't lose them," he muttered. "Lord, please help me. Please protect everyone at the House, especially my sister and Lily. I'm sorry for how I treated her."

He had acted as though he didn't care when Lily had told him she wouldn't be coming to stay at his house. But he had cared. He understood why she had refused to go with him. After how he'd constantly ignored her over the past few days, she'd probably grown tired of him and felt more comfortable staying with Rachel. How he wished that he had insisted she come along. If only he'd treated her better, she would have followed him home, and she wouldn't be in the situation she was in now.

He moaned. He felt like throwing up as fear coiled around him, threatening to suffocate him. He would give anything to tell her how he truly felt about her and to hide nothing from her. He had been trying to keep his distance to give him time to process his feelings, but he should have learned from his late wife's death that life was short. Why had he wasted so much time that he could have spent making his feelings known to Lily? Now, it might be too late to do so.

"Lord, if you save her, I promise I'll tell her how much I love her."

Faye was dead and gone, and as much as he had loved her, he had to move on. She would have been happy that he had found someone who he loved with all his heart. Yes, it was barely a year since she'd died, but he couldn't help how he felt about Lily. As for Josh and the promise he had made to him, he would have to explain to his son that sometimes things did not always pan out the way people thought they would. Josh would understand... someday. Hopefully, sooner rather than later.

"Lily! Rachel! Lord, please protect them. Please help them." He picked up his phone again and dialed Lily's number, his hand shaking. It rang and rang, but she didn't answer.

***

Rachel's eyes widened as Mike opened the gate of the House of Refuge and yelled, "Your time is up! We're coming into the House!"

A gunshot pierced the air, and Rachel bit her lip. Upstairs, women screamed in fear, closet doors shut loudly, and feet scampered about.

Rachel sighed and stared out the window again. Keith stood at her side, peering out. Daniel stood at the door, his gun drawn and pointed toward it. Olivia, Davina, and Lily were sitting on one of the sofas in the common room. Davina and Olivia wept.

Lily came to stand behind Rachel and put her arm around her.

Rachel looked back at Olivia and Davina and said, "It's time to go out." She had given Emily to one of the women upstairs to hide her along with Olivia's boys. They would have to go out — she, Olivia, and Davina — and find another excuse to give to Mike as to why they couldn't bring out the children. Who knew what Mike would do?

"We need to go out now, ladies," she said again. "Mike and his men will come in any moment now, and we can't afford to let that happen."

Keith shook his head and said, "I can't let you go."

"I have no choice."

Mike yelled again, "Your time is up! We are coming in."

Rachel began to move toward the door and then

froze when a loud voice said, "No, you aren't going into that house!" Her mouth fell open, and she could not believe her ears. That voice. It couldn't be. She turned to Keith. His eyes were as round as dinner plates. "Is that...? It can't be."

Keith nodded slowly. "After spending hours in his study for days, talking with him, I would recognize that voice in my sleep."

"But how is he alive?" Rachel asked, and then screamed as a series of gunshots exploded simultaneously.

Olivia yelled, "We need to go. They're coming in!"

Davina wept.

Rachel covered her mouth and shook her head. "They're not coming in, Olivia. Someone else has come to fight Mike on our behalf. Dennis Hamilton." Another series of gunshots sounded, and Rachel jumped.

Olivia gasped and rushed to the window. "How can that be? Dennis Hamilton is dead!"

The house seemed to shake as gunshots rang continuously. Rachel's mind traveled back to that fateful day when Dennis Hamilton and his men had fought with her stepfather and his men. Dennis had won that battle, but God had won the war. How was Dennis even still alive? Had he been living in Fallow Creek all this time?

Daniel turned to them and said sharply, "You all need to step away from that window! A stray bullet might hit you." He looked at Davina, who was still sitting on the sofa, looking at the wall with a vacant stare. He went over to her and put his arm around her shoulder.

Rachel sat down on the sofa and squeezed her eyes shut. She prayed earnestly for victory over Mike, but she wasn't even sure if Dennis Hamilton was truly here to save them. For all she knew, once he was finished with Mike, he and his men would come into the House and finish them all off.

"Rachel!" Lily's eyes were wide. "I think Dennis Hamilton was the person Taylor was talking about when he said he knew a man around here who he could ask about my parents."

Rachel blinked. "That means Dennis Hamilton has been living in Fallow Creek for some time now, and I didn't even know," she said, shivering.

"Yes," Lily nodded. "I think Taylor knew Dennis was here in Fallow Creek. I think he was the one who called Dennis to help us. You said Dennis's first wife is in the House. That might have been enough incentive for him to agree to help."

Rachel nodded. "You're right, Lily. Taylor must have called Dennis. And that means he knew Dennis has been in Fallow Creek all this while."

Another hail of gunshots crackled through the air, and Davina wrapped her arms around Daniel. Keith came and sat on the left side of Rachel and put his hand around her waist. "Let's hope that Dennis is really here to help us," he said.

"I think he is," Rachel said, and then pressed her lips tightly together, fear coursing through her as more gunshots sounded. It reminded her of the day Dennis Hamilton had kidnapped them and her stepfather had ambushed them on the way to his house. She and Keith had sat in the car wondering about the outcome of the gun battle taking place around them, knowing that whichever way it went, they were still in danger. This time, she believed Taylor had called Dennis and his team to help them, but Dennis Hamilton was just as insane as Mike was. And after everything that had happened months ago, he must hate her as much as Mike did. Who knew what he would do after all this was over?

The gunshots suddenly stopped, and for almost ten minutes, silence reigned. Some of the women began to come down the stairs, but Daniel told them to go up and hide again. They were not out of danger yet. Until they knew that Mike and his men had been subdued and defeated, they still had to hide.

Mike's voice suddenly boomed in the air again. He sounded like he was inside the grounds of the house. "So, you called Dennis Hamilton to defeat me. Well, you all lost. I have captured him and destroyed his men. Now, I won't say this again. All my wives and children, including Rachel, are to come out now, or we come in there and kill everyone. Don't make me come in there, because once I do, that will be the end of you all."

"Let's go, Olivia," Rachel said. "And you, Davina."

Lily held Rachel's hand. "You can't go! He'll kill you."

"Yes, Rachel," Keith said. "And if you all go without the children, you know what Mike will do."

"We have to try. We can't send the children out there," Rachel said. "Who knows what sight will be waiting for us outside?" She shuddered. "I'm pretty sure it's not something we want to expose the children to."

Keith shook his head and whispered, "I can't let you go, Rachel."

She caressed his cheek tenderly. "Don't be so afraid, Keith. I don't think Mike will kill us. Just as we've said, Mike likes to collect property of all kinds, and he sees us as his property. It's unlikely he'll kill us."

"You can't be sure of that," Keith gazed at her.

"We have to take our chances. For the sake of all the women here. You know I have no choice, Keith." Her heart broke as she reached out and hugged him tightly. Tears fell down her cheeks. Keith pulled away slightly. "I promise, Rachel. I will find a way to get you out."

Daniel and Davina hugged. "Keith and I will look for a way to free you all," he said.

Rachel stood up, and Olivia did, too. Davina looked like she was about to pass out as she slowly walked to the door. She rushed back to Daniel, and he held her tightly. Keith came to Rachel, took her in his arms, and kissed her. "I love you with all my heart," he said. "Daniel and I will find a way to rescue you."

She smiled sadly and touched his cheek. "I love you, too," she said. She blinked back the tears threatening to fall down her cheeks again and pulled away from Keith. She walked to the door, and Olivia and Davina followed. The three of them walked out of the House of Refuge and out the gate.

Rachel's stomach turned with revulsion as she looked around her. There were men lying on the ground, clearly dead. Dennis Hamilton was some distance away on his knees, one of Mike's guards hovering over him. His hands were bound and his mouth gagged. Mike glared at her and then at Olivia and Davina. "Where are my children?" he barked.

Rachel looked around her and pointed at the bodies on the ground. "Mike, look at this place. We knew this was the kind of thing we would see when we came out here. We didn't want the kids to see all this."

Mike charged at Rachel. She stood her ground but looked away from him. He stopped just in front of her, let out a yell of frustration, and backed away again. "Okay, then! We will clear out all the bodies. And then my children will be brought out. No excuses!"

Olivia said, "Let me just go into the house and check on the children. When it's safe for them to come out, I'll bring them all out and then we can go home, Mike."

She started to move away, and Mike spat out, "Stay right there!" He turned to Rachel and shook his head. "I know you called the police." He looked at Olivia and then at Rachel again. "We aren't going home. We're leaving this town once the kids come out."

Rachel's heart began to thud in panic. She'd been hoping that somehow the police would arrive soon and rescue them, but if they left town, that would be the end. She might never see Keith again. *Lord, please help us.* She couldn't let Emily come out here or follow Mike out of Fallow Creek. There had to be a solution.

Mike said, "My men have removed all the bodies. Now all my children can come out." He barked at one of his men. "Go and get my kids, all three of them. You know them, don't you?"

"No," Rachel began to panic. Once the kids came out, there would be no more reason for delay. Mike would take them all away. And he still might not spare the women here or her husband. She had to find a way to stall him. "Let me go and get them."

He laughed. "You think I don't know what your plans are. You're not going anywhere." Mike nodded at his man again, and the man began to move towards the House.

"Please, Mike. Look at him." She pointed at the beefy, scary-looking guard holding a gun. "He's a goon with a gun. He'll scare the kids. Please, let us go in and get them."

Mike glared at her and called his man back. "You can go. Just you, Rachel, but I'm giving you fifteen minutes to get all my children out here. Is that understood?"

"Yes," she said quickly. She started to go in, but he called her back. She groaned and turned around.

"Alan will go with you." She opened her mouth to protest, but Mike shook his head. "Alan will follow you. I don't want you playing any games."

"But he'll scare the kids."

"The kids know him already," Mike said. "Now you go with her, Alan. Remember, you have fifteen minutes." He called Alan aside, and Rachel strained her ears to hear what he was saying to his guard. "When my kids are out, send the signal, and we'll come in and finish those women off. Okay?"

Alan nodded.

Rachel's blood ran cold, and she almost threw up.

"Now go," Mike said loudly.

Rachel turned around again and marched to the door of the House of Refuge, Alan behind her. She opened the door and blinked at Daniel. Hopefully, he would understand what she couldn't say out loud to him. She opened the door wide and entered, and the guard followed right behind.

Daniel immediately put the gun to the guard's head once he was inside the house and the door was shut. "Drop your gun now!" Daniel ordered. The man obeyed, and Daniel kicked the gun aside. "Keith, take his gun." He looked at Lily. "You and Rachel, get strong ropes and tie him up."

Rachel hurried over to Keith, and they hugged. She whispered in his ear because she didn't want to scare Lily and the others, "Mike doesn't plan to let any of the women live." She told him what Mike had said to his guard.

"Then we can't let that one out of our sight," he said. "And you certainly can't go out to meet him again. We need to pray for a miracle, Rachel."

Rachel nodded. She left the common room with Lily to find rope. Mike had given her fifteen minutes to bring his children out, but there was no way she was going to do that. Which meant they barely had fifteen minutes to find a solution, or there would be a huge disaster. She prayed with all her heart that God would give them an idea of how to escape before Mike's patience ran out.

EIGHTEEN

Rachel finished tying the guard's hands while Daniel stood over him, the gun pointed at him. "Keith, get his gun. We might need you to use it later." Daniel picked up the guard's gun from the floor and put it in Keith's hand.

Keith shook his head. He looked horrified as he stared at the weapon. He dropped it onto the coffee table. "I'm not holding that," he said.

Daniel snorted, and Rachel said to Lily, "Have you ever noticed a back gate or something like that through which we can escape this House? I haven't, but you also lived here."

Lily shook her head. "There's no way to escape through the back. And the fences are really high and have barbed wire."

"That's true," Rachel said. "It's the way the Restoration House was built so that no one could escape from it."

"Yes," Lily said. "I also saw Mike's goons patrolling the back of the house. We can't..." She gasped.

"What is it?" Rachel asked.

"Taylor told me that your grandfather also built most of the homes in Fallow Creek."

"Yes." Rachel nodded and looked inquisitively at Lily.

"But I know Taylor built some of the buildings, too. Was the Restoration House built by Taylor or your grandfather?"

Rachel frowned. "My grandfather built most of the homes and the older buildings in Fallow Creek. But the newer ones, like the town hall and the Restoration..." She sucked in her breath sharply. "Taylor was the one who was commissioned to build the Restoration House years ago. A smaller building was on this land before Dennis Hamilton told Taylor to build this larger House."

Lily nodded. "That means Taylor might know every nook and cranny of this place."

"He probably does," Rachel said slowly, her heart racing with hope. "He's a very detail-oriented person. This House was built a long time ago, but he might just remember if there's something like a secret escape route."

Lily said with urgency in her voice, "Let's call him. We have very little time before Mike becomes suspicious and comes in here with his men." Her eyes traveled around the common room. "Where's my phone?" she asked, and then grunted. "I left it in your apartment, Rachel."

"I'll call him with mine." She picked up her phone from the sofa and groaned. The battery was dead.

"Let's use mine," Keith said and picked up his phone. Taylor's phone began to ring, and then his voice came on the other end of the line. "Taylor!"

"Keith!" Taylor sounded scared. "Are my sister and Lily okay? Has Mike Cadwell been subdued?"

"Rachel and Lily are fine, Taylor. But Mike Cadwell defeated Dennis Hamilton. I take it you're the one who called Dennis."

"Yes," Taylor said, groaning.

Rachel sighed. That meant Taylor had known Dennis Hamilton was alive all this while but hadn't told her. There was no time to ask him about it right now.

Keith went on. "Mike still insists that Rachel and his kids go with him. He's planning to leave Fallow Creek to some secret location." Keith glanced at Lily and lowered his voice. "And he's not planning to spare anyone here, either."

"No... oh no...! That man is mad! Can I talk to Lily and Rachel?"

"Yes. They have something to ask you anyway."

Rachel took the phone from Keith. "Taylor!"

"Rachel! Are you okay? Thank God you're alive. Please don't go anywhere with Mike Cadwell. Hopefully the police will arrive soon."

"We don't know when that will be. Mike has given me fifteen minutes." She glanced at the clock on the wall. "Ten minutes now. Listen, Taylor. We thought of something. You built the Restoration House years ago. Do you remember if there's any secret passage or door where we can escape without being seen by Mike and his men?"

For a few seconds, Taylor said nothing, and then he said, "It was such a long time ago..." There was a brief silence on the other end, and then Taylor spoke again, "Wait! I remember adding a *secret* door and telling my builders to build an escape route. A tunnel. Dennis didn't tell me to do that, but I just thought it might be needed one day. I'd forgotten all about it."

"Where is this secret door?" Rachel asked, her hope soaring.

"It's in the common room…"

"Here in the common room?" Rachel looked around her. "I've never noticed any secret door."

"Yes, Rachel. That's because it's a secret door. Move the large bookshelf that's against the wall."

Rachel blinked. "Can it be moved? It's huge." Before Taylor could say anything, she said, "Don't worry about answering that. I think we'll all manage to move it." Keith and Daniel were already on opposite ends of the bookshelf. Lily went and stood beside Keith, and Rachel went to the other end and placed the phone on the edge of the sofa. She stood next to Daniel, and together they began to struggle to move the bookshelf forward. It took a lot of pushing and effort, but they finally managed to shift it forward.

Panting, Rachel picked up Keith's phone again and said, "We've moved it, Taylor." She frowned as she looked at the wall behind the bookshelf. She could see no clear edges that indicated any door or passage. All she could see was smooth painted wall in front of her. "Are you sure this is the location of the secret door?" she asked. "Maybe someone like Dennis Hamilton discovered it some time ago and had it sealed."

"No," Taylor said. "I had the wall plastered that way so no one would know there was a secret passage… but it's there for sure."

"So how do we find it?" Rachel asked impatiently.

"You don't," Taylor said. "I do."

"How?"

"With an electronic device I have here that's... You know what, don't worry about all that. I'll open the door from here." He sounded like he was walking fast, even running. "Let me find it. I haven't seen that thing in years, but I know where I kept it." There was silence for a few seconds more, and then Rachel gasped as the wall in front of her suddenly moved back, and a big empty space gaped at them. Lily's mouth was wide open, her eyes as big as dinner plates, while Keith stood shaking his head, a look of wonder on his face.

Daniel said, "Let's start evacuating everyone. What are we still waiting for?"

"It's open?" Taylor asked.

"Yes," Rachel answered, astonished. "So where does this lead?"

"There's a long passageway that leads to a flight of stairs that goes underground to a tunnel. It's a very long walk down the tunnel but it ends at the edge of Fallow Creek, near the river."

Rachel shivered slightly as she remembered the awful events that had taken place almost a year ago at that river. That day had been etched in her mind, and she was sure she would never forget it. Neither would she forget this one. She looked at Keith and said, "That place still gives me nightmares."

"I'll drive there right now with my children," Taylor said. "I'll be waiting there for all of you."

"But what about Davina?" Daniel asked, looking at Rachel. "There's no way I can leave here without her."

"And Olivia." Rachel said. "She is with mad

Mike."

"Who?" Taylor asked. He didn't wait for an answer. "Is Lily there? Can I speak to her?"

Rachel handed Lily Keith's phone.

Lily looked uncertain as she took the phone from Rachel. "Hello, Taylor?"

"Oh, Lily!" Taylor sounded both relieved and worried. "I'm so glad you're safe. I'm really sorry for how I've treated you these past few days. For ignoring you. I thought... There's no time to tell you everything I want to. You will have to get out of there now! I'll be waiting."

Lily nodded as though he could see her. She pressed the phone to her ear, overcome with emotion. "Lily, I have so much to tell you. I can't wait to see you."

Lily smiled. "Taylor, I..."

"No, Lily! There's no time to talk! You need to leave that house! We'll talk as soon as you're all safe." He ended the call, and Lily looked at Rachel.

"We have to go now," she said.

"I'm not leaving without Davina," Daniel said again.

"I certainly can't leave when the lives of all the women here are on the line," Rachel said. "We have to get them all out quietly through this secret door without Mike suspecting anything."

Keith said, "Rachel, I will stay and try to get them all out and also try to stall Mike. You and Lily can go with the children."

Rachel shook her head vehemently. "No. These women are my responsibility. I'm not leaving them when Mike is looming outside like the devil himself. I will help you and Daniel get them all out before I leave this house."

Lily glanced at the clock on the wall. "We have five minutes more," she said, with a tremble in her voice. "Whatever we plan to do, we need to do it now."

"Let's start getting the women out," Rachel said. "We have to make sure they're all quiet so Mike doesn't find out what our plans are. He might tarry longer than five extra minutes for the kids, but not much longer than that. Once we get everyone to the edge of town, we can take them all to the police station in Prospect."

"We're going to walk that long distance?" Keith asked.

"Yes, if we have to." Rachel shrugged.

"And what about Olivia and Davina?" Daniel asked. "How are we going to get them away from Mike?"

Rachel said, "I'm not really sure how we're going to do that. We might have to find another way to stall Mike, though that will be dangerous." She turned to Lily. "Mike might storm in here while we're trying to get the women out if our time runs out. You will take Emily and Olivia's boys with you now."

"I'm not leaving without you," Lily said.

"Yes, you are. You're going now. You have to get the kids safely to Taylor."

Lily looked up the stairs and said, "Let me go get them." She left quickly.

Rachel looked at Daniel. He was looking out the window, his gun pointed out. She looked up at the clock on the wall, and her heart began to pound again. Any moment now, Mike and his men would come storming in. "Daniel, Keith, please start to evacuate the women."

Daniel nodded.

Keith smiled and kissed her, and then went off with Daniel.

Lily made her way down the stairs holding Emily, with Olivia's kids in front of her. She reached Rachel, and Rachel hugged her tightly, and then kissed Emily's cheek. Rachel swallowed the sob that rose in her throat and said to Lily, "Please take care of my Emily and these precious boys. We'll meet up with you as soon as possible. Now go!" she ordered.

Lily went.

NINETEEN

Lily turned on the flashlight she'd taken from a room in the House and shone the light into the passageway. She stepped in, carrying Emily in her arms. Olivia's children walked by her side down the empty passageway. They got to the end and went down the flight of stairs into a cavernous tunnel.

Emily chattered continuously as they made their way down the tunnel. Soon, the boys began to whine and complain. They didn't want to go on walking.

"We have to keep walking," Lily said to them, her heart pounding with concern and fear. She didn't know how long they were going to walk down this tunnel or when they were going to finally be able to come out on the other side.

The farther they walked, the more tired Lily got. She shifted Emily to her other side and carried the flashlight in her right hand. Emily stopped chattering and began to whimper. Lily tried to talk to her to find out what was wrong, but it didn't help. Soon she began to wail.

Lily's head pounded. She felt like crying along with Emily. She was tired from the long walk. The boys were already slowing down and constantly complaining. They told her they wanted to stop and rest, but she kept telling them they couldn't stop. They had to keep moving.

They continued to walk, and Lily wondered if this tunnel was ever going to end. She shifted Emily to her other side again and then finally put the little girl down. Emily wailed even louder, and Lily tried to soothe her again. The boys kept complaining, and then, finally, they refused to go on. Emily was exhausted, and Lily knew that in spite of the danger they faced, they had to stop for a while in order to rest. None of them could take another step forward.

They stopped, and Lily leaned her back on the cement wall and slid to the ground. She sat Emily on her lap while the boys sat on either side of her. She took deep breaths as she held Emily to herself. Soon, Emily stopped crying and began to play with her fingers.

The boys started to bicker loudly, and Lily said, "We have to be quiet." They stopped talking for about a minute and then began arguing again.

She sighed and allowed her mind to go back to what Taylor had told her over the phone. He had apologized for how he had ignored her for days. He had also told her he wanted to say something to her. What was it he wanted to tell her? Maybe he was going to tell her how he felt about her. Maybe he would let her know that he felt the same way about her that she did about him.

She sighed again. Or maybe he wanted to tell

her that he liked her, but not in the way she liked him. She didn't know what he was going to say, but whatever it was, she longed to see him again.

She stood up. They had to keep moving. She looked down at the boys. "We have to go, boys," she said. She held Emily's hand and began to move again. She blinked and looked back. The boys were still sitting down with stubborn expressions on their faces.

"Boys, we have to go now!" she said exasperatedly.

"We're tired," the older one said.

She sighed and then brushed aside the frustration she felt. Stooping down to look them in the eye, she realized she didn't even know their names. She focused on the older one and said softly, "I'm Lily. What's your name, buddy?"

"Will," he answered.

She smiled and faced the younger one and asked him what his name was. He didn't answer for a short while, but then he said, "Jeremy."

She nodded. "Will and Jeremy, you have an idea of what's happening upstairs, don't you? I know you're tired and hungry, but it's very important for us to move forward and get to the other end of this tunnel."

"I want my mom," Jeremy said.

"Yes," Lily looked into his eyes. "I know. That's why we have to get to the other end. The sooner we do, the sooner you can be reunited with your mom." She didn't know if that was true, but she had to keep them moving. It would be what Olivia would want.

Will stood up and looked down at his brother. "Let's go, Jeremy," he said.

Jeremy huffed and stood up as well.

"Thank you," Lily said, and allowed the boys to walk in front of her. She held Emily's little hand tightly as the ground was slightly slippery. Her mind returned to Taylor as they walked. The days they had spent in Tuscon getting to know each other all over again had been amazing though difficult. If only he had not completely ignored her once they'd arrived in California. If only she had not spent those days in Arizona falling hopelessly in love with him, she would not feel the way she did now. What if they didn't make it through this and she never saw him again?

She gasped and held Emily's hand tighter when the little girl almost slipped and fell. Emily began to cry again, and Lily picked her up and settled her on her hip.

They all continued to walk again, and soon she began to grow too weary and too numb to even think. Emily felt like a ton of bricks on her hip. The boys turned to her and told her they were tired and hungry again. When she said nothing, they began to vehemently complain. Jeremy started to cry, and she bit her lip. She knew what would come next. Emily would start to cry again, too.

Emily let out a loud wail, and Lily sighed. Once again, she felt like crying. She whispered encouraging words to Emily, and when she calmed down, Lily put Emily down, reached out for Jeremy, and hugged him tightly. Jeremy stopped crying, and she said to him, "Just a little while longer, Jeremy. Soon we'll be on the other side."

She didn't know what else to say to encourage them. They really had no choice but to go on walking.

Will turned around and looked up at her. "Where's our mom?" He looked worried.

Lily searched her mind trying to figure out what to say to him and then told him his mother was safe. "You'll see her soon." She felt slightly bad about what she'd told him. She wasn't sure Olivia *was* safe, as she was with Mike right now. Since his kids had not been brought out to him, who knew what he would do to Olivia? Lily shuddered. There was nothing else she could have said to Will.

They continued to walk again in silence. After a while, she picked up Emily as the toddler began to walk slowly, clearly weary. And then she nearly dropped Emily as a loud gunshot rang through the air. Screams followed, and Lily winced as fear gripped her. The boys put their hands around her and looked up at her with frightened eyes.

"It's okay, boys," she said to them. "Let's keep going." She held Emily tightly while she prayed silently, asking the Lord to protect Rachel and all the people upstairs. She jerked her head up as another gunshot rang through the air, followed by more screams. The children began to cry again. She tried to comfort them, but she didn't know exactly what to say except to tell them they had to move even faster now.

Will and Jeremy stopped moving again, and Jeremy sat on the floor, kicking his feet and wailing.

Lily put her hand on her head and groaned. "Lord, please help me!" She looked down at Jeremy as he threw a huge tantrum, and then shook her head, feeling completely drained. *Lord, when are we going to get to the other end of this tunnel?*

She took Jeremy by the hand and pulled him up. He tried to resist, but she forced him to his feet. Once again, she looked him in the eye and said, "Jeremy, remember what I told you. There are bad men up there. We need to move as fast as we can. Please."

Jeremy stopped crying and wiped the tears from his eyes.

They walked on, and Lily gasped as she saw natural light streaming into the tunnel a short distance away. The boys began to move faster, and she hurried after them. Emily began to chatter again. The nearer they got to the light, the brighter it became. She sighed with relief when she saw they were approaching the other end of the tunnel. "Finally," she said. She could get the kids to safety now.

At last, they reached the other end, and Lily whispered a prayer of thanks to God. Just before they stepped out, she spotted two of Mike's men standing a few feet away, their eyes roving around the area. Her heart sank. Mike must have decided that someone in the house would find some way to escape and sent these men to the edge of town to make sure no one did.

She told the boys to get back and then pressed her back against the wall, praying they had not been seen. After a few minutes, she took a deep breath, stepped slightly away from the wall, and glanced outside. Her eyes traveled around, trying to find any sign of Taylor or his car, but she saw nothing. Just before she moved back to hide again, Emily let out a loud wail, and Lily froze for a few seconds. The guards turned around, and their eyes met hers.

Her heart stopped, and she began to hyperventilate as they made their way toward her. She stepped back and yelled, "Run, boys! Run!"

The boys ran back into the tunnel and so did she. More gunshots rang out above them and more screams followed. The boys stopped running and turned to stare at her in confusion and panic. She stopped. They couldn't go back up, but they couldn't go out of the tunnel either. She immediately turned the flashlight off and told the boys to continue to move as fast as they could in the darkness. They had no other choice.

She swept Emily into her arms and began to move as fast as she could in the darkness, and then she shrieked when one of the boys screamed. She quickly turned the flashlight on. Will had tripped and fallen. He held his leg, crying out in pain.

She bent down to look at his leg, her heart beating fast. What were they going to do if Will couldn't stand? Her heart began to drum with fear as the men who were pursuing them shouted and blocked the entrance to the tunnel.

"All of you, come out now!" they yelled. She blinked as the sound of a car drew nearer. She sucked in her breath sharply as Taylor's voice boomed, "Both of you, stop right there! Drop your guns now and turn around slowly."

Lily stood up and went to peer out of the entrance. Her heart raced as the men dropped their guns and moved toward Taylor. He had a gun pointed at them, and she was surprised by that, but grateful to see him. They kept walking toward him, and then he told them to stop.

Her heart jumped into her throat as one of the

men slowly put his hand behind his back and began to pull out another gun. "Taylor!" she screamed. "Watch out!"

A gun exploded, and the guard dropped to the ground. In a split second, the other guard pointed a gun at Taylor, his hand on the trigger. Taylor was not paying attention to him, his eyes on the other man who had fallen. She gasped and flung the flashlight in her hand at the man with all her might. His gun went off as the flashlight hit him on the head. He fell to the ground and lay there, unconscious.

She turned to look at Taylor, fear gripping her, and sighed with relief. He was okay. He beckoned to her, and she held up her hand. She turned around and said, "Come on, boys!"

They refused to move, looking terrified. She looked down at Will. He was standing on his feet. "Thank God," she whispered. Hopefully, he would be able to walk. She went and took his hand and lifted Emily up with her right arm. "Let's go, Jeremy," she said. "It's okay."

The boys still looked frightened as they walked to Taylor, but Emily seemed unbothered by the violence they had just witnessed, as she clearly understood none of it.

They neared the men on the ground, and Lily herded the boys to her other side. She looked down at the one Taylor had shot. Blood oozed from his leg, but he was alive. He groaned as he looked up at Taylor, who still had a gun pointed at him.

Overwhelming relief ran through her as she reached Taylor. She fell into his arms, and he hugged her and Emily together, and then he pulled back slightly to look her in the eye.

"Thank God you're safe, Lily," he said and kissed her cheek. "What would I have done if anything had happened to you?" His eyes grew soft as he gazed at her, and then he cupped her cheeks and fixed his eyes on her lips. Her knees grew weak. He was going to kiss her.

She blinked when he pulled back and saw he was looking at Olivia's children. The boys still looked scared, and Lily said, "We have to get them to safety."

Taylor nodded. "Take them to the car and shut the doors." He opened the trunk of the car and brought out a first aid kit. He quickly began to tend to the bleeding man's leg.

She led the boys to the car, still carrying Emily in her arms. After they all got into the car, she strapped on their seatbelts and got into the passenger seat. Taylor got into the car minutes later and turned to her. "The men will be all right. I tied up their hands and took their weapons. Rachel and Keith will find them once they're out of the House."

Lily nodded and turned to look at Emily and the boys to make sure they were okay. She turned back to Taylor as he started the car. He reversed while she gazed at him. She felt a pang in her heart as she recalled how he had looked at her tenderly moments ago and the kiss they had almost shared. Disappointment flooded her, but she pushed the feeling aside. She had to focus on getting the children to safety.

They finally got to the plane, and Lily quickly got Emily and the boys out of the car. She carried Emily to the plane while Taylor and the boys followed her. The pilot was up front, and Joshua and Bree sat buckled at the back of the plane. Bree began to bump up in her seat when she saw her father, while Josh's eyes focused on Olivia's boys. He completely ignored Lily.

Lily put Emily down, and Emily immediately headed straight for Bree. Lily chuckled when Emily wrapped her arms around her younger cousin and tried to lift her up.

Bree scowled at Emily, no doubt to show her she would have none of it and then began to mumble when Emily did not let up. She stopped mumbling, pointed her tiny finger at Emily, and started to chatter non-stop in her baby voice, clearly scolding her cousin who did not understand the meaning of personal space.

In spite of her recent ordeal, Lily roared with laughter. Taylor and the boys were laughing too as they all watched the babies. She finally turned to look at Taylor again and gasped when he strode to her and swept her into his arms. He kissed her, sending bolts of pleasure through her, and she returned his kiss ardently.

"Dad! Stop it!"

Taylor pulled away slightly and looked down at Josh. He was looking at both of them with outrage, but Olivia's boys were grinning. Taylor stepped away from Lily, lifted Josh up, and carried him to a seat at the back of the plane. He sat Josh in the middle seat and took the window seat next to him. When he beckoned to Lily, she frowned.

"Come and sit with us, Lily," he said.

Josh began to grumble while she mouthed, "Are you sure?"

"Yes," he said loudly. "I've never been surer of anything."

She went and sat beside Josh in the aisle seat so that Josh was sitting in the middle of her and Taylor. He stared at her with daggers in his eyes and then turned to look at Taylor. When Taylor took her hand and kissed it, she couldn't help grinning. She looked down at Josh's frowning face and stopped smiling.

Taylor said to Josh, "I put you in the center so you know you will always be at the center of my life. You and Bree. The thing is, you'll have to share with Lily now."

Josh grumbled some more, and Taylor said, "Listen, Josh. Just because I have fallen in love with someone new, doesn't mean I love you any less." Lily blinked, and she felt as though the sun had just risen in her heart. He'd said that he was in love with her.

His eyes stayed on Josh. "When Bree came into our lives, didn't you have to share me with her? But did my love for you grow any less?"

Josh shook his head.

Taylor lifted his eyes to look at Lily. His gaze swept her entire face, and he gave her a tender smile. "I love Lily with all my heart, but I love you and Bree, too. I could never stop loving you." He looked at Lily again and said, "If you just give Lily a chance, you'll come to love her as much as I do," he smiled, "because she's so easy to fall in love with."

Lily felt her heart soaring. She couldn't keep her eyes off Taylor, even knowing Josh might complain about it again. She felt as though she were a child again and she had just been given the one gift she wanted most in all the world.

Josh sighed, and a look of resignation appeared on his face. He looked at Lily, but this time, he didn't scowl at her. He turned back to Taylor and said, "Okay, Dad. I'll give her a chance, but please don't kiss her again when I'm around. Please."

Taylor chuckled. He leaned over Joshua and took Lily's face in his hands. "Do you mean like this?" He kissed Lily soundly.

Josh groaned. "Dad, stop it!" He shook his head and laughed.

Taylor began to laugh as well, and Lily joined in. When they finally stopped, Josh said, "Can I go and play with those boys?"

"Sure," Taylor grinned and ruffled his hair. "But we will soon take off, so you'll have to be ready to sit and buckle up your seatbelt, okay?"

Josh nodded.

After he left, Taylor took the seat Josh had vacated and took Lily's hand in his. "I am so glad you're safe and right here with me," he said. The smile melted off his face, and he looked worried again. "I hope Rachel and Keith will be able to get out of the House safely."

Lily sighed. "I hope so, too." Fear gripped her again as she remembered the gunshots and screams she had heard coming from up in the House.

"I wish we could wait for them here," Taylor threaded his fingers through hers, "but we have to get the kids out of here as quickly as possible."

Lily's thoughts kept rotating between the gunshots and Mike Cadwell's many threats. She prayed in her heart that the Lord would protect Rachel and everyone in the House.

Taylor craned his neck and looked over at the children. "I hope all of them are buckled in," he said.

Lily went to check on the kids. She buckled in the boys. Emily and Bree were already strapped into their seats. She came back and sat next to Taylor. "They're all seated and buckled in," she said.

"Dave, we are ready to go!" Taylor called out.

The plane began to taxi down the runway and, once again, Lily's mind went back to Rachel and Keith and all the people in the House. She took a deep breath and prayed silently for God's protection. Taylor had gone through so much, losing his wife just months ago. Losing his sister too would be a disaster.

"Are you okay?" he asked, gazing at her with concern.

"Yes. I'm fine... especially now that I'm with you."

"I love being with you," he said tenderly.

She fixed her gaze on him and opened her mouth to tell him she loved being with him too, but he leaned in and covered her mouth with his. He kissed her slowly and deliberately, taking her breath away. When he finally pulled back, her brain was muddled and she couldn't think properly. She finally found her words and said, "Josh will be angry if he sees us, Taylor."

He chuckled. "Well, Josh isn't looking, so I can kiss you as much as I want." He claimed her lips again before she could reply, and she settled in for a long trip full of sweet kisses.

TWENTY

About a dozen women had gone through the large hole in the wall when Mike's voice boomed, "Your time is up! Rachel, come out of the House right now with my kids or you'll be blamed for whatever happens next."

Rachel gritted her teeth as anger and fear ran through her. She trembled when a gunshot exploded in the air. Women screamed and rushed into the secret passageway. She, Keith, and Daniel tried to calm them down so there would not be a stampede.

Daniel went to the window and opened the curtains. He looked back at Rachel and Keith and said, "They're coming in."

Rachel put her hand on her forehead as fear threatened to smother her. She exhaled and tried to put her fear away. "Mike won't start shooting if he believes his kids are still in the house. That might buy us a bit more time." She looked at the front door. They had tried to barricade it by not only locking it but piling furniture against it

"They have equipment of some kind," Daniel said, still looking through the window. "I think it's for breaking down the door. That furniture won't be able to keep them out for too long."

"How many men are there?" Keith asked.

"Apart from Mike, there are about four of them. I think there are three more at the back of the House."

"We need to place more things against the door," Keith said.

Rachel nodded. "But I still think as long as I stay in here and don't bring out the kids it'll buy us more time."

Another gunshot rang through the air, and once again the women screamed. Confusion broke out, and some of the women blocked the secret passage, delaying escape. Rachel tried to bring back order, while Keith and Daniel went to gather more furniture to place against the door.

Another round of gunshots sounded, and a bullet shattered one of the windows. Daniel quickly moved away from the window for only an instant and then raised his gun, preparing to shoot.

"Don't shoot, Daniel!" Rachel said. "It'll cause a shoot-out and endanger everyone still in the House."

Rachel looked back when she heard a loud pounding at the door. Daniel turned around and told her that the men were now trying to break the door open. She took a deep breath to try to calm her fears and began to breathe easier when they were able to finally get all the women out of the House through the secret door.

The front door began to crack open and all

the furniture they had piled against it started to topple over. "Let's go!" Rachel screamed as another loud bang pushed the door open further. "They're coming in!"

The last woman went through, and Rachel rushed into the passageway, followed by Keith, then Daniel. They heard a deafening sound and then Mike's voice inside the common room. Gunshots went off again, and Rachel sucked in her breath. "It's like Mike doesn't even care if his children are in here or not," she said.

"Maybe he's guessed that they've been sent off already," Keith said.

They raced down the stairs and hurried through the tunnel. Rachel whispered harshly, her heart knocking in fear, "I think they've found Taylor's secret passage."

"They're right behind us," Daniel said. "We need to hurry!"

It was dark in the tunnel, but they rushed forward anyway. Rachel's eyes began to grow accustomed to the darkness, and she saw the other women were not too far ahead. Loud footsteps pounded behind them, getting closer and closer.

"Rachel and Keith, you both can go on with the women," Daniel said. "I'll stay and try to delay Mike and his men."

"No, Daniel!" Rachel shook her head. "They'll kill you."

He waved her off. "Go! There's no time. Someone has to stay and stall Mike and his men."

Keith took Rachel's hand, and they hurried off, leaving Daniel behind. They ran faster, catching up to the women, but they couldn't run any further as the crowd of women stretched on before them. Another round of shots sounded, followed by a loud groan of pain.

Rachel winced. "That was Daniel. I hope they haven't killed him."

They kept walking fast, unable to run because of the crowd of women in front of them. Rachel felt more and more helpless as the footsteps behind gained on them. If they didn't start to run now, the men might catch up to them. And yet the women seemed too confused and frightened to move any faster.

Mike yelled, "My men are stationed all around Fallow Creek, even at the border. I have given them orders to kill anyone they see. Tell me where my kids are right now, Rachel, and I might consider sparing them."

Rachel shut her eyes in horror and yelled, "Mike, your kids aren't here. With all this madness caused by you, I sent them away first."

There was silence for a few seconds, and Mike shouted again, "Then you come to me. Alone and willingly! I promise to spare everyone's life, including your friend's here, if you come. If not, he dies."

Keith held her hand. "No, Rachel. Mike can't be trusted. If you go to him, he still might harm the women and Daniel."

Rachel wove her fingers through Keith's. "That might be, but we can't take any chances. There might be a chance he'll let the women go if I go and meet him. But if I don't, there'll be no chance for them or Daniel at all."

Daniel screamed again, and Rachel bit her lip.

"Come to me, Rachel!" Mike said. "I won't hurt you. You're mine. You know I love you."

"She's not yours!" Keith shouted. "She'll never be yours!"

"I guess, then, that the blood of your friend right here will be on both your hands. And we'll also kill every single woman that we see. Is that what you want?"

Keith screamed in outrage, and Rachel shut her eyes. "Lord, this can't be happening. Please help us." She placed her hand on Keith's cheek. She couldn't see his face clearly, but she felt him trembling with rage and fear for her. "I have to go to him. It might save the lives of everyone."

"No! We'll find another way!"

She caressed his cheek. "There is no other way, Keith," she said tenderly.

He pulled her into his arms and hugged her tightly.

For a long moment, Rachel held on to Keith. *Lord, I don't want to leave him. I don't want to go to Mike.* But she had no choice.

Keith pulled back, cupped her cheeks, and kissed her. She tasted his salty tears as they kissed. He was crying. She felt like sobbing loudly. She wrapped her arms around her husband and kissed him like a dying woman. Which she probably was. Even if Mike didn't kill her, staying with him would still be a living death, especially when she would be separated from the man she loved.

She finally pulled away from Keith and sighed. "I have to go," she said and turned around.

He took hold of her hand, and she turned back to him. "I love you, Rachel," he said. "I'll try to find a way to get you away from Mike."

She smiled sadly and pressed her lips together to keep from sobbing. Tears began to flow down her cheeks. She had to leave now or she never would, and then she would share the blame in whatever Mike and his men did. Slowly, she removed her hand from Keith's and hurried away.

She walked quickly to find Mike, afraid he may have killed Daniel already. When she finally reached him and his men, she stopped. Mike had a large flashlight, and it illuminated the area where they stood. She looked down and sighed with relief. Daniel was kneeling on the floor, his hands tied behind his back. Blood streamed down his head to his cheeks, but he was alive.

She looked at Mike and spat out, "You beast! Let Daniel go. I'm right here!" She sighed and then pleaded, "Please stop this murderous pursuit and let everyone go. It's not them you want. It's me."

Mike chuckled. "First, you will have to lead me to where my children are, and then I'll tell my men not to harm any of your women."

"I don't know where they are, Mike! I sent them off with a friend, but I don't know where she went with them. They're all safe, though. I can promise you that. Once you stop this evil pursuit of yours, they can all return to you."

Mike yanked her hair and pulled her to him. She screamed, and he grabbed her hand. "I don't believe you, Rachel! You will lead me to where my children are right now!"

"I'm telling you the truth, Mike. I don't know where they are."

He looked at his men, all three of them, and said,

"Rachel will lead me to my children. You three are to make sure no one gets past you. The other men are on the other side of wherever this tunnel leads, I'm sure. They'll make sure no one escapes." He looked down at Rachel and said, "You'll lead me now to where Emily and my sons are, and if you try to play any games," he raised his cell phone, "I'll call my men and give them orders to start shooting everyone. Is that understood?"

Rachel glared at him, her stomach boiling with anger.

"Is that understood?" he repeated.

"Yes!"

"Now, let's go." He pulled her along with him, and they kept walking in silence until they got to the secret entrance again. They walked out into the common room. As he pulled her toward the door, sirens began to scream through the air, and she gasped. Mike jerked her back from the door. He pulled her to the window, drew back the curtains slightly, and cursed. "The police!" he spat out.

Rachel's heart soared with hope as she stared out the window. Police cars, about five of them, were parking in front of the House of Refuge. Their sirens wailed as police officers jumped out of their cars, pointing their guns at the house. One of the officers, a policewoman, raised a loudspeaker to her lips. "Come out with your hands raised!"

Mike held the gun to Rachel's back. "Open the door and tell them that everything is alright. Tell them it was a false alarm. That a disgruntled neighbor was the one who called them."

She moved slowly, and he pressed the gun into her back and held out his phone to her. "Play no games, Rachel, or I'll call my men. I just need to say a word to them, and they'll know to start shooting. You don't want that, do you?"

"No," she said.

"Then do as I've told you... and you better sound convincing." He stepped back slightly, hiding behind the door as she slowly opened it. She looked at him, and he held up his phone to her. He muttered, "Tell them everything is fine, with a smile on your face."

She opened the door and stepped out of the house.

The female police officer blinked and looked at Rachel. "Are you okay, ma'am?"

Rachel pressed her lips together and nodded. "Yes." She forced a smile. "Yes, I'm fine. Everything is fine."

"Are you sure?"

For a brief moment, Rachel didn't know what to say. She was not fine, and everything was not okay, but if she made a mistake now, it would end in disaster. She had a split second to make a decision. She could defy Mike and let the police know the truth and then have a calamity on her hands, or follow Mike's orders and who knew what would happen after that? She nodded. "I'm fine. Thank you." She blinked rapidly at the female police officer, hoping the woman would understand what she was trying to tell her.

Another officer came and stood beside the policewoman. She smiled again and backed away slowly.

"Okay, ma'am," the policewoman said. "Since you're okay and everything seems alright, we'll leave. Have a good day."

"Thank you," Rachel said, her heart drumming. She turned around and walked into the house. *Lord, I hope they understood my message.* She shut the door and faced Mike. "I've done what you told me to," she said.

He lowered his hand, his phone at his side, and pointed his gun at her. "Now, tell me where…?" His eyes widened in astonishment as the door flew open and the policewoman barged into the house. She pointed the gun at Mike. "Put down your weapon and raise your hands where I can see them!"

The surprised look on Mike's face melted away, replaced by rage. Rachel screamed as Mike pulled the trigger of his gun and an explosion sounded. She gasped as pain tore through her waist, and she fell to the floor. A loud thud sounded beside her as Mike crashed down next to her. Blood oozed from his chest.

She looked down at herself and saw blood pouring from her side. She began to feel herself drifting away. "Lord, help me," she whispered. Keith's face appeared clearly in her mind. Overwhelming sadness settled over her. If she died, he would be devastated. "Lord, please be with Keith and protect my Emily."

Two more police officers entered the house, and the policewoman knelt by her. She brushed Rachel's hair from her face and looked up at another officer. "Call nine-one-one, now!"

Rachel shut her eyes as the policewoman said, "It's okay, ma'am. I think it's just a flesh wound. You'll be okay."

Rachel nodded, but fear poured through her as

the darkness kept encroaching. The woman had said she would be fine, but Rachel wasn't sure if she was saying that to make her feel better or if it was the truth. She certainly didn't feel like she was going to be okay. She felt as though life was oozing out of her.

She tried to keep her eyes open, but she couldn't anymore. She mustered all her strength and pointed at the secret entrance. "They're all in there," she said weakly. She took a deep breath as she began to slip away. "Lord, be with Keith and Emily," she whispered again, and then everything went black.

TWENTY-ONE

Lily sat in the common room in the House of Refuge, Bree seated on her lap. Beside her on the sofa were Taylor, Rachel, with Emily in her arms, and Keith. Patricia, Dennis Hamilton's first wife, sat on the sofa in front of them, listening intently to what Taylor was saying. From time to time, she asked him a question, but she mostly listened.

Apart from them, no one else was here, but Lily could hear the voices of the residents of the House chatting and laughing. She could not help smiling at that. One month ago, the atmosphere in the House had been totally different after the scary events that had taken place involving Mike and his men. The house had worn a dreary look for weeks, but then, gradually, normalcy had returned, and now the place was bustling with activity.

Thankfully, no one had been hurt except for Rachel, but she was fine now. The police had arrived, and everyone had been saved. The bullet that had hit Rachel had only grazed her side; she'd needed a minor surgery, but she was up and about a week later.

It wasn't only the House of Refuge that was bustling with activity. A few of the residents of Fallow Creek had also returned, and Rachel had graciously given them their former homes back. Unfortunately, Lily's parents were not among the people who had returned, and neither was her sister.

She looked down at Bree, who had dozed off on her lap, and sighed sadly as she thought about her family. Taylor had made calls and had followed leads that ended with nothing. She had visited the returning residents of Fallow Creek with Taylor, but none of them knew where her parents or her sister were. The fear that she might never find them constantly ate at her, but she had not given up, and thankfully Taylor hadn't either.

He had vowed to keep looking for them with her, and she was eternally grateful to him for that. She turned to look at him as he talked with Patricia, Rachel, and Keith. His handsome face scrunched in concentration as he listened to what Keith was saying. How she loved him! He made her world better. Apart from her sadness at her parents' and sister's absence, she was as happy as she could ever be now that they were officially together in a steady relationship. She still chose to stay at the House of Refuge, and he'd agreed it was the right thing to do. There was no point putting themselves through all that temptation if she moved into his house. Their desire for one another was as strong as ever.

She sighed sadly as her eyes remained on him. There were two things that kept her from being the happiest woman in the world. The first was, of course, the fact that she didn't know where her parents were, but the second had to do with Taylor. He was perfect to her, but there was still a part of him she wanted, and which he held back from her. Without question, he loved her, but she wanted more. She wanted to marry him.

But it wasn't possible now. It felt as though he was still mourning his wife. Not that she blamed him. It was barely a year since Faye had died. He wasn't ready yet to fully commit to her. She sighed again. She would take whatever he gave her now, even though it hurt that he couldn't give her the one thing she wanted most.

She shut her eyes in frustration. When would he stop mourning his wife, anyway? She immediately felt awful for thinking that way. *Give the man some time, Lily.*

But how much time did he need? How long would she have to wait to become fully his, and he hers? She loved him enough to wait for him forever, but it would be great if they could get married now. She ached to be with him the way a husband and wife were meant to be.

You're being really selfish, Lily. Let the man be.

She ran her fingers through her hair and pressed all her frustrations away. She focused on the conversation her friends were having. Taylor was telling Patricia about how his workers had found her husband, Dennis, in the river. He had already told Lily, Rachel, and Keith the story.

"Dennis told me that when the flood came, it carried him and the squad team that were with him into the river. It kept pulling them farther and farther away from shore. He said he and his men struggled to stay above water, but gradually they grew tired, and the next thing he knew, he was drowning." Taylor brushed his hair back from his face in that peculiar way of his that made Lily's heart pound. "As your husband began to drown, he said he heard a voice tell him that he would be given another chance to do the right thing. The voice told him he would be saved and so would the other men."

Patricia's mouth was open, and she looked shocked as she listened to Taylor.

"Dennis said that somehow he began to rise and rise until his head popped out of the water, and he saw a vessel coming his way. My vessel. I had left Fallow Creek at that time, but I still had some business there and that particular vessel, I think, was transporting some of my equipment out of Fallow Creek. Some of the men on the vessel saw Dennis and the squad team fighting for their lives and rescued them. Many of them had swallowed a lot of water, but they all lived thanks to the quick intervention of my men on the vessel."

He went on. "I was called as soon as they were rescued. Dennis told me he had nowhere to go, and even though I thought that strange, I told my men that when they were feeling better, Dennis and his men could be taken to the emergency house I had built near the border. There was enough food to last them for a long time, and they stayed there."

Taylor shut his eyes briefly and then opened them. "Because of my wife's death, I didn't want to know about anything that was happening in Fallow Creek at the time, and Dennis offered no explanations as to why he wasn't going back to his own house. I knew he was in some kind of trouble, but that was all I knew. I've been helping him out from time to time, sending food and other basic necessities for him and his men."

"But why did you not tell me, or anyone?" Patricia asked.

"I wanted nothing to do with anyone here. I wasn't even picking up my sister's calls."

"So Dennis lied to you and didn't tell you he'd stolen what belonged to Rachel?" Patricia asked.

"Yes. I didn't find out the whole truth until Rachel told me about it. I would've stopped helping him, but I knew in my heart that it was what God wanted me to do."

Patricia nodded again.

Taylor leaned forward and gazed at Patricia. He said tenderly, "Dennis is still at that house now, in case you want to see him."

Patricia shook her head. "No! I don't want to see him. He pretended to be dead all these months. As far as I'm concerned, he's dead to me."

Lily understood the woman's anger. She shuddered as she remembered once again the day she'd found out Dennis was planning to marry her. If she had agreed, she would have been, according to Sofia, a sister wife to this woman. She would have been a widow for months, only to have her dead husband come back to life. She could not fathom how her life would have been now. She was overwhelmed with gratitude to God for leading her in a different direction. The worst part was that she would never have had the chance to be with Taylor. The thought was horrifying to her.

Taylor smiled at Patricia. "I understand how you

feel. You don't have to see him now anyway."

Patricia got up and thanked Taylor for telling her everything she wanted to know about Dennis. "And thank you for all you did for him," she said in a voice heavy with emotion. "I am truly grateful."

"It was no problem," Taylor said, beaming at the woman.

Patricia left the common room.

Their conversation moved to the occupants of the House. A few kids now also lived in the House of Refuge with their mothers. Amongst them were Olivia's boys and Olivia. She had refused to go back to Mike's after he'd died.

"Olivia and her boys are doing okay under the circumstances," Rachel said. "I'm glad she's free from Mike, though it's unfortunate that he had to die for that to happen. She suffered a great deal with him."

"She loved him, though," Keith said.

Rachel threaded her fingers through her husband's. "I'm glad that I don't have that kind of toxic love. The man I love actually loves me back." She smiled widely at Keith, and he smiled back at her.

"I'm so happy everyone is safe now," Lily said. "I just wish I knew where my parents and my sister were."

Rachel took Lily's hand, squeezed it, and smiled encouragingly at her. "I'm sure they're okay, wherever they are. You'll find them eventually. I'm sure of that."

"Thank you," Lily said.

Will and Jeremy ran into the common room screaming and laughing. Josh ran in chasing them.

The three boys ran around the common room while the adults watched. Rachel smiled broadly, Keith looked amused, and Taylor looked exasperated as he gazed at Josh.

Emily started bouncing on Rachel's lap, clearly wanting to be free so she could run around with the boys. Rachel held her tightly and shook her head. "No, Emily, you're not running around with those rascals. You'll fall and hurt yourself."

Lily chuckled as Emily strained to get away from her mother. Clearly, what Rachel had said meant nothing to her. Bree suddenly woke up, probably because of all the noise the boys were making, and began to wail. Lily rubbed her back and spoke softly to her to try to calm her down.

Olivia came into the common room and apologized profusely for her boys' disturbance. She grabbed them by the hands and pulled them out of the common room. Josh moaned, turning and fixing his gaze on Bree. He ran up to Lily, grinning, and Bree immediately stopped crying. She stared at her brother and raised her hands, clearly wanting Josh to carry her.

"Can Bree come and build LEGO with me?" Josh asked Lily with a sweet smile.

"Sure, Josh," Lily smiled at him. She let go of Bree, and the toddler slipped off her lap and toddled after her brother. Lily smiled and turned to Taylor. He was grinning at her, and she knew exactly what was on his mind. Josh was gradually losing the belligerent attitude he'd had toward her. He still didn't want his father kissing her in his presence, but he'd come to terms with the fact that she was here to stay. She hoped they would become close one day.

Taylor whispered, "Lily, can you take a walk with me?"

Her heart began to pound, and she nodded. She stood up just as he did and took his hand when he held it out to her.

"We just want to go for a walk. We'll be back," Taylor said to Rachel and Keith.

Keith waved them away. "Go, guys. We need our alone time, anyway." He gave Rachel an impish smile, and Taylor shook his head.

Lily left the house hand in hand with Taylor. Daniel and Davina were at the gate whispering to each other, obviously smitten with one another. Lily greeted them both briefly and followed Taylor out the gate.

They walked through Fallow Creek holding hands, silently enjoying each other's company. Lily looked from house to house as they walked. Already, the town was not as abandoned as it had been a month ago, though many houses were still empty.

Taylor finally stopped, and Lily did too. He stood in front of her and took her other hand. "Lily, I'm sorry that I haven't been able to find your parents or your sister yet."

"It's not your fault, Taylor. It's no one's fault."

"We won't stop looking for them, Lily. Until we find them, we will not give up."

"Yes," she said. "Thank you, Taylor."

He beamed, and they continued to walk through town until they came to the front of his house. She looked up at his house in surprise. She hadn't even realized they were going in that direction. He stopped her once more at the gate and fixed his gaze on her. "I know you have two main things you want to see come to pass, Lily," he said. "One of them is to find your parents and sister, and the other is to travel the world."

No. Three, Taylor. The third is to marry you. She chuckled to cover the pain she felt and said, "You know me so well."

"I haven't been able to help with the first... yet, but the second I might be able to help with." He put his hand into his pocket and, for a split moment, she thought he was going to bring out an engagement ring. When he brought out two slips of paper and a brochure, she sighed with disappointment.

Why would you think he was about to propose, Lily? she scolded herself.

He held out the slips of paper and brochure to her, and she took them from him. "What is this?" she asked. Her heart leapt as she scanned the papers. "Two tickets for a world cruise?"

"Yes." He smiled. "And we can keep looking for your parents while we take the cruise."

She flew into his arms and hugged him tightly. He pulled away. "Lily, you haven't looked at the brochure."

She smiled and opened the brochure. She began to flip through it and looked up at Taylor and shook her head. "This says that you booked a cruise for two, but with just one room." Her mouth dropped open, and she said, "This says the room has a big cozy bed for two." She shook her head as she looked at him. "Taylor, you know we can't stay in a room with just one bed!"

He shrugged. "Why not?"

"Taylor... please, I'm serious. You have to rebook this. We haven't kept away from temptation for this long only for you to book a world cruise and have us stay in the same room. You know what will happen. It would be..." He placed a finger on her lips, silencing her.

"Shh... this brings me to my other surprise."

"What other surprise?" She gasped when he brought a tiny box out of his other pocket and held it out to her. When he knelt down before her and opened the box, her heart stopped beating. Inside the box was a huge diamond ring.

A sob rose in her throat, and he said, "Lily Hunter, I love you with all of me." He grinned and winked at her. She shook her head at the mischievous smile he gave her. "Will you be my wife so we can take that cruise together and finally be able to share a room as a couple?" He pointed at the brochure. "Say yes, Lily. If you need more convincing, look at that bed. It looks inviting, doesn't it? I can't imagine how it would..."

"Stop!" She laughed out loud. She couldn't stop giggling at the look on his face. Finally, she calmed down and said, "So, you want to marry me just so we can go on a world cruise and share a bed that looks inviting?" She covered her mouth so she wouldn't burst out laughing again.

He nodded, a serious look on his face.

She laughed again. "Okay then, in that case, I will marry you. I need a travel buddy anyway."

"Great!" he exclaimed. "Now, all we need to do is to start packing, because we're going to get married as soon as possible."

She giggled. "You have all this planned out."

"Yes, I do. We'll be married before the end of the month so we can go on the cruise together. I just can't wait to take that cruise."

She laughed again. Her heart flooded with joy as she gazed at him. She felt she would die of happiness at any moment now. She took his hand and pulled him to his feet, her heart racing. It felt like her heart was about to crash out of her chest. His gaze took her breath away, and tears filled her eyes.

In a voice laden with emotion, he whispered, "I love you, Lily Hunter. I can't wait to spend the rest of my life with you."

She threw her arms around him and kissed him. Her dream was finally going to come true. Soon, she could love him with all of her. She smiled as she breathed in the musky scent of his cologne.

He pulled slightly away from her, his eyes glazed with such desire that her stomach flipped. He looked up at his house longingly and shook his head. "We'd better go back to the House of Refuge," he said.

She giggled as he firmly turned her around and led her away from the house.

She was bursting with their good news as they headed to the House of Refuge. Once they got there, she would tell Rachel, Keith, and everyone else she saw that they were now engaged. God had brought triumph out of tragedy and hope out of despair.

As they walked with their hands linked, she felt like she was walking on clouds. The moment seemed sacred, wonderful, and a little sad because her parents and sister were not here to witness her engagement. But even though she didn't know where they were, she was not alone in the world.

God had given her a new family — a ready-made one, made up of a man who loved her dearly and two precious children she could now call her own.

A LOOK AT:
CHASING AFTER DESTINY

A STORY OF FORGIVING THOSE WHO HAVE DONE WRONG AND BRINGING LIGHT TO THE DARKNESS – THE DESTINY SERIES IS CHRISTIAN ROMANCE, SUSPENSE AND INTRIGUE AT ITS BEST.

Sofia Ross thinks her boyfriend, George Davidson — a married man — is about to finally ask her to marry him and leave his wife. But instead, he tells her he must break up with her. She not only loses the man she has loved for the past five years, but also her job, her Tucson penthouse, and her car, all which he provided.

Not knowing what else to do, Sofia tries to end her life with a handful of pills, luckily her friend Edith is there, and Sofia survives. But the depression resurfaces, and Sofia attempts again right as her friend Lily is calling. Sofia explains how she feels empty and has nothing to live for. Lily tells her Jesus will give her the love she is looking for.

Eventually, a supernatural peace settles over Sofia, and she knows that whatever has happened, God will help her through it.

COMING JULY 2020

ABOUT THE AUTHOR

Like the characters in her stories, Emma Easter juggles a range of identities.

In the low-income community where she works, Easter is known as a family medicine physician who treats patients of all ages and backgrounds.

College friends see her as an accomplished musician, having studied and mastered five classical instruments—but behind closed doors, she's just as comfortable rocking an air guitar to Creed. And when she isn't giving her heart, soul, and sanity to her three young children she's indulging in her most secret identity of all: meeting new characters, crafting fresh plots, and exploring every corner of her imagination.

Across all these different roles, one cohesive thread has tied everything together: her faith and love of Jesus Christ.

Find more great titles by Emma Easter and Christian Kindle News at https://christiankindlenews.com/our-authors/emma-easter/